FALLING FOR MY EX'S BROTHER

A SECOND CHANCE ROMANCE

ELLA SLOANE

Copyright © 2023 by Ella Sloane

All rights reserved.

No part of this book may be reproduced in any form or by any electronic or mechanical means, including information storage and retrieval systems, without written permission from the author, except for the use of brief quotations in a book review.

1

LANA

I knew I should look away, but the dark stubble lining the man's sharp jaw and the perfect shape of his nose and cheekbones had me rooted in place. I sat staring at this gorgeous stranger, unable to tear my eyes away.

He was in the car next to mine, looking down at his lap, unaware of my gaze.

I'd never been quite so struck by how handsome someone was. At least not to the point that I lost track of what I was doing. I kept glancing at the driver's window as I walked between our cars.

I finally managed to drag my attention away, not wanting to be caught openly gawking.

As I tried to pull the gift and the casserole I'd made out of my passenger side, his door swung open, making impact with mine. I gasped at the sharp crack and pushed my door halfway closed.

"Oh!" I exclaimed.

"Shoot, sorry about that," he said, his voice deep and rich.

I turned and my eyes landed on the handsome man I'd

been admiring seconds earlier. His eyes met mine and a hint of a smile played on his lips, making my stomach do a weird flip.

He was even more good-looking up close.

For a moment, as I looked into his soft brown eyes framed by perfect, dark eyebrows, I forgot what the heck I'd been doing or thinking about.

I swallowed hard, struggling to form coherent words.

"That's okay," I finally managed, flashing a small smile in return.

He smiled a little sheepishly. "I was worried about being late. Not paying attention. Sorry, I didn't mean to startle you."

He straightened to his full height, and my eyes followed his up until I was craning my neck to look at him. I wondered if my brain was going to come back online for the rest of the night.

He was well over six feet tall, dark brown hair, and so well-built. His fitted shirt showed off his thick chest and biceps, and I couldn't help but notice the way his muscles flexed as he shut his door.

An intricate tattoo wrapped around his arm. The black ink contrasted nicely against his tan skin. I could see hints of more tattoos peeking out from the neckline of his t-shirt, making me wonder what other body art he was hiding underneath his clothes.

I imagined running my fingers over each marking. I had never wanted to tear a shirt off a man more than I did at that moment.

Normally, I would've been a little intimidated by a man like him if it wasn't for his soft smile and boyish twinkle in his eyes.

My purse slid off my shoulder and hit the ground. He

Falling For My Ex's Brother

immediately picked it up and handed it to me. My fingers brushed his as I took it, and either I felt an electric jolt of attraction or something in my brain was about to pop.

I pressed my back against my closed car door. It seemed like there was barely more than a few inches between us. And I felt in danger of swooning and falling forward against him. Especially since he kept staring into my eyes, his brows drawn down in a slight frown.

I quickly assessed for any damage from our doors colliding.

"My car's fine," I blurted. "No damage that I can see. Yours?"

My voice came out a little too high and too tight. It probably didn't surprise him. He must have had that effect on a lot of women.

I wanted to reach out and touch his chest. To see if it was as firm and muscular as it looked through his shirt.

He gave a quick look at his car door. "Mine's fine too," he said, one side of his lips turning up.

Oh yes. Yes, it is.

"It wasn't all your fault," I said. "I was worried about being late too. Hate running behind. It makes me feel panicky, so I didn't notice you until it was too late."

That was such a lie. I noticed him, all right. Part of the reason I had been running late was *because* I noticed him. But it sounded reasonable, at least.

He gazed at me for a few seconds, his head slightly tilting to one side as if assessing me. He held his hand toward me. "Dylan Easton."

I took his hand, and it was as warm and firm as I'd expected. A little callused and rough, but just the right amount. The men I dated usually had softer hands, and I wondered what I had been missing out on all this time. As he leaned in close, I caught a whiff of his woodsy, masculine scent.

I'd never felt so attracted to anyone before, especially not to someone a little rough and rugged. Meeting him might have opened up a whole new type for me.

I realized I was standing there gawking at him and squeezing his hand.

"Lana Murphy," I replied as I gestured past him toward my car door. "Excuse me."

I tried to casually slip by him in the tight space, but my foot caught on his and I stumbled forward.

Oh no. Not now. Don't fall now.

I let out a startled yelp and stretched out my arms, hoping to steady myself before I hit the ground. But Dylan moved fast, catching me and pulling me back up. The jerky movement sent me crashing right into his firm chest. His strong hands gripped my hips to steady me.

Oh god, I wanted to melt into the pavement.

"Whoa there," he said with a little chuckle, holding me against him. His grip felt strong yet gentle. "You okay?" he asked.

I blinked up at him, embarrassingly aware of how I was pressed against his muscular frame. His chest rose as his eyes locked with mine. My hands were clinging to his thick muscular arms. God, they felt so good.

"Sorry. I'm such a klutz," I said, feeling my cheeks flush.

He released me from his hold, and I immediately missed his warm hands on my body. I smoothed my hair and clothes, trying to regain composure. Something about this guy made me feel like a blubbering mess.

His eyes glinted with amusement as he looked down at me. "Don't apologize. I don't mind a beautiful woman falling into my arms," he said with a grin.

I was simultaneously mortified and thrilled at his reaction, even if it was an obvious pickup line. I looked up at him, arching an eyebrow, and stifled a laughter.

He let out a soft chuckle and then made a face, wincing playfully. "Wow. That sounded so much smoother in my head."

I had to laugh at his own admission of the less than subtle line.

"At least you know how to flatter a girl after you save her from face-planting. Does that line work on most women?" I teased as I smiled cheekily.

"Oh, yeah." He nodded exaggeratedly, in mock seriousness. "Every single time. Women love a good pickup line, right?"

I laughed again, shaking my head.

He laughed with me, his caramel eyes twinkling. Then he leaned in slightly and added, "In case it wasn't clear, it really wasn't a pickup line."

"I wouldn't be offended if it was." I pressed my lips together, rolling them in.

Was I flirting? More importantly, would *he* think I was flirting?

His eyes dropped to my mouth before meeting my gaze again.

This was the part where he was supposed to ask for my number or go our separate ways, but neither of us moved or said anything. We stood there looking at each other for what felt like an eternity.

"Thanks for breaking my fall," I said with a smile, finally breaking the silence.

"Anytime," he replied.

"I should, um . . ." I gestured at my car door again, managing to sidestep him this time without tripping. I thought maybe he would start walking away, but there he stood in my periphery, still just inches from me. Was he waiting for me? I hoped he was.

As I bent into my car to get the packages, my ass brushed against him. My face heated in a blush, and I stood quickly, not daring to look at him, in fear that I might spontaneously combust.

My hands were full, so I tried to close my door with my elbow. My purse slid off my shoulder again and hit the ground as it dangled from the long strap on my forearm. This unbalanced the hold I had on everything. I nearly dropped the casserole, which was uncomfortably warm on the bottom.

"Let me get that," he said softly, as he took the casserole and the gift bag from me in one smooth motion.

He kneed my door shut, bringing his body closer to mine. Our faces were only inches apart, his breath warm on my forehead. The confident curl of his lips told me he noticed the effect he had on me.

I cleared my throat, pulse racing. "Th-thank you."

"My pleasure," he said, smiling down at me.

"You're here for the party?" he asked. "For Dave Easton?"

"Yes. Are you–" I hadn't put the names together. Probably because my brain was still recovering from how hot he was. "You must be one of his grandkids! He and my Grandpa James are close friends, so Grandpa invited me to come."

"We're going the same way then," he said, giving me a sexy, crooked smile.

His brown eyes crinkled at the corners when he smiled like that, making my knees weak.

Get a grip, Lana.

"We are," I said, swallowing hard. I was thrilled that we were both headed to the party, and to have more time to get to know him. My heart started drumming in my chest in anticipation.

I reached for the gift and casserole he'd saved me from dropping.

"I've got it," he said, stepping back so I could walk out from between our cars and head inside.

"Thanks, I said, almost giggling like a schoolgirl. "I guess chivalry isn't dead."

He laughed. "What if I said the food smelled good, and I just didn't want to see you drop it on the ground?"

Dylan winked at me, and my stomach fluttered. Lots of my parts fluttered.

"I'd say that at least you're honest." I brushed off the bottom of my purse and hoisted it back onto my shoulder.

When we reached the front door of Crystal Fountains Senior Home, despite carrying all my things, Dylan still managed to open the door for me.

I walked through the door and I glanced back to catch his eyes moving up quickly from my behind.

My face heated. He was checking me out. I'd never felt so damn giddy about a man ogling my ass.

The look on his face told me he liked what he saw and that he knew he'd been caught. But he held my gaze, a small smile playing on his lips.

I liked that he didn't turn away and pretend that he wasn't looking like most men would've done. Something about the way his confident eyes held mine was like a challenge.

Or a promise, I hoped.

"It's in the dining room, right?" I asked.

"Yep. And as far I can tell, my grandpa still has no idea. Your grandpa was tasked with keeping him in his room while everything was set up. Probably another round of Gin Rummy."

I followed him to the dining room, where a few dishes waited on a table and another small round one held a gift bag and several cards.

The staff had blown up some balloons and secured them to the middle of a few tables to give the room a festive look.

"I hope he likes the gift I got him. I'm a little nervous he might think it's lame," I said after Dylan put my things down.

"What did you get him?" Dylan asked, leaning in, his chest brushing against my back.

I let him peek in the gift bag. It was a little back cushion for his wheelchair that read 'Still calling the shots'. I hoped he'd get the reference to his bar owner days. I'd only met Dave a few times, so I wasn't sure if he'd like it.

Dylan glanced down at me and raised his eyebrows.

"Oh no," I said, cringing. "Is it that bad? You can be honest. Grandpa told me he used to own a bar."

"It's not quite as bad as my pickup line," he replied, his lips pressed together, suppressing a smile.

I covered my forehead with my hand and groaned. I knew I should've played it safe and just gotten him a mug.

"I'm kidding." Dylan chuckled softly, nudging my arm. "Don't worry, he's going to love it. It's such a thoughtful gift."

I turned to look up at his mischievous grin, and I playfully pretended to elbow him.

"Are you sure?" I asked, narrowing my eyes at him.

He nodded, his smile softening. "I actually own the bar now, and I would love it. I think it's perfect." The sincerity in his voice put my doubts to rest.

One of the staff members carried a cake from the kitchen and needed to put it on the table behind us.

Dylan put his hand on my arm to move us out of the way. I felt ridiculous at the thrill I got from that unexpected touch.

We seemed to be standing in everyone's way, so we helped set up the napkins and plastic picnicware, then we moved to stand against the wall. Dylan leaned close enough to me that our arms touched.

"It's a shame we didn't run into each other before, while we were visiting our grandpas," I said without thinking.

Dylan turned, his shoulder against the wall, his arms still crossed.

"It really is," he said with a half-grin. "We could have been gambling in their card games all this time."

I swallowed hard, very aware of Dylan's intense gaze on me.

I turned to match his stance and nodded.

"Yep," I said, grinning back. "I'm not a very good gambler, though. And Grandpa James likes to cheat at cards. He'd probably have wiped me out."

"I've got a great poker face. We could have secretly paired up and held our own, I'll bet." Dylan gently bumped my arm with his hand.

A sound as sharp as a shot rang out. I jumped forward and grabbed Dylan. His arms wrapped around me protectively as he looked around for the source of the noise.

"It's okay, just a balloon," he assured me, his voice calm and steady.

I exhaled with a laugh, feeling silly for my reaction. Maybe being that close to someone as sexy as Dylan was making me jumpy.

A couple of the nurses laughed. One picked up the limp blue latex and tossed it into the trash.

"Sorry, didn't mean to grab you like that," I said, shaking my head. "I don't know what came over me."

"It's okay, it was just a natural reflex," Dylan said with an easy grin. He gently released me from his grasp. "You do seem to keep ending up in my arms today. It must be fate."

We shared a look at his intentional pickup line this time and both laughed. I stepped back reluctantly.

"Fate or my jumpiness. Or my clumsy feet," I added. "You must think I'm so ridiculous."

"Not at all, maybe I tripped you on purpose," he said, a playful smile on his lips.

"You did not," I scoffed, looking at him incredulously. I narrowed my eyes at him and smiled. "Did you?"

"You'll never know." He shrugged and let out a low chuckle. "But I would have definitely popped a balloon myself if I'd known it would get you to jump into my arms again," he added, his voice low and husky.

I licked my lips, noticing the way his eyes tracked the movement.

I was trying to figure out what to say back when a staff member said, "James is bringing Dave down the hall right now. Get ready!"

DYLAN

"We're not really going to *yell*-yell 'surprise', are we?" Lana asked, her hands clasped in front of her chin.

She looked like an excited kid waiting for her own party. Her blonde hair was tied up with loose strands framing her gorgeous face, and her baby blue eyes sparkled with anticipation.

I loved a pretty set of blue eyes. And I loved curvy hips that I could sink my fingers into. The tight leggings Lana wore showed off her perfect ass and shapely thighs. She was a fucking knockout. I couldn't take my eyes off her in the parking lot as we walked in together.

Yes, I admired the way her ass moved with each step as she walked in front of me. I was a red-blooded man.

But there was something else about her besides her looks that I liked too.

From the minute I'd hit my car door into hers, it had been hard to look away. I'd never been at a loss for words when talking to a woman, but I hadn't been able to come up with anything to say. So I stood there, gawking at her like an idiot.

As we stood between our cars, I'd thought maybe I knew her from somewhere. Maybe I met her a long time ago.

I'd taken in every beautiful feature, wracking my brain about why she seemed so familiar. By the time we got inside, I realized I didn't know her.

She only seemed familiar because she was like the perfect combination of everything that attracted me to a woman.

I was tempted to look for a straight pin, a knife, anything to pop another balloon just to have her body pressed against mine again.

I realized she was staring at me, waiting for an answer. I cleared my throat.

"I don't think it's wise to scare the hell out of someone who just turned eighty."

She nodded. And then her grandpa appeared, pushing my grandpa in his wheelchair.

The staff clearly didn't worry about giving an eighty-year-old a sudden heart attack, because they screamed *surprise* like they were at gunpoint.

He clapped his hands together and smiled as he pretended to try to punch James for keeping the secret.

Lana laughed next to me, looking delighted at how happy they both were.

As food and cake were doled out, and our grandpas smiled about us finally meeting, I could barely take my eyes off Lana.

"Dylan thinks you two should let us in on some of your gambling," Lana said, pulling me out of my fugue. "He thinks he's got a good poker face."

Grandpa shook his head. "You're welcome to join us. But you know your grandpa cheats, right?"

They laughed, and I went back to watching her smile at

her grandpa and mine. She had mine charmed, but that didn't surprise me. She seemed like someone who everybody probably liked.

And any man with eyes certainly had to notice what a stunning woman she was.

Another balloon popped. Lana flinched along with everybody else, but unfortunately, she was too far away to jump into my arms.

Not that she would have done that again anyway. But a man could hope.

She smiled and looked at me, hopefully thinking along the same lines. As a couple other party guests came to talk to my grandpa, I moved closer to Lana.

"Did the staff lose control while blowing up these balloons, or what?" she asked.

"Too bad you were so far away that time," I said.

She chewed on her bottom lip as she glanced up at me. "I agree."

I wanted to tell her I could put my arms around her and keep them there, just in case another one popped.

"Maybe you should stay a little closer, just in case another one goes up?" I offered instead.

"Maybe I should." Her smile wiped away the doubts I had.

I didn't see how I could let the party end without doing my best to make sure I was going to see Lana again.

"Can I call you sometime?" I asked.

I wasn't at my smoothest, but something about Lana disarmed me. If she'd been just another beautiful woman that I met at a bar or out somewhere, I'd have been more suave. But the sense that there was something special about her left me a little unsure of myself.

"Yeah. Okay," she said, smiling as she took my phone to

put in her number. She handed my phone back with a huge grin. And her eyes focused on my hand as I took it.

On my wedding band.

Her huge grin faded and a scowl took its place.

2

DYLAN

"I guess it's a good idea to exchange numbers," Lana said quickly, her gaze darting away. She started glancing around the room, as if she was looking for an excuse to get away. "In case one of us looks closer later and needs insurance information."

"I guess. But also, in case you want to meet here for a visit, eager to lose some money to a couple of old coots. And me." I put on my best sly grin. "Or meet for coffee or dinner or something. Without a couple of old coots."

Her smile was tighter than before.

"Sure. Sure thing," she said, but I could tell she was being polite and had no intention of ever answering my call.

God damn it.

"Lana, I know what you must–"

"Hey!" My brother Todd ran up to us. "Sorry, I'm late. I got tied up at work at the last minute with a client. I got here as fast as I could. Did I miss much?"

The whole time he spoke to me, he was looking at Lana. I could see the stars form in his eyes.

Todd was twenty-five, five years younger than me, probably closer to Lana's age. And he'd dated more women at twenty-five than I had.

He was young and hip, with a sense of humor that made most people like him. At least until they got to know him. And right then, I didn't want him to have a chance to get to know Lana.

"You missed the surprise," I grumbled. "You should at least go let him know you're here." I motioned toward Grandpa, where a little white-haired lady was giving him a kiss on the cheek. I looked at Todd expectantly, hoping he'd clue in. I needed a moment alone with Lana to explain myself. To explain my ring.

Todd hesitated, looking at Grandpa and then back at Lana before flashing her a smile.

"Be right back," he said to Lana, not me. "Don't go anywhere."

If he realized I was interested in Lana, he didn't show it. Maybe because he knew I was still technically married and that I hadn't been looking to date yet.

Todd was probably going to monopolize the rest of Lana's time, so if I was going to tell her I was in the process of a divorce, I had to do it then. I wanted to make sure she'd welcome my call because I absolutely had to see this woman again.

Lana turned away, starting to follow in the direction of where Todd was headed.

"Lana–" She turned back to me, her eyes laced with a hard edge that wasn't there before.

"Mr. Easton?" a nurse with bright red hair said as she touched my shoulder. "Can I talk to you for a minute about David? It's important."

I tried my best to hide my frustration, but I couldn't hold back the sharp exhale that escaped my lungs.

For fuck's sake. Could people stop interrupting us?

I held up my hand and started to tell the nurse that I'd speak with her in a minute, but Lana saw the opportunity and swiftly made her exit.

"Excuse me," Lana said. I quickly turned back to her, but she was already headed back to our grandfathers without another glance in my direction.

I should have taken my wedding ring off the day Marie told me she wanted a divorce, but at first I'd hoped to save the marriage.

Then I just forgot about it. I hadn't been worried about it because I hadn't been looking or flirting.

I had no desire to date yet. Not until today.

Who would've thought I'd meet the woman of my dreams at a senior home?

I should have told her that my divorce would be final, probably within a month or two. That my marriage had been over long before my wife cheated on me. We had lived separate lives for the past year and were finally officially calling it quits.

Even if I did tell her about the pending divorce, without giving any details, I knew she'd probably smile tightly and nod.

A lot of cheating, married men trotted out that line.

But in my case, it was true.

I wanted to go after her and explain myself, but she was already engrossed in a conversation with Todd. He bumped his shoulder against hers and said something she laughed at.

I followed the nurse out of the dining room, giving Lana one last look, hoping like hell I hadn't just blown my chance.

LANA

I stood next to Todd, who made a few jokes he included me in with a light shoulder bump. After he'd given his grandpa a hug, he turned to me.

"Since my rude brother didn't introduce us, I'm Todd, the better-looking brother." Todd stuck his hand out and flashed a charming grin at me.

Todd was tall and lean, wearing an impeccably tailored dark grey suit. He had handsome, chiseled features like Dylan and short sandy blonde hair neatly styled into place. While Dylan radiated a rugged, masculine charm, Todd was more polished and refined. Both men were attractive in their own, very different ways.

"I couldn't just abandon a customer in the middle of a sale," he said, looking around the room, "or I'd have made it on time."

Ordinarily, I'd have been a little flustered at how good-looking he was. But I'd just spent half an hour next to Dylan, marveling at how handsome and sexy he was. Even gave him my number. I really thought we'd had a connection.

Then I saw his wedding band. My stomach churned at the thought. At least I dodged a bullet there. I felt bad for his wife, wherever she was.

"Nice to meet you, Todd. My Grandpa James invited me," I said as I shook his hand. "I'm Lana."

"Lana. Wow. A gorgeous woman like you comes here and somehow, I've missed you every time? Life truly isn't fair," he said, grinning widely.

I snorted and he laughed. It was a little too obvious, but Todd's light tone and smile somehow made it seem charming.

I may have latched onto his charm a little harder than I should have, because focusing on Todd and our grandpas laughing together was keeping me from dwelling on how foolish I felt.

Why did I let myself think someone like Dylan might be interested in me *and* a decent guy? How often did that happen?

There was usually something wrong with the men who showed that much interest. And I usually didn't let my guard down so easily as I had done with Dylan.

But there was something about him that felt familiar. Something that put me at ease. I guess I couldn't have been more wrong about him.

"So, tell me about yourself, Lana. I'll bet you're a creative type," Todd said, holding his hands up like he was framing me into a photograph. "Artist. Singer. Model."

I knew how I looked. I was no slouch, but model was pushing it. I was average height and average build. My thighs rubbed together when I walked and certain areas jiggled with each step in a way I'd been self-conscious about when I was younger.

But I'd grown to appreciate my figure over the years and

thought I looked pretty damn cute even though I was never going to be the type of gorgeous woman who turned every head. Still, I was confident enough to know some men found me desirable.

"Nailed it in one!" I said, clapping my hands together. "But you probably cheated. Saw me on the covers of last month's Vogue, Vanity Fair, and Elle, so you knew the answer going in."

"You caught me." He winked and laughed. All I could think about was how my breath caught in my throat when Dylan winked at me earlier. "Do you do anything but grace the covers of high-fashion magazines?"

"I go to school and work at a diner. You know, for fun. In my spare time, when I'm not walking red carpets." I took a piece of cake a staff member offered me on a tiny paper plate.

"What are you studying?" He asked.

"Marketing. It's my last semester so I'll be getting my degree soon," I replied.

As I struggled through school and scraped by financially, I couldn't wait to graduate and begin my real career. I'd applied to every scholarship and grant program I qualified for but they still weren't enough to cover my tuition. I had to rely on student loans and working at the diner to cover the rest.

"I think I can guess what you do too," I admitted.

"Go for it." Todd stuffed a huge forkful of cake into his mouth.

He'd already said he was in sales. And as smooth as he was, there was no way he was doing sales with small commissions. He seemed like someone who could talk headless people into buying hats.

"You sell something expensive. Tech equipment. Solar panels. Or maybe cars. Definitely something high-end."

Todd made an impressed sound. "You got me. I'm a salesman at the Audi dealership on the south side of town. I guess you're a model, server, student, *and* a psychic, huh?"

"I'm going to add that to my resume tonight." We smiled at each other and ate cake.

Todd leaned in, whispering as if sharing a secret.

"I won't tell Dylan, but between us two, who do you find more charming?"

I burst into laughter. "You guys have a competition going or something?"

"Of course," he responded, winking. "The Easton brothers' charm-off."

I rolled my eyes, laughing. "I'll take the fifth on this one."

He chuckled, nudging me lightly with his shoulder. "Fair enough. I'll ask again later after I've had the proper time to win you over."

I wanted to reply that his brother had already won me over until he got caught in a lie, but I couldn't say that. Out of the corner of my eye, I noticed that Dylan and the nurse who'd called him away were back and standing just outside the dining room doors in deep conversation.

He glanced into the room and met my gaze. Before I could look away, he turned his attention to his brother, his expression darkening. Then he looked at me again with a little smile of acknowledgment.

I returned it quickly then turned back to Todd. Dylan was the one who made my stomach do flip-flops, but I couldn't get that wedding band out of my mind.

Wouldn't get it out of my mind. How could he flirt so blatantly when he was married?

I felt as deflated as the balloon that had popped and

startled me enough to latch onto Dylan earlier. No matter how excited I'd been when he wanted to exchange numbers, there was no chance in hell I'd fool around with a married man.

"So, Lana. Since you're psychic and all," Todd said, "can you guess what I'm going to ask you next?"

I focused my attention back on Todd and played along. And it did actually make me feel a little less disappointed.

3

DYLAN

I glanced from Todd's happy face to Lana's. He was chattering away next to her, turning on the charm like he did with everyone, especially beautiful women.

I shook my head, pushing down the jealousy that was creeping up.

I liked her. I really liked her. More than I had anyone in a long time. And there she was, lighting up like a firefly for my younger brother.

I knew I'd blown it. The minute she saw my ring, she'd shut down.

"It's not really an issue right now, but I thought I should let you know," Sarah said, slipping her hand into her pocket.

She'd worked at Crystal Fountains since before my grandpa started living there. She was also the one who communicated most of the bad news to me. I liked her, but I always had to brace myself when she wanted to talk to me.

"I appreciate it, Sarah. Thanks for letting me know." I patted her shoulder, then I glanced into the dining room to look at my grandpa.

The news wasn't anything I hadn't been expecting. He'd started to sometimes forget the names of the nurses, usually when he woke up. It came back to him, but the forgetting was new.

"Well, let's get back to the party, shall we? Dave looks like he's having fun," Sarah said, laughing as she looked toward the group.

Grandpa danced in his wheelchair with a couple ladies as James stood behind, pushing and spinning him to the music. They were having a blast. While I was glad to see their fun, I couldn't ignore my lingering irritation watching Todd and Lana.

Taking a deep breath, I made my way back to rejoin the celebration. Before I could reach them, Mrs. Mills wheeled up to me and stopped me to tell me what a good grandson I was, always coming to visit my grandpa. Then Mrs. Jameson walked over and joined her.

We'd had the same conversation a hundred times before. But Mrs. Mills rarely got visitors, despite having a large family. I didn't have the heart to cut her short. So I let her say the same things she always said to me. I held her hand when she took mine. I gave her the time she clearly needed.

But I couldn't help glancing over at Todd and Lana while I listened.

He kept laughing, leaning in close, touching her arm.

God damn it. Worse than that, Lana was giving those same vibes back to him, making it pretty clear she was interested.

If only I'd taken my damn ring off. That could be me.

"You take care now, honey," Mrs. Mills said, squeezing my hand.

"You too, ma'am." I took Mrs. Jameson's hand quickly too, then I headed toward Todd and Lana.

Hell, maybe I had it all wrong.

Maybe her attention would have turned from me to Todd the minute he walked in no matter what. They seemed to be hitting it off, so maybe she'd have liked him better anyway.

Then Lana looked at me over Todd's shoulder, and I thought maybe I was wrong.

I stood there while Todd flirted in front of me, and I tried to pretend to be more interested in everything else. I shook my head when Todd asked if there was a problem.

I talked to Grandpa for a little while, then chatted with James, all the while listening to Todd putting the moves on Lana.

Todd laughed at something Lana said, touching her arm lightly as he responded.

"That's crazy! You really told your boss off like that? I wish I could have seen his face," Todd said.

Lana laughed, clearly enjoying her conversation with Todd.

"Well, someone had to stand up to him. He was being a complete jerk."

"I love that you're not afraid to speak your mind," Todd said, gazing into her eyes. "Beautiful and strong."

"Oh stop," Lana scoffed, a sweet blush creeping up her cheeks.

"Just telling the truth," Todd winked. "You'll have to tell me more about it over dinner sometime."

She paused, looking unsure of how to respond. "Um yeah, that sounds like fun," Lana said.

"Great, it's a date then." She opened her mouth to say

something, but Todd continued on. "I know this amazing Italian place downtown. Best lasagna you've ever tasted."

"I love Italian," Lana said. Todd grinned, knowing he had closed the deal.

"Me too," Todd lied smoothly.

I rolled my eyes.

Todd was more of a sushi type of guy.

But he probably sensed Lana was more of an Italian kind of girl. He was good at reading people. Part of what made him a top salesman at his job.

I couldn't listen to this bullshit anymore. I turned my attention to Grandpa, trying to focus on anything but Todd and Lana.

I didn't have another moment alone with her. I had little choice but to decide that maybe it was for the best.

Lana might have been the kind of distraction I didn't need.

She clearly liked Todd. And I still wasn't officially divorced. Telling her I was in the middle of one might not have changed anything. She could still have walked away. I was technically married, and that alone could have turned her off.

But it was damn hard to stop looking at her and wishing things were different.

Later, I talked to a couple of the residents for a few minutes. When I turned around, Lana was gone.

She'd left without even saying goodbye to me.

If I needed confirmation that she was no longer interested, there it was.

Todd approached me with that shit-eating grin of his plastered across his face.

"Hey, brother," he greeted, his voice laced with smug satisfaction. "I got her number."

He waved his phone. I wanted to slap it out of his hand.

"Just debating whether to call her tonight or tomorrow. I don't want to seem desperate, but I cannot wait to take her out."

I clenched my jaw muscles, trying not to blurt that I'd gotten her number too. First.

"That's great," I said flatly, not meaning a word of it.

"Lana said to say that it was nice meeting you," Todd said, sipping his punch.

"That all she said?"

He looked up, like he was trying hard to remember.

"Oh yeah. She said it would be nice to meet your wife next time." He waved his hand playfully. "Something like that," he said with a snort. Then he smoothed his tie down with his hand. "She's really something, huh?"

"Yeah. Seems to be," I grumbled, taking a drink. "You didn't tell her I was in the middle of a divorce?"

"Nah, didn't feel like it was my place or story to tell. And Grandpa was there. You didn't tell him yet, right?"

I sighed and nodded. That would have to be a conversation for another visit.

"What did the nurse want to talk to you about earlier?" Todd looked at our grandpa. "Anything wrong?"

"Getting a little more forgetful, that's all. You should come see him more often. Before things get worse." I started picking up empty cups and plates from the tables to distract myself.

Todd joined me. "Yeah, I will. So do you think I should take Lana to dinner and a movie, or come up with a more unique first date? The zoo. Or a picnic in the park. Maybe paintball."

He was talking to himself more at the end than me, and I was fucking glad he didn't expect an answer.

The last thing I wanted to do was give him advice on how to impress Lana. Not when I was still kicking myself for missing out on my chance.

4

LANA

THREE MONTHS LATER

Todd and I pulled into the parking lot of the senior home, and I noticed Dylan's car was there. We were going to take our grandfathers to the park to have lunch and sit outside in the fresh air for a while.

In the three months since Dave's birthday, his memory problems had gotten slowly but steadily worse. My grandpa's memory wasn't so great either, and Dave's slowly declining health was hard for him too. We thought the outing would do them both some good.

"I didn't know Dylan was coming today," I said, my brows dipping in a slight frown.

"Didn't I mention that?" Todd said. "It was his idea, actually."

No, he hadn't mentioned that. Had I known, I would've made different arrangements to take Grandpa on his outing.

I really didn't want to spend the entire day dodging Dylan. It was going to be awkward as hell.

Todd had called before I'd even made it home from his grandfather's party. I thought maybe we could hang out casually. He seemed like someone I could be friends with. He had an endearing goofiness about him that made me laugh.

We saw each other a few times over the first couple weeks, then we started hanging out almost every day after that.

Even though Todd was handsome, charming, and obviously a great catch, I didn't feel the connection with him like I had with Dylan. Not at first, anyway. But the more we hung out and as I got to know him better, we connected in a different way. He was sweet and fun to be around. We always had a good time together. Sure, he was a little flaky and irresponsible at times, but he obviously had a good heart.

Todd was quickly becoming someone important to me, but I wasn't sure if he was the one. We were still getting to know each other.

When I got out and joined Todd, he put his arm around me and kissed my temple.

As we walked toward the doors, I spotted Dylan through the glass. He looked like he was brooding, worrying about something, maybe even angry.

I'd seen Dylan a few times since I'd been dating Todd, but only in passing. We'd never really had any time alone without Todd or one of our grandfathers nearby.

Not that I had anything to say to him after the day we'd met. In fact, I hoped I wouldn't ever have to see him again.

It just made things more awkward with Todd. I never told him about how I'd given Dylan my phone number.

Telling Todd that his brother was a cheater and a liar

wasn't a path I wanted to go down. I decided it was simply better to avoid the topic altogether.

But every time I did see Dylan, I felt the undeniable pull that I'd felt the day we'd met. I thought maybe he felt it too, judging from the way he'd stare at me.

It was ridiculous. He was married. And I was with Todd.

Even from across the room, his presence affected me in a way that no other man ever had. I didn't want to feel it because it was usually followed by a wave of guilt right after. I should feel this way about my boyfriend, shouldn't I?

Twenty minutes later, we were at the park near the lake where several ducks swam around, oblivious to all the people watching them.

Grandpa and Dave sat at a picnic table near a few benches, with my grandpa complaining loudly about being so hungry he might have to catch a duck and build a campfire to cook it.

I laughed and kissed the top of his head. "Spare the ducks, Grandpa. We're going to get lunch right there." I pointed at a nearby food truck. "Let me know what you want, and I'll go get it now."

"I'll come with to help carry," Dylan said, falling into step next to me as I headed off with the food order.

I looked around for Todd, hoping he would come instead so that I didn't have to be alone with Dylan.

I spotted Todd off in the distance, talking on his phone. Again. He'd been distracted lately, always walking away to take calls or respond to texts.

"You don't have to," I said curtly, hoping he'd take the hint.

"I don't mind," Dylan replied with a soft smile that made my stomach flutter. I hated that my body reacted to him that way.

"Thanks," I said, a little awkwardly before heading to the food trucks.

Just having him walk next to me reminded me of the day we'd met, standing so close between our cars.

The physical pull was unmistakable. I wondered if he felt it too. And somehow, he'd only gotten better looking in the last few months, though he looked a little tired around the eyes.

After placing the order, Dylan and I sat on a nearby bench to wait. He put his hand on his thigh—a thigh that looked amazing in the faded denim jeans he wore—and I had to stare at it for a minute before I realized what was hitting me wrong.

He wasn't wearing his wedding ring. His finger still showed where it had been, the skin slightly paler, as if he'd only taken it off recently.

Dylan noticed me looking at his hand and lifted it, slowly moving his fingers as he stared at it.

"I wonder when that mark will go away?" he said with a soft laugh. "I guess five years is a long time to be hidden from the sun." He rubbed the paler ring of skin, like he was trying to wipe away the difference.

"Five years, huh?" I said, feeling numb.

I'd never asked Todd about Dylan's wife, and he'd never offered any information.

"Yeah. The divorce will be final before we hit six," he said, his voice low.

Oh. Divorce.

"What happened?" I asked, my mind swirling.

He sighed. "It was a long time coming." Then he met my gaze. "The divorce was already in motion three months ago, when we met. I just hadn't taken my ring off yet."

My stomach knotted, and my chest felt tight.

He was getting a divorce when we met? Would it have mattered if he had told me that day? I wasn't sure.

Divorces were messy and ugly. I saw it firsthand with my parents. My dad had cheated on my mom several times before she finally filed for divorce. He always apologized, begged, told her he would change. She'd given him enough chances, and he failed her every time. I was little, but I remember the arguments and how sad my mom had been.

I wasn't sure if could see myself dating a man who had yet to finalize his divorce. But at least I would've known that he wasn't trying to pull one over on me. Here I was all this time, thinking he was some cheating asshole.

"Todd really seems crazy about you," he said, interrupting my thought. "And vice-versa."

I didn't know what to say to that. I was still reeling from the fact that Dylan was going through a divorce when we met.

And now he was talking about his brother's feelings for me.

"Todd's a great guy," I said, forcing a smile.

Dylan nodded, his gaze assessing me.

"So things are going well?" He narrowed his eyes, and I tried not to show how much his dark eyes affected me. Was it my imagination, or did he look like he was hoping I'd say no?

My mind was racing. How were things with Todd? They were good, weren't they?

"Pretty well, I guess." I tried to smile and hoped it didn't look as false as it felt. "He's a lot of fun."

"That he is," Dylan said, and it didn't sound like approval. "Lots of fun."

Todd's voice rang out, interrupting our conversation.

"There you guys are! Let's eat over by the pond." He

waved us over impatiently. Dylan held my gaze a moment longer before getting up to grab the food and drinks.

I followed, my heart pounding in my chest. I couldn't shake off the feeling of guilt or the attraction I had for Dylan.

We settled on the grass to eat. When Dylan casually sat beside me, my skin prickled with awareness of how close he was.

I tried to focus on my food, nodding along to the conversation flowing around me.

"You okay? You seem quiet," Todd said, jolting me from my thoughts.

"Hmm? Oh, I'm fine," I said too brightly. "Just spacing out, I guess."

I avoided looking at Dylan, though I could feel his eyes on me. Todd frowned slightly but let it go, turning back to the others.

Being around Dylan felt like playing with fire, especially now that I knew the truth. But it was impossible to resist the flame drawing me closer, no matter how I tried to fight it. I couldn't help but wonder what it would be like between me and Dylan, had things played out differently that day we'd met.

After the conversation with Dylan in the park, I tried to act normal as we spent the rest of the afternoon sightseeing downtown.

Our grandfathers wanted to do a little shopping, so we got Dave's wheelchair out of the trunk and leisurely walked down the street in the main business district.

The sidewalks had a steady stream of people as we strolled through the city. It was a pleasant day, so plenty of people were out enjoying the nice weather.

A few different people stopped to talk to Todd, keeping

him behind while we kept walking. He was a master networker, always looking for the next big opportunity, so he was often running into somebody he knew.

Once, he disappeared for twenty minutes and caught up with us later. The Mercedes dealership was trying to lure him away from Audi, he said, because he pulled such high numbers on a monthly basis.

As he talked about that, Dylan nodded and said some encouraging things. But when he kept talking about it and about how much more money he could make, Dylan looked at me and rolled his eyes.

We both laughed softly and tried to pretend we were amused about something else.

Todd stopped to talk to someone again and waved us on. I gave up on the idea that he'd be actually spending time with us.

I tried not to let my irritation show. This was a day for Grandpa and Dave to enjoy and I wouldn't let it dampen the mood.

Todd had done his own thing all day. I also noticed that Dylan hadn't left my side. And I didn't miss how every time Todd got close to me or showed me some attention, Dylan got quiet, sometimes even glaring at him.

Dylan fell into step beside me, hands tucked casually in his pockets.

"Gorgeous today," he commented.

I snuck a glance in his direction to see him gazing at me.

He cleared his throat, "It's a nice day for walking around."

I felt my face heat up as I nodded. "Yeah, perfect day for exploring the city," I managed to reply breezily.

I admired his broad shoulders and the way his shirt clung to his muscular frame.

Stop ogling him. You're with Todd.

As we squeezed past the large tour group getting out of a bus, Dylan gently nudged me towards the buildings, away from the busy street. His arm brushed against my back, and my body shuddered at the touch.

Before I knew it, he was walking on the street side while I was closer to the buildings, shielded from the traffic.

I glanced up at him, but he just continued chatting casually with his broad frame angled slightly towards me. Though he didn't stand quite as close to me as he had the day we'd met.

It was a simple gesture, but I appreciated how thoughtful he was without making a big show of it. I couldn't remember the last time a man had taken such care to make sure I felt safe.

He was still carrying the bag of things my grandpa bought at the drugstore after taking it from my hand when I needed to retie my shoe. I'd gone to take it back, but he'd waved me off.

He kept stepping up in little ways when Todd didn't even seem to notice. Or care. The difference between them was painfully obvious.

Two brothers couldn't be any more different than they were. I'd been right in my first impressions of both of them. Dylan was the storm to Todd's sunshiny day. The steady rock to Todd's airy, fluffy clouds.

And I felt so guilty for wanting the brother who seemed intent on quietly caring for me in all the small ways that mattered. I missed how carefree and uninhibited Dylan had been the day of the party. How he stood close to me and leaned in. How he smiled at me and joked around.

Now, he was so different. Reserved. Distant. Like he was holding back and putting a barrier between us. As he should be. I was his brother's girlfriend. I should be wanting him to do that, right?

We approached a new art gallery my grandpa wanted to go into. After Grandpa pushed Dave into the gallery, Dylan held the door for me to walk in.

"More of that chivalry, huh?" I said. "You can't blame it on my hands being full this time."

"You caught me," he said with a broad smile as I walked through the doorway and glanced back at him.

It reminded me of the last time he had held the door open for me.

Stop it. What the hell was wrong with me?

Later, when we were going through the gallery, Todd finally joined us. Dave needed to use the bathroom, so Todd and Dylan went with him in case he needed help getting out of his wheelchair.

For the first time, Grandpa and I were alone, looking at a sculpture of something . . . lumpy.

"What is that supposed to be?" he asked, squinting at the title card.

I read it out loud. "Deconstruction of Emotional Resistance."

"What the *hell*?" he said softly, the pitch going up at the end. I laughed a little too loudly, but his sentiment matching mine perfectly caught me off guard.

"I have no idea, Grandpa."

"It's no God damn statue of David, that's for sure," he whispered, and we both laughed again. He took my hand and held it as we slowly walked through more impenetrable works of art.

"Lana, it's fun watching both your admirers trying to impress you." His tone was playful, but his eyes were serious.

I scoffed. "What? You know I'm dating Todd, right?"

"I know. And he's buzzing around like a bee, hoping you'll notice how popular and in-demand he is."

Was that what he was doing? I was starting to think he was just self-absorbed and being rude. But I wasn't going to say that out loud.

"He's a busy guy," I said instead.

"Maybe he doesn't realize that his brother's picking up the slack for him, doing all the things he should be doing." Grandpa smiled at me, then squinted at a painting that was, unbelievably, all one color. "It's amusing to watch. Except it's not that fun to see Dylan so moody sometimes. Especially when he thinks Todd is neglecting you."

"You must be really bored to be coming up with such tall tales," I said, teasing him. "They're just brothers, and you know how brothers are. Nothing more to it than that."

He looked at me skeptically and said, "I know there's no rivalry quite like the one you can have with a brother." Then he squeezed my hand and raised his eyebrows. "But Dave and I both wonder if you're with the wrong one."

The guys came back, saving me from having to say anything. Todd wrapped his arms around my waist and kissed me on the cheek. I smiled up at him and then caught Dylan glaring as I looked back.

5

DYLAN

Todd walked up to Lana and put his arms around her from behind. And I wanted to drop him like a rock.

He'd been on his damn phone nearly the entire day. I was close to snatching it out of his hand and throwing it in the nearest trashcan. We started making our way through the museum when I saw him make another call.

"Can you get off the damn phone for five seconds?" I glared at Todd and crossed my arms. "You can't possibly be selling cars over a call."

He shushed me and turned his back to finish his conversation while Lana was talking about a wire sculpture with our grandfathers.

"I'm not selling cars," Todd finally said when he hung up. "I have other business deals to worry about, you know."

I gritted my teeth. "Yeah? So that was *your dealer*?"

"Lay off it, Dylan," he spat out, glaring at me.

Todd had always been a heavy drinker and a casual drug user. He smoked pot, which didn't really bother me. It had never really interfered with his life.

But when he did coke, he became a real asshole and

started letting things slip. I wondered if he'd gotten back into that. Or something worse.

There was a time when he got trashed every night to the point of unconsciousness, not remembering what he did or how he got home.

By some miracle, he was able to get clean and his life back on track. He was doing really well for a while, but I worried that he was back to his old habits again.

"You're here to spend time with Grandpa. You haven't said more than two words to him all day," I snapped. "Not to mention you've been completely ignoring Lana."

Todd frowned as he glanced over at Lana, his jaw ticking. "She's fine Dylan. Mind your damn business."

I took a deep breath and turned away to look at the art, trying to calm myself down.

When I turned to him, he had an arm around Lana's waist. And he checked his phone five times in the course of a few minutes.

"That's the ugliest thing I've ever seen," Grandpa said about an abstract painting all in browns and blacks. I had to agree with him.

Todd tried to explain its artistic merit, like he fucking knew anything about art. He sounded like a know-it-all, and the look on Lana's face made it clear she thought the same thing.

Then Todd kissed her, and all I wanted to do was get between them to make sure that didn't happen again.

I'd fully intended to take my grandpa back to the senior center after he got tired. I had a meeting with Brent a little later, but I'd given myself time to make an afternoon of this outing.

I wasn't going to make it. Being around Todd and Lana together was driving me fucking crazy.

I had to get the hell out of there.

When Todd ignored her, it pissed me off. When he paid attention to her, I wanted to yank him away. The only thing that made it enjoyable, aside from seeing Grandpa enjoying himself, was being near Lana.

If Todd hadn't been there, I could have pretended they weren't together. I might have made it through the day that way.

"I need to meet Brent at the bar, but I had a great time, Grandpa," I said, giving him a hug. It felt like shit to leave early, but it was better than staying there watching Todd kiss Lana. The guilt of leaving was better than that, by a mile.

"Can you get him settled?" I asked Todd, who was already on his phone.

Todd nodded but held his finger to his lips so I wouldn't interrupt his conversation. Probably his drug dealer again. I wanted to slap the phone right out of his hand, but I bit my lip and turned to Lana instead.

"It was great to see you again." I put my hand on her shoulder, realizing I hadn't thought about what she might need. "Do you need any help getting James back and settled?"

It might have been wishful thinking on my part, but I thought she looked disappointed. "No, I've got it. You go on to your meeting."

"It can wait, if you need some help." Damn it, why didn't I ask before I said I had to go? "A few minutes won't matter."

"I'm fine. But thanks. And Todd's here." She took a deep breath and let it out in a rush. I think she knew Todd might as well not have even been there. She gave me her sweet little smile. "Really great to see you too."

I walked to my car, pissed at myself. But mostly pissed at

Falling For My Ex's Brother 43

Todd because it seemed like he didn't appreciate how lucky he was to have a woman like Lana.

∼

"What do you think?" Brent asked, pushing some glossy photographs toward me, then combing his fingers into his beard. "I know it doesn't look like much, but this would be the taproom, and this could be a place for merchandising, where we sell T-shirts, can cozies, keychains, that type of thing."

We sat at my bar, Brent with his file folder of photos and documents spread out in front of him. He'd taken photos of a property that he thought would be perfect for the brewery we'd been talking about opening for months.

"Looks promising," I said, wishing my heart was actually in the conversation.

But I couldn't stop thinking about Lana and how good she'd looked in the park. How great it had felt to be near her again.

How pissed I was that Todd was dating her.

It should have been me.

Fingers snapped in front of my face, startling me back to the present moment. "Yo, Dylan. Am I losing you?" Brent asked with a laugh.

"Sorry man. Been a long day."

"Clearly. How's he doing?" Brent asked.

He obviously thought it had been long because of my grandpa. I'd known Brent most of my life, and I'd told him about Grandpa's slowly failing memory. He'd even gone with me a couple of times to visit.

"About as you'd expect. Really good spirits though. He

was fine." I took a long drink of beer and sighed. "Todd and his—his girlfriend were there too. And her grandpa."

Brent nodded knowingly. I hadn't really told him about Lana. But he knew Todd almost as well as he knew me. "He showing his ass?" Brent said with a smirk.

I shrugged. "Isn't that what little brothers do? Let me see those other pictures again."

I shuffled through the photographs, wanting to change the subject and get my mind off Todd and Lana. Unfortunately, another subject I didn't want to talk about came up.

"How soon do you think it'll be before the divorce is final?" Brent asked. "Not to push or anything. I know it sucks. But I also know you can't really invest in this until you know how the numbers are going to come out."

I raked my fingers through my hair. "I'd really hoped I wouldn't have to sell this bar, but my wife's lawyer is apparently more skilled than mine."

We both had a bitter laugh about that. Brent had been divorced for a year. He knew what it was like to get raked over the coals.

"Until the sale's in-progress, probably with a final offer on the table, I don't really know what I have to play with. I can't pin my banker down until I know where I'll stand. I know I can get the financing, just not how much."

We talked a little more about my financial situation. Then a text came in from Todd.

> Thanks for helping us get them back to the nursing home, bro. Appreciate it.

"You cheeky little shit," I grumbled, then I showed Brent when he raised an eyebrow. "He got on my last nerve today."

I texted back.

> I told you I was leaving. You could have said something if you could pry the phone away from your ear for two seconds.

Brent and I started talking again until a text came back from Todd.

> We should do this again in a week or two.

Watch him alternately ignore Lana and then hang all over her? I didn't fucking think so.

> We'll see.

And I left it at that.

As long as they were dating, I thought I was probably going to have to stay away from them. An outing with one of them and our grandpas would be okay, as long as they didn't talk about each other the whole time.

But I wasn't sure I could trust myself alone with Lana. It had been hard enough not to confess my feelings at the damn food truck when she noticed my missing ring.

"God, I'm going to miss this place," Brent said suddenly, looking up at the ceiling. "I mean, it'll still be here, but it won't be the same if it's not in your family. Are you going to tell Dave?"

"I already did. He understands." When I'd inherited the bar from my grandpa, he'd insisted that I keep him up to date on what was happening all the time. It had been his pride and joy, a business he'd built from the ground up. But the older he got, the less interest he had in knowing the details. It had gone from his main purpose in life to something from his past. "He agreed it was a shame, but that you had to do what you had to do."

"I'm glad he's taking it that well." Brent raised his glass. "To The Cliffside Bar. I hope whoever the new owners are, they keep the place classy."

I toasted to that and hoped the same.

"Hey, when it sells, we should have a party. A big send-off, you know? The regulars would love that."

I agreed. And as much as I knew I needed to stay away from Lana, I'd love to have her there. To see the bar that Grandpa and I had worked so hard on and really turned into something great.

Damn it, she's not yours.

My short happiness about the party soured as I imagined Todd there too, drinking more than he should and kissing the girl that should have been mine.

6

LANA

I checked my phone for the tenth time. Todd should have been there to pick me up thirty minutes earlier, when I ended my shift and closed up the diner for the night. I tried his number again, but it went to voicemail after several rings.

A gust of wind blew rain into my face.

"Damn it!" I moved to stand closer against the building, but the small awning didn't help when the wind seemed to blow in every direction.

If the weather got much worse, I was going to unlock the diner and go inside to wait.

I called and got his voicemail again. "If this is your way of punishing me, Todd, it's childish. You shouldn't offer to pick me up if you're not going to be here."

With a huff, I hung up. We had a fight the other day over him partying too much lately. I thought we were ok after making up but maybe I was wrong.

Or had something happened to him? Maybe he got in a car accident on his way over. I suddenly felt a pang of regret for leaving him that message.

The wind picked up even more, and the rain beat down harder. I dialed Todd one more time. Please pick up.

"Lana?" The deep, gruff voice made my breath catch.

"Dylan? Where's Todd? Is something wrong?" All the worst-case scenarios that would cause Dylan to answer his brother's phone ran through my mind.

"He's right here, Lana. He's fine. Just...sleeping." Annoyance came through clearly in Dylan's voice. I had a feeling he meant to say 'passed out'. "It's late. Is everything ok?"

"Um, yeah I guess so. I got off work half an hour ago, and he was supposed to pick me up. I'm—"

"You're at the diner? You're not outside alone, are you?"

"Yeah, I've been out here figuring he'd show up any minute." I swallowed hard, the roughness in Dylan's voice doing things to my insides.

"I'm on my way," he said.

"What?"

"It's at 4th and Vine, right? Uptown? I'm coming to get you. But go inside while you wait. I don't want you out there this late at night by yourself." Something slammed, maybe his door, then I heard an engine rumble to life. "It's going to take some time in this weather."

"You don't have to do that, I can grab a cab..."

"I'm on my way," he said. "Go on inside and lock the doors."

"Okay," I said, but I thought he'd already hung up. The storm only got worse, so I took his advice and unlocked the door to step inside. I'd see him pull up through the glass front of the building, and it was a lot dryer and warmer in there.

The tension that had run through me at Todd not showing up was gone. It was like the uncertainty of not knowing where he was had been replaced by the certainty that Dylan was coming. I had a feeling he did the things he said he'd do, unlike his brother.

I immediately felt guilty about how excited I was to see Dylan. To see him alone again.

Then I crushed that guilt into a little ball and threw it away.

It was Todd's fault that it was happening at all, so I tried not to feel too bad about it.

Headlights appeared, and a rush of relief mixed with excitement flowed through me. I went outside and was about to lock the door behind me when the wind whipped up so hard that it pushed me into the building.

Suddenly, Dylan's large body enveloped mine from behind and shielded me from the wind.

"Go back inside!" Dylan said, pulling the door open and guiding me through the doorway.

"Holy—" A trash can slammed into the glass of the diner and disappeared. The rain and wind made it impossible to see beyond the sidewalk. "I've never seen wind like this," I said.

"Me neither. Let's get away from the glass until this passes." He pulled me away from the windows and toward the back of the diner.

A large broken branch slammed against the door, so we hurried into the back.

The storeroom didn't have tables or chairs, but there was a very short bench along one wall barely big enough for two people. I turned on the light, and we sat.

I shivered at the contact with the cold bench.

"Here." He slipped off his burgundy hoodie, holding it out for me.

"Oh no, that's ok..." I started saying as I waved him off,

but he gave me a look that said he wouldn't take no for an answer.

He wrapped it around my shoulders and tugged the front closed. His warmth and masculine scent surrounded me, and I found myself pulling it tighter around my body, getting lost in his presence. It was the closest I'd ever get to feeling him.

"Thanks," I said with a small smile.

The storm raged on outside, but inside the diner, it was almost peaceful. We sat in silence, listening to the rain falling against the roof and walls of the diner.

Then the light started flickering, threatening to go off.

DYLAN

"I didn't think Oregon had tornadoes," she said, looking at the lights.

"It's pretty rare. This probably isn't one, just a storm." Lana looked worried. "Don't be nervous. We'll be okay."

Then I patted her hand, which was a mistake. I needed to remind myself not to touch her, because it only made me want to keep touching her.

I wasn't worried about the storm as much as I was of sitting that close to Lana. It'd be hard not to give my feelings away. Not when she was this close. Just the two of us.

God, I wanted her.

"I'm sorry he left you stranded like that," I said. "Makes me want to kick his ass when he wakes up."

"Makes me want that too," she said with a soft laugh, and then looked at her hands. Her smile faded. "As long as he's safe. I was getting worried."

"He's safe at home," I said, squeezing her hand. There I went, putting my hand on her again.

"Was he out again tonight? He's been going out a lot more than usual," Lana said.

"Yeah, I've noticed that too."

"Do you think everything's ok with him?" she asked, concern filling her eyes.

"I don't know," I answered honestly, shaking my head.

I wondered how much she knew about Todd's history. I didn't want to scare her, but I also didn't want her to be blindsided.

"I hope so. He's been doing really well for a while now."

"Oh...was there a time when he wasn't?" She asked, eyebrows drawn together.

I nodded. "There was. When he was younger. And then he got his act together." I paused, debating whether or not to tell her the whole story. I felt like I should explain Todd's behavior. Not that I was making excuses for him, but I wanted her to at least know why he did the things he did. "It wasn't easy for him growing up without our parents."

She looked down, nodding. "He doesn't talk about them. I only know that they both died when he was young. I know it's been hard for him."

"Todd was only three when Mom died," I began.

Lana gave me a sympathetic look. "I'm so sorry," she said.

"I remember the day our parents told me mom's cancer returned. Mom fought hard but eventually..." I trailed off, not wanting to relive the painful memory.

"It must have been tough for you too," Lana said softly.

I shrugged. "It was. But I was older. I had some memories of her. Todd barely knew her."

I gave her a sad smile. "Dad did his best to raise us. He was always working, doing the best he could for us."

Lana stayed silent, listening intently.

I took a shaky breath. "Then Dad got in a car accident. He was gone by the time help arrived."

Lana reached over and squeezed my hand, then let go slowly.

"I can't imagine growing up without parents," Lana said, shaking her head.

"It was rough. It sent Todd over the edge. He started acting out, getting into trouble. I tried to keep him on the straight and narrow after I dropped out of college. But I was working all the time at Grandpa's bar. I didn't see what was happening to Todd. He fell in with the wrong crowd. Started getting into alcohol and drugs."

"You did the best you could."

I shook my head. "Maybe, but it wasn't enough. I feel like I failed Todd."

"Don't be so hard on yourself," Lana said gently. "And he turned out okay. He's doing better now, right?"

I sighed. "Yeah, he was able to get his life back on track. It just worries me when I start seeing the same behavior again. I hope he has it under control."

Lana nodded. "You're a good big brother. Todd is lucky to have you."

"He's lucky to have you too," I said softly, wishing that it was me instead of Todd who had Lana by his side. "Sorry, I didn't mean to get all heavy on you."

"It's okay," Lana said with a small smile. "I'm glad you felt comfortable enough to share that with me."

I cleared my throat. "Are things going ok with you guys?"

She blinked fast. Nodded. Swallowed hard. "Things have been a little up and down, but that's normal right? Todd's a good guy."

"Yeah, he is. When he wants to be."

Lana flashed me a tight smile. She straightened and wrapped her arms around herself as she let out a deep breath.

"Enough about Todd. So what about your folks? Are they around here?" I asked.

She shook her head softly. "No, my mom passed away a few years ago," she said with a sad look. "Stroke. And my dad left us when I was little. We don't really keep in touch."

I remained quiet, unsure of how to respond. Our eyes met in silent understanding. Neither of our experiences had been easy. I offered a small smile.

She sighed and continued, "So it's just me and Grandpa. I wish he had more visitors, but it's just me. I try to go see him as much as I can." Then she smiled at me warmly. "I'm glad he has Dave. It's nice that they have each other."

"Yeah, those two are trouble when they're together," I chuckled, hoping to lighten the mood. "James is quite the wingman. Can you imagine if they were friends in their younger days?"

"The ladies wouldn't have stood a chance," she smiled, her eyes sparkling. "Didn't know Dave was so popular with the ladies. I hope you took notes."

"Notes?" I scoffed playfully. "Please. Who needs notes when you have hands-on experience. I worked with the man in a bar for ten years. Taught me all his best moves."

"Oh, so that's where you learned all those smooth pickup lines."

I clutched my chest, feigning hurt. "How dare you? That was some of my best material."

She let out a sweet laugh, and I wanted to hear more of it. I caught myself getting lost in her smile. Before my brain could catch up with my heart, my hand was tucking that stray lock of hair behind her ear.

I mentally kicked myself as she stiffened at my touch.

Stop touching her.

"How have you been?" she asked, clearing her throat pointedly.

A sweet blush spilled across her cheeks, tempting me to feel the warmth under my fingers.

I rubbed the back of my neck instead.

"Good, I guess. Busy," I said honestly. "The divorce is all but final if her lawyer would stop nitpicking everything. It's been a nightmare, and I'm ready for it to be over."

"I can't even imagine," she said. "It's so sad when people split up, especially when they can't be civil afterward."

"Oh, we're civil enough. She's just got a shark lawyer she won't say no to." I leaned my head back against the wall. "I'm not even mad at her anymore. I just want the whole thing behind me."

Lana was looking at me with surprise, so I shrugged. "We got married too young. I was twenty-four, and she was only twenty-one. So when things started going south, I guess she wasn't mature enough to deal with it. And she cheated. It upset me at first, but then I realized I didn't even care that much. It had been over in my heart for a long time anyway."

Lana shook her head. "Wait, she cheated on *you*?"

"Wonders never cease, huh?"

I had to laugh at her baffled expression. A moment of silence stretched between us.

Then she sighed heavily and rested her head on my shoulder. I wanted nothing more than to wrap my arms around her.

Lana snapped her head up, like she'd done something wrong. "Sorry."

"It's okay. Rest. You look like you've had a long day." I held my breath until her temple touched my shoulder again.

"I am really tired. I've been taking extra shifts, trying to cashflow my way through this last semester and keep my student loans from getting out of hand. I did a double shift yesterday, and one this morning too. Just need a good night's rest." She inhaled deeply and relaxed against me a little more.

After a few minutes, Lana's breathing was deep and steady. She'd fallen asleep. I leaned my head against hers, inhaling the flowery scent of her hair.

Lana stirred slightly, murmuring something softly. I instinctively put my arms around her and she nuzzled against my chest.

"I regret not calling you," I whispered, knowing she couldn't hear me. "Explaining the ring. I regret that so fucking much."

Todd didn't deserve Lana. And if I'd had any idea that he might treat her this way, I wouldn't have held my tongue. I'd have made a move early on.

I should never have let the fact that he was my brother stand in my way.

Lana's phone vibrated. She opened her eyes and realized she'd fallen asleep on my shoulder.

She straightened with a deep sniff and looked at her phone. It chimed with a voicemail and she played it on speakerphone.

"Sorry about that, Lana," Todd said, slurring like he was still drunk. "I'll leave right now and come get you."

I quickly dialed Todd before he had a chance to do anything stupid. "I picked her up and I'm taking her home. Don't you dare get behind the wheel, Todd."

Todd argued but eventually gave in.

I listened closely and no longer heard the wind howling, so I opened the storeroom door and went as far as the front counter. It was still raining and a little windy, but the worst of it seemed to have passed.

Lana turned to me. "Thanks for coming to get me. And being such a good pillow."

"I don't mind," I said softly. "You clearly needed it."

"Oh here," she said, slipping out of my hoodie.

I pulled it back around her. "Keep it on."

I put my hands on her shoulders and gazed into her eyes. I wanted so badly in that moment to kiss her, to tell her how I really felt. How much I wished I hadn't let her slip away that day. And I thought I saw the same sentiment reflected in her eyes.

Thunder boomed, and that made it easier to back away.

"Come on, let's get you home," I said, pulling the hood over her head.

As much as it pained me, I had to respect her relationship with Todd until she ended things herself. Anything between us before that point would be a betrayal I couldn't live with.

So for now, I could only savor these stolen moments of closeness, as tempting as Lana was.

Tonight, simply being next to her felt like enough.

7

DYLAN

I looked around my bar, taking it all in one last time. I was finally selling this place. My divorce had drained my finances, and the settlement required I sell my most valuable asset. This bar.

This place held so many memories, both good and bad.

But it was time to move on. I needed a fresh start.

I stood behind the bar and drew a beer for one of the longtime regulars.

"Here you go, Chuck. Thanks for coming."

"It's the end of an era. I'm sure going to miss you guys," he said, raising his glass to me.

I rarely ever bartended, but since this was the final night I would actually own the place, I personally gave some of the longtime customers their drinks. And the first two drinks were on the house, so we had a pretty good going-away crowd.

I drew a beer for another customer and saw Lana and James come in the door. Todd hopped up from the table where he sat with Grandpa and went to greet her.

I looked away as he kissed her. Otherwise, I wasn't sure I

could stop myself from throwing a beer bottle at Todd's head.

James sat at the table next to Grandpa, and Todd sat again too. But Lana walked up to the bar with a bright smile. My pulse quickened.

"Hey. Barkeep!" she said, smacking her fist down onto the wood. "Line 'em up!"

I smiled and said, "Your gramps actually wants a beer?"

"Yep. So make that two." She grinned and held up two fingers in a V.

"What kind?"

"Whatever's on tap is fine." Lana leaned on the bar as I poured beer into two glasses. "Are you doing ok? Todd said you weren't thrilled about having to sell the place."

I sighed heavily, both that Todd talked to her about me, and because no, I wasn't.

I shrugged. "No, but some things can't be helped. I've accepted it. Ready to move on. It's good to see everyone. I wanted to celebrate this place one last time, you know? It deserves a big sendoff."

Lana smiled warmly, and I felt myself letting down my guard. I couldn't help it. When she looked at me like that, I forgot all the reasons I needed to keep my distance.

Todd appeared behind Lana, snaking an arm around her waist. She leaned back into him, giggling as he kissed her cheek. Jealousy simmered inside me.

"Come on, babe. Let's go sit," Todd said as he pulled her toward the table.

Lana looked at me and smiled. Such a fucking *beautiful* smile.

"I hope you won't be too busy bartending to come over and visit," she said as she pushed away from the bar.

"Nope," I said, passing her two full glasses. "Just wanted

to give some regulars a bit of personal attention. I'll be over when I can."

Fucking liar. I had no intention of sitting with them.

I had to do my best to stay away from Lana. It's been over a month since the last time I saw her at the diner. I had come dangerously close to crossing the line and saying something I knew I'd regret.

If Todd had been anybody else, I wouldn't have cared. I'd have done my damnedest to win her over and fuck how he felt.

But Todd was my little brother. And he was completely in love with her. I just couldn't hurt him by doing anything to ruin what they had going on between them.

I nodded and smiled as friends and regulars stopped by the bar to chat, but it was getting harder to focus. My eyes kept drifting to Lana's spot across the room.

The effort of staying away from her all night was slowly killing me.

I busied myself restocking glasses, trying not to stare at the woman I couldn't have.

She looked amazing tonight. The skin tight jeans she wore hugged every curve. And her hair was up in a loose bun with soft curls that framed her beautiful face.

"You're cleaning that thing enough to wear a hole in it," James chuckled as he sidled up to the bar. "What's got you so distracted tonight?"

"Just trying to get used to the fact this will be our last night here."

"Gonna miss this place, huh?" He asked.

I nodded. "Yeah, it's been good to me over the years. Time for a change though."

James gave me a knowing look. "Time to get over a certain someone too?" He inclined his head towards Lana.

I shrugged, avoiding his gaze. "What do you mean?"

"I've seen the way you look at Lana when you think no one else is watching," James said gently. "And how moony you get when she's around. Face it, son. You've got it bad for her."

Before I could respond, James held up a hand. "But I get it, she's with Todd."

I met his sympathetic gaze.

"Yeah, it's...complicated. But it doesn't matter. Nothing can happen between us." Saying the words aloud only made the situation more real.

James nodded. "For what it's worth, I've seen the way Lana looks at you sometimes too when she thinks no one is watching. Makes me wonder if the feelings aren't entirely one-sided."

He gave me a meaningful look before heading back into the party.

My eyes drifted to Lana, laughing with Todd across the room.

The sight made my chest tighten. I quickly looked away.

I couldn't avoid their table all night, though. I wouldn't, because Grandpa deserved better than that. But I could make myself scarce when Todd and Lana were there.

When the music started, Lana and Todd got up to dance, so I stopped at the table for a few minutes to visit and get Grandpa a drink.

The nurses said beer wouldn't be good for him because of his medication. He didn't know Sarah had taken me aside and said one beer wouldn't hurt anything.

I surprised him with a glass of that instead of his diet soda, and he lit up like it was Christmas.

He took a swig and let out a sigh. "Damn, that's good."

We both chuckled. "How are you holding up, kid?" Grandpa asked, giving me a pat on the back.

"I'll be fine, Pops. What about you? This place means a lot more to you than anyone," I said, looking down. My throat tightened just saying it. "I'm sorry I couldn't save it."

"Ah don't you worry about me," he brushed it off. "And don't you get down on yourself. I know you fought like hell for this bar."

I frowned down at the table. "It wasn't enough though."

Grandpa squeezed my shoulder. "There's more to life than four walls, Dylan. Like how you're doing after that hellish divorce. That lawyer really put you through the wringer."

"It was rough but it's behind me now. I'm moving on."

I glanced up to see Todd all over Lana across the room. He looked so damn happy. I should be happy for him, shouldn't I?

Grandpa followed my stare. "Good to hear you're moving forward, son. Seems like you spent your whole life making sure Todd was taken care of. Maybe it's your time focus on you for once."

I gave him a stiff smile and nodded. Lana was headed back to the table, so I got up and walked back to the bar to talk to some of the regulars instead. Todd came a moment later.

"Hey, come over to the table," he said, tugging on my arm.

"In a few minutes," I said.

"Try now," Todd said, then he pulled his hand out of his pocket and opened it, using his body to keep other people from seeing what he had.

A fucking ring box. This had to be some sort of a sick joke.

Apparently, the universe wanted to torture me today.

He was going to ask Lana to marry him.

In my fucking bar.

In *front* of me.

"Todd," I said, my tone low.

I had to stop and carefully measure my words. Because *don't you fucking dare* would have been hard to explain.

Instead, I said, "You've been dating for barely five months. Rushing it much?"

"When you know, you know," he said.

His eyes looked a little glassy, maybe from the alcohol, maybe from something stronger.

"How high are you?" I asked softly.

"Not so high that I don't know what I'm doing. High on love, how about that? Come on to the table. I want my family there. Even the assholes," he said with a wink. I shoved him with a laugh.

What else could I do? I couldn't tell him not to propose. He was my little brother but a grown man.

If he was going to do it, I sure as hell didn't want to see it.

God, it was ridiculous to be that hung up on someone I wasn't even with. But from the moment we'd met, she stuck inside me in a way no one else had.

He looked at me with big, sappy eyes, so I dropped my shoulders and followed him to the table. I stood a few feet behind Grandpa, my arms crossed.

That was as close as I was willing to get.

LANA

Aside from my few minutes at the bar, I hadn't talked to Dylan all night. I should have felt relieved. All being near Dylan did was make me feel guilty about how much I wanted him.

On the way back from the dance floor, I'd watched him get up from the table and walk away as he saw me approaching.

He was avoiding me.

And Dylan had no reason to do that unless he was trying to stay away from me for the same reasons I should have tried to avoid him.

He just had the willpower I didn't seem to have.

Knowing that made it worse. It made me wish things had been different the day we'd met. And it thrilled me like nothing else did to think that Dylan might want me too.

But as I watched woman after woman approach him, I thought maybe I was wrong. Maybe the electricity I felt between us was just one sided. Just my hopeful imagination.

A lot of women probably felt that with Dylan. So many

put their hands on his arms. He obviously knew those women and was comfortable with them.

Others, he seemed to be meeting for the first time, but he was warm and affectionate with them.

And they ate it up. Like I did.

Maybe he was kind and attentive to many of them. I wasn't special.

I wondered if Dylan was actually enjoying himself tonight or just putting on a good front.

Lost in thought, I didn't hear Todd come up behind me. He wrapped his arms around my waist, nuzzling my neck. I stiffened in surprise.

"There you are," he murmured against my skin. "What are you doing hiding back here all alone?"

I turned in his arms to face him. "Sorry, just needed a minute to breathe. It's pretty packed in here."

Todd studied my face, his brow furrowing. "Is everything okay?"

"Yeah, of course!" I said brightly. "Just overwhelmed by the crowd. I'm fine."

"Good," he said, planting a kiss on my temple. "Let's go sit at the table. I'll be right there."

Todd went to talk to Dylan, and a moment later, they walked back toward the table where I sat with Grandpa and Dave.

Dylan stood a few feet away, glaring at Todd. Then Todd moved to sit again, but as he went down, he bypassed the chair and dropped to one knee, fumbling for something in his pocket.

My heart stopped.
Oh my God. No.
NO.

I stared down at him in shock, my mouth falling open. Marriage had never even been discussed. Not even close.

I hoped he would see the unspoken answer on my face and stop before it was too late. That didn't happen.

"Lana, I know this is fast. But I know a good thing when I see it, and I don't see any point in putting this off."

"Todd," I said, shaking my head a little. "Honey—"

He opened a ring box in front of me. It was a round solitaire ringed by sapphires. It was lovely, and a huge chunk of a ring. It probably cost a few months of income, at least.

"I love you, Lana. Will you marry me?"

His smile was so sweet. I wanted to cry. The tears wouldn't be from joy, but from guilt.

"Todd ... it's—it's beautiful. But—"

"Here," he said, plucking the ring out and taking my hand to slip it on my finger.

I pulled my hand away slowly to keep him from doing that.

"We've never talked about marriage. I wish we could have discussed this first, Todd."

My face felt like it was going to start smoking any second. He hadn't made a huge spectacle of us, but some people seated nearby were watching. And waiting for my answer. And both our grandfathers watched intently.

Neither had been smiling when he got down on his knee. They didn't look happy about it. They looked ... concerned.

"Well," Todd said, clearly flustered. "I thought a surprise would be more romantic." He kept smiling. "Isn't it?"

I stammered, trying to say *no* and *maybe* and *for some people* all at the same time.

My heart ached at his hopeful look.

Get up off your knee, damn it.

The volume of the music in the bar went up suddenly, making it harder for other people to hear our discussion.

I looked to the bar. Dylan stood at the controls and had clearly been the one to turn it up. His expression was hard as he gave me a quick nod.

There he was, coming to my rescue again.

"Are you—are you saying no?" Todd asked, his nervous laughter breaking my heart just a little.

"No," I said, wrapping his hand in both of mine. "I mean, I'm just not . . . not ready for something like that. It's not no, it's . . . not yet. It's just such a big step. I'm so sorry." I squeezed his hand.

Todd looked stunned. I knew he'd seen this night unfolding very differently. Todd nodded, attempting a brave smile though his eyes were sad.

"It's okay. I clearly misread things between us," he said as he cleared his throat.

Todd laughed and shoved the ring box into his pocket. "Not the *worst* night of my life, at least."

"Todd, I'm sorry. You just caught me—"

"Everybody," Todd said loudly as he stood and held his glass of beer in his hands.

My gaze met Dylan's, and I could see he was as worried about what Todd was going to say as I was.

Todd spoke above the music. "Now that my little show's over," he said, still trying to laugh it off, "I wanted to say congratulations to my brother Dylan. I know congratulations is a strange thing to say when selling a business you didn't want to sell, but it's for the future. Congratulations on making a fresh start. Here's hoping for your success, brother."

He held his beer toward Dylan and took a big drink as most of the crowd said *hear, hear* and other nice things.

Relief washed over me. I caught Dylan staring at me with that same look of *thank god* on his face.

My grandpa reached over and put his hand over mine. He closed his eyes and nodded, telling me without speaking that I'd done the right thing.

I had. I knew it in my bones.

I'd hurt Todd even though I hadn't meant to, but saying yes just to avoid an embarrassing moment in public would have been the wrong thing.

I could feel Dylan staring at me from behind the bar, so I looked his way. He'd just watched me turn down his brother's proposal.

In the few seconds we stared at each other, I felt more desire, more heat building in my body, than I had in the months I'd been with Todd.

Dylan didn't come to the table for the rest of the party. I hadn't really expected he would.

8

DYLAN

I sighed as I saw the living room in shambles. Todd was passed out face down on the couch, still in his clothes from the night before.

This was becoming Todd's new normal.

I knew he was going through some stuff after Lana turned down his proposal a few weeks ago, but it was starting to escalate quickly.

He had been drinking every night and missing work. He was going to get fired soon if he kept this up. I started seeing the same patterns from the last time he was in it deep. I hoped this would be a short phase and he'd get his life back on track.

It was hard to see my brother so broken up but I couldn't deny the relief I felt when she didn't say yes. And the guilt I felt was just as strong.

I slammed down my coffee mug, trying to wake up Todd. He stirred with a groan.

"Morning asshole," I said sarcastically as Todd slowly sat up, cradling his head in his hands. "Have a good night?"

"Ughh, too loud," Todd moaned. "What time is it?"

Falling For My Ex's Brother

"It's almost 10 am," I said. "Here."

I pressed a glass of water into Todd's trembling hands. He downed half the glass and sighed.

"Thanks," he mumbled, not meeting my eyes.

I sat down in the armchair across from the couch, facing him directly. "So, want to tell me where you were last night?" I asked.

Todd squinted at me over his glass. "What are you, my dad? Lay off, man."

I sighed, trying to keep my cool. "I'm just worried about you."

"I'm fine," Todd grumbled.

"Todd, you're out of control," I replied.

Todd shrugged, his bloodshot eyes focused on the floor.

I tried a different approach.

"Get your shit together, or you'll lose Lana," I warned.

At the mention of Lana's name, Todd's head jerked up.

Todd jumped to his feet, wobbling a bit. "Like you know anything about our relationship," he spat.

I stood up too, anger building inside me now. "You don't know what you have, Todd. You don't treat her the way she deserves. She's going to realize that one day and leave your ass."

Todd laughed bitterly. "Take relationship advice from you?"

I gritted my teeth at his implication about my failed marriage.

"Don't turn this around on me," I growled. "I'm trying to help because I care about you."

Todd let out a harsh laugh. "Sure, big bro swooping in to save the day. Did you kiss Lana to make her feel better about me too?"

I flinched at his accusation. If he only knew how much I'd held back.

"Don't think I haven't noticed the way you look at her," Todd spat, his eyes narrowing.

"Are you fucking kidding me?" Todd knew it. He knew I was into Lana, but I'd never do anything to jeopardize his relationship with her. "But you keep this shit up, and I sure as hell won't hold back the next time I see Lana."

Todd slammed his cup down on the table, spilling water all over.

"Don't say her fucking name!" he burst out.

For a second I thought he might actually take a swing at me. But then his face crumpled.

"Lana deserves so much better than me," he said quietly, sinking back down on the couch. "I tried, Dylan. I really wanted to be the guy she needed."

Seeing Todd look so broken made my chest constrict. I sat down next to him with a heavy sigh.

"I know you tried," I said gently. "But you can't drink your problems away. You have to work at a relationship. Make it a priority if you guys are having issues. If it's not right, then make a clean break and move on. Trust me, I learned that the hard way."

I thought of my ex-wife and felt a twist of regret. We had dragged on our relationship longer than we should have. We both would've been happier ending things sooner.

Todd dropped his head in his hands again. "I just wish I could fix this," he said. "Make Lana happy, be better..."

"Then be better. Get yourself clean. You've done it once, you can do it again." I squeezed his shoulder. "You know I'm here for you. You don't have to do it alone."

My heart ached for him. Under all the lashing out, Todd was still the vulnerable kid I grew up protecting.

With Todd being five years younger than me, the impact of losing our parents was bigger for him. It had messed up him. He feared rejection and had a boatload of insecurities. Lana turning him down had brought a lot of that back for him.

That wasn't her fault. Maybe I hadn't been supportive enough.

Todd didn't respond or lift his head. I stood up with a sigh, realizing he probably needed space to process.

"I'm heading out," I told him. "Text me if you need anything, okay?"

Todd just gave a half-hearted grunt in response. I hoped I had gotten through to him at least a little, but only time would tell. As frustrated as I was with Todd lately, I knew it came from a place of deep hurt and insecurity.

But he had to be the one to decide to change. Brothers or not, he had to walk his own path.

LANA

I watched with concern as Todd downed another shot at the bar with his friends. My heart ached with guilt. I'd never meant to hurt him.

As Todd ordered another round, I squeezed his arm. "Hey, I'm gonna step outside for some air." He waved me off, reaching again for his freshly refilled glass.

I wove through the crowded bar until the cool night air hit my face. Taking a deep breath, I leaned against the brick wall and stared up at the night sky.

My emotions felt tangled and confused. I wasn't sure where our relationship was headed anymore or if was worth saving. Things had been tense between us ever since I rejected his proposal a couple weeks ago. I felt awful, but I didn't think I should take all the blame.

Marriage wasn't something to pop onto someone. And not after five months of dating. It was a romantic notion, but to me it seemed like one more irresponsible, spontaneous thing Todd did to go with the rest.

Maybe he thought an engagement would somehow keep us together despite the problems we were starting to have.

He'd been drinking more, becoming moodier and more unreliable. He started partying almost daily and missing work.

I'd noticed Todd's behavior changing since around the night of the storm at the diner. We were getting comfortable in our relationship, and I began to see different sides of him. Like he had been on good behavior to show me the best version of himself, hiding all the hurt and ugliness he had buried deep down inside.

Todd always had a smile on his face, ready with a witty joke to make me laugh. Even with his friends. He was the guy that everyone wanted to be around. Always down for some fun at a moment's notice.

On some level, I always had a feeling that I didn't really know the real Todd. Sometimes, I felt him opening up to me but his walls were back up before I could really get through to the real him.

It must have been exhausting. The effort he must have been putting in to keep up the façade that he had everything under control. That thought alone made my chest ache.

I still cared deeply for Todd, but I was starting to think this was the beginning of the end for us. Still, I didn't want to leave him when he was hurting. Not when I could see that he was on the brink of falling apart. I felt partly responsible to make sure he made it out of this slump, to stick by his side through it.

Especially now that I knew how deep his hurt went.

After Dylan had told me about their parents, I understood that Todd's drinking went much deeper than what appeared to be just harmless partying. The door swung open again and Todd sauntered out, blinking against the bright street lights.

"There you are," he said, draping an arm around my shoulder. "What are you doing out here? Everything ok?"

"Yeah, just getting some air." I sighed heavily.

He cupped my face in his hands and kissed me softly. He wasn't quite drunk yet, but I could sense he was getting there.

"Todd, let's get out of here," I said, hoping he'd be swayed easily tonight. "We can go back to my place, order some food. Have a night in."

"Leave so soon? It's Mike's birthday and we just got here not too long ago," he replied. "Come on, let's go back inside. One more drink and then we can go home."

One turned into two, and then two into a lot more. Soon enough, Todd was stumbling around with his friends who were just as drunk.

I didn't want to be there, but I couldn't just leave him in that condition. I had to make sure he got home safely at least.

I finally got Todd in the car with the help of one of his more responsible friends, who managed not to get trashed like the rest of them.

The drive was quiet. Todd stared out the window, exhaling a deep breath. He held his forehead and squeezed his eyes shut like he was in pain.

At a red light, I touched his arm gently. "Hey, you okay?"

Todd reached for my hand. "I'm sorry, babe."

He looked over at me with glassy eyes, a sad expression on his face.

"I love you, Lana. Please don't give up on me. On us. I promise I'll be better."

I blinked back sudden tears. We had a lot to talk about and I didn't even know where to begin.

"We'll talk tomorrow," I replied, squeezing his hand.

He slumped against the window, closing his eyes. We drove the rest of the way in silence.

9

DYLAN

Brent had set me up on a blind date. I finally agreed after he asked me for the fourth time. He'd been trying to get me out of my rut.

Little did he know, it wasn't my ex-wife I was hung up on. It was my brother's girlfriend.

Kristen was gorgeous, funny, and perfectly pleasant, but to be honest, I wasn't very invested. There was no real spark there.

Not like there had been with Lana.

I nodded and smiled as Kristen chatted, but I was waiting for our date to end.

I went to use the restroom and on my way back, I spotted a woman that looked like Lana sitting at the bar. I stopped and stared because I wasn't sure if it was just my imagination dreaming up the woman that I wanted so badly.

Then I laughed to myself when I realized it *was* Lana. She was wearing a little black dress that hugged her every curve.

I could only see her back, but well...I would recognize that back from anywhere. I could feel myself getting hard as

I my eyes stayed glued to her figure. I took a deep breath, trying to get my shit together.

It looked like she was waiting for someone, glancing around and checking her phone periodically.

Then as if sensing me, she turned and zeroed in on where I was standing.

Our eyes met from across the crowded restaurant.

I lifted my hand in a wave and she smiled back, her eyes lighting up in recognition.

I assumed she was waiting for Todd. For his sake, I hoped he would show up tonight. As I made my way over to her, I couldn't help but feel a little guilty for wanting her so badly.

"Hey," I said, leaning against the bar next to her.

She turned to me with a big smile. "Hey yourself."

"Waiting for Todd?" I asked, knowing well that she was.

She sighed, a small frown forming on her face. "He should be here soon. I came a little early so it's really my fault for waiting this long."

I nodded knowingly.

"What about you?" she asked, her gaze quickly assessing my attire. Her eyebrows rose, I hoped in appreciation. "On a hot date?"

I grimaced. "On a blind date, actually."

Lana laughed softly. "And?"

I rubbed the back of my neck, debating how honest to be. "And... she's nice."

Lana quirked a perfect eyebrow. "Just nice?"

"Well, if you really want to know, she's beautiful and smart," I replied honestly.

Lana glanced down and smiled softly. It might have been my wishful thinking, but I thought she looked disappointed.

"That's great. Sounds like you're a lucky guy."

We looked at each other for a moment. Something in her expression made my chest tighten. She looked so sad, sitting there alone.

She finally dropped her eyes and cleared her throat. "Well, I should let you get back to your date. Todd will probably be here soon."

"Right, yeah." I tapped the bar counter. "It was great seeing you, Lana."

I walked slowly back to my table, wishing it was me that she was waiting for. Not that I would have ever kept her waiting.

I sat back down across from Kristen, trying to focus on the rest of our date. But it was no use. My mind kept drifting back to the bar where Lana sat alone. Was she still there by herself?

"Dylan?" Kristen asked, noticing I'd trailed off mid-sentence.

"I'm so sorry," I said, lightly shaking my head. "I just have a lot on my mind today."

Kristen nodded, her expression neutral. I felt a twinge of guilt for not giving her my full attention, but my mind was on Lana.

She sat alone, nursing a drink, waiting for my brother who was running late. I knew in my gut that he was out partying again, and that he likely wouldn't show.

The night would end with Lana in tears.

I'd been keeping my distance, trying to respect their relationship, but the sight of her all alone gnawed at me.

As if reading my mind, Kristen gave a small sigh and said, "Well Dylan, this has been...nice, but I should probably get going."

I tried to look disappointed. "Oh really? So soon?"

She gave me a wry look. "Yes, clearly you're not feeling this date."

I winced, knowing I deserved that. "You're right. I'm sorry for being a lousy date."

Kristen softened, seeming to sense my sincerity. "No worries. I get it. We can call it a night."

After seeing Kristen safely into an Uber, I lingered on the curb. Lana was still sitting alone when I had glanced at the bar on our way out.

Part of me wanted to go back inside and keep Lana company, but I knew that would be walking a fine line. A line that could be easily blurred.

I decided to head home and gave Lana a last look through the restaurant windows. And what I saw made my blood boil.

10

LANA

"Hey, beautiful. You look lonely. Who's keeping you waiting?" I turned toward the voice to see a man next to me. He was good looking, maybe in his mid-thirties, and probably into his fourth or fifth drink, judging by his glassy eyes and slight slur in his speech. He leaned in, his shoulder touching mine.

"I'm just waiting for my boyfriend," I replied leaning away, hoping he'd take the hint and leave me alone.

It didn't work. He glanced around and leaned in even closer.

"Sorry to break it to you sweetheart, but I don't think he's going to show," he smirked. "But whoever he is, he's an idiot for keeping a gorgeous thing like you waiting around."

This guy was giving me the total creeps. But I had to agree with him on the part about the idiot keeping me waiting.

Todd was now running over thirty minutes late. He texted me five minutes ago, saying he was about to leave, so I decided to give him another ten minutes to get here. His work wasn't too far. Where the hell was he?

"Let me buy you a drink," he said, his gaze dropping down to my cleavage.

I huffed in annoyance and scooted away from him.

"No, I'm good." I snapped, turning my head in the other direction.

"Aw, come on. I promise to be on good behavior." He slid his hand up my arm. I flinched away, getting ready to tell him to fuck off.

But before I had a chance to tell him where to shove it, I heard him grunt loudly. I whipped my head around to see the creep stumbling back, his face contorted in pain.

I felt a firm hand wrap around my waist and a kiss on my temple. I was flooded with relief and a bit of surprise that Todd had finally shown up.

"Hey babe, sorry I kept you waiting," said a deep voice that sounded nothing like Todd. My body clenched at the unexpected voice. The voice I knew too well.

Dylan.

"Who the hell are you?" Dylan spat, glaring at the man who was clutching his wrist, blinking in pain.

Dylan's large hand covered my arm where the man had touched, rubbing soothing circles like he knew I needed his touch to replace the memory.

"Oh, hi," I said, shooting him a grateful look. "He was just leaving."

Taking the hint, the man backed off, nursing his wrist in his other hand.

"No problem, I'm going," he muttered.

As soon as he was gone, I let out a nervous sigh.

"Thanks. He would not take a hint."

Dylan didn't move from where he stood glued to me, his arm still around my waist. He watched the man until he disappeared around the corner.

His eyes finally shifted down to me, his face just inches from mine.

"Are you okay?" He asked, his eyebrows knitted together with concern.

"I'm fine now." I smiled weakly, trying to ignore the way my body was responding to his closeness. His eyes searched my face, like he was trying to decide whether I was telling the truth or not.

"That guy was an asshole," he rumbled low, letting his hand slip away.

"Guess I looked like an easy target, sitting at a bar alone for so long," I said.

Dylan's jaw twitched as he shook his head.

"No Todd yet?" he asked, taking the stool next to me.

I checked my phone and sighed. "Nope. But that's Todd, always running late. He said he'd be here soon."

"Well, I'm happy to play your fake boyfriend until your real one shows," Dylan offered with a small smile.

Those words made my chest ache. How I wished the roles were reversed.

My real boyfriend. Todd didn't even feel like one anymore.

"Thanks," I replied, laughing softly. "I would take you up on that offer, but I don't want to keep you from your date."

"She left when she realized it wasn't going anywhere," Dylan said.

"Oh, that's too bad," I said, trying to sound sympathetic though a part of me was inwardly celebrating. Just then my phone buzzed on the bar counter.

It was Todd saying his work friends invited him out and I should join them at the bar they were headed to across town.

Was he serious?

Tonight was supposed to be a celebration for finally completing my last semester and getting my degree.

It was a big night for me. Todd had been so proud, so excited to take me out to celebrate. He had wanted to make up for his behavior from the other night out.

I was not in the mood to be out with his rowdy friends. Especially not after I've sat here for over thirty minutes, waiting for him to show.

My eyes stung, tears starting to form, but I blinked them away.

"I'm guessing Todd's not coming," Dylan said quietly. I couldn't look at him. I couldn't bear to see the pity in his eyes.

I shook my head, swallowing down the knot in my throat. "No, he wants me to meet him at another bar."

I looked down at my drink and tried to suppress the anger that was rising. I could feel Dylan's eyes watching me.

He could probably see the emotions brewing inside me. He knew I had no intention of meeting Todd there.

I was about to tell Dylan I was heading home when he asked, "Do you like chocolate?"

I frowned in confusion and turned to him. He looked back at me with such an earnest expression, the random question threw me off even more.

"What?" I asked, blinking rapidly.

He laughed, shaking his head.

"Come on, I'm taking you out." Dylan motioned to the bartender to close out my tab.

He meant he felt sorry for the poor girl who got stood up by his brother, so he was throwing her a bone.

"What? Dylan, you don't have to-," I started saying.

"Hey." He softly tugged my wrist, stopping my sorry attempt at trying to come up with an excuse. He seemed to sense what I was thinking. "I want to. So let me. And you look hot as hell. I'm not letting you waste that outfit."

He winked at me and I thought my face was going to go up in flames. Dylan dropped some cash for my drinks and held out his hand, palm facing up.

"Let's go," he said, waiting expectantly as I sat there debating whether I should head home or take Dylan's hand and salvage the night.

The truth was, I didn't want to go home. I had come out for a night out with Todd, but the thought of spending time with Dylan was more appealing by the second.

"Just two friends catching up," Dylan said, his hand still held out for me to take. "What do you say? I know a great place for dessert. Or drinks. Or whatever will make you happy tonight."

How could I say no to that? I deserved to celebrate my achievement tonight.

"Okay," I said as I slipped my hand into his. "Dylan?"

"Yeah," he replied, closing his fingers over mine.

"I love chocolate."

I hopped off the stool and let Dylan lead me out of the restaurant.

∽

Dylan and I walked over to a nearby restaurant called Marcella's. It was a charming little Italian place with a mellow vibe.

The sweet smell of fresh bread and cheese hung in the air, making my stomach rumble. We were seated at a small table tucked away in the corner.

We ate dinner as we chatted and caught up. The server came to clear our plates and asked if we wanted dessert.

"Have you ever tried a brookie explosion?" Dylan asked, turning to me.

I narrowed my eyes and smiled. "No, I haven't. What is it?"

His face went deadpan.

"What is it? Only the best thing you'll ever taste. It's life changing."

I laughed as Dylan put in the order with our server.

"So, how's the dating scene these days?" I asked, regretting immediately after I'd said it.

I wasn't sure if I even wanted to know his answer. I assumed his divorce was final and now he was officially back on the market, dating around.

Dylan chuckled, "I wouldn't know. I'm not really in the scene. Today was my first date."

I rolled my lips, secretly happy that he wasn't dating.

"What happened with your date tonight?" I asked. "I thought she was beautiful and smart. And I know you must have had her charmed."

He watched me, running his fingers along his jaw. I squirmed under his intense gaze.

"She wasn't my type," he replied, the corner of his lips turning up.

I rolled my eyes and scoffed. "You don't like beautiful and smart women?"

He laughed, his eye crinkling in the corners.

"Of course, I do. I know one, in fact. She's perfect," he said, his smile softening. "But she's taken."

I inhaled deeply as I bit my lower lip. Our gazes stayed locked on each other for a moment.

Just then, the server brought our dessert. My eyes went wide as I took in the impressive dessert. It was fresh baked brownies and chocolate chip cookies swirled together, served warm in a pan, topped with a heaping scoop of ice cream.

We each took a forkful, but Dylan waited, watching me as I took a bite.

"Wow," I said, covering my mouth as I savored the rich flavors. "Just wow. That's amazing."

Dylan raised his eyebrows and a huge grin spread across his handsome face.

He was right. It was one of the best things I'd ever tasted. Rich, decadent, warm gooeyness.

I took another bite and closed my eyes.

"Mmm. So good," I said, as I exhaled slowly.

When I opened my eyes, Dylan was staring at me, his eyes slightly hooded. He licked his lips.

My face heated. I laughed and wiped my lips with my napkin. "Sorry, got a little carried away there."

He smiled back at me, "Don't mind me. Should I leave you two alone?"

We talked and laughed and soon, I forgot that I was feeling so awful just an hour ago. Dylan had managed to come to save the day again.

Dylan must've noticed how much I was enjoying the dessert because he let me dig into the rest after he took a few bites.

"Oh god, take this thing away from me," I said laughing as I eyed the last bite left on the plate. "You were right. This thing is dangerous."

"Told you," he said, grinning.

Then he scooped the last bite onto his fork and held it in front of me.

"Please. Spare a girl the embarrassment," I said as I covered my face, unable to stop smiling. "I ate pretty much the whole thing by myself."

"Knock it off. You did not." He chuckled, gently prying my hand away from my face. "Stop being polite. You don't have to with me."

His smile was sweet and genuine, his eyes twinkling. He leaned in and brought the fork closer to my mouth, not letting go of my hand. "Here."

How could I say no to this gorgeous man feeding me chocolate? I rolled my eyes and leaned forward. His gaze dropped to my mouth as I parted my lips, taking the last morsel off his fork.

He rolled his lip and then smiled softly as he looked down at the table. I thought he looked a little sad, and it suddenly made my chest ache.

"So, what's next for you?" I asked, breaking the awkward moment.

Dylan shrugged. "Still trying to figure out some things. It's been kind of a rough year."

I nodded. His divorce had taken a toll, even if he downplayed it. I wanted nothing more than to comfort him, but I didn't know how he'd receive that.

"But the brewery is looking promising. We found a really cool spot for it. It's a huge warehouse with space for outdoor seating. Brent and I are going to look at it next week."

"How exciting! How far out is the opening?"

Dylan inhaled deeply, looking up as he thought. "Probably not for a while. It'll take close to a year to get everything up and running. We have a lot of work ahead of us."

"Well, I'll be your best customer," I said. "Or if you need help, I can be a barmaid too."

It wasn't likely that Todd and I would still be together by then, but I'd still go and show my support.

"I'd love that," Dylan replied, laughing. "I'm going to hold you to it."

"I'll be disappointed if you don't." And I meant it. "I know you're going to build something amazing Dylan. I just know it."

"Thanks, I hope so," he replied, his smile softening. "So, how's school? You said it was you were almost done with the last semester."

"Yeah, I just finished this week actually. I finally got my degree." I smiled proudly.

Dylan raised his eyebrows in surprise.

"Lana, that's amazing! Congratulations." He reached out and squeezed my hand on the table. "I'm so happy for you. What are you doing to celebrate the big milestone?"

"This is my celebration," I replied. "Tonight."

Dylan's smile faded as he understood why I was dressed up and waiting for Todd. He sat back in his chair and sighed, releasing my hand.

"I'm so sorry," he said, gazing at me with apologetic eyes. "I can't believe Todd would do that."

"Dylan, please don't apologize for Todd. I already feel so lucky to be here with you. Always coming to my rescue out of nowhere, like some sort of superhero." I laughed, trying to lighten the mood.

He didn't laugh with me. He just kept looking at me with the same sad eyes.

"We should've gone somewhere nicer. I should've asked where you wanted to go."

My chest tightened. I wasn't expecting this reaction from him. I started to regret saying anything at all.

"Dylan, stop. I love it here." I reached for his hand, holding it in both of mine. "Really. I really do. I would've picked a place just like it."

I hoped my sincerity came through. I really meant every

word. I couldn't have imagined a better way to celebrate. He looked down and shook his head.

"I'm going to kick his ass," he muttered to himself and let out a big sigh. "Are you okay? After, you know..." He trailed off, but I knew he meant Todd's proposal.

"Oh, yeah I'm okay. Just wasn't expecting it." I hugged my arms. "It didn't feel right to say yes. I feel so bad."

"Don't feel bad. You did the right thing. You deserve to be happy, Lana."

I sighed. "He took it harder than I expected. It's been rough lately. I feel responsible..." I bit my lip.

Dylan's brow furrowed with concern. "You're not responsible for how he copes. We just need to look out for him."

I nodded in agreement with him, but I couldn't shake the feeling that it was partly my fault.

We sat there in silence for what felt like an eternity, the mention of Todd breaking the moment.

"We should probably get going," I finally said.

We made our way back to the bar where my car was parked.

"Lana..." Dylan said, catching my wrist. I held my breath as I looked up at him.

"I just wanted to say, for what it's worth..." He hesitated, seeming to hold back what he wanted to say. "Maybe this is out of line. But I need you to know, you deserve someone who cherishes you. Who sees how incredible you are. Be with someone that makes you happy. Don't settle for anything less."

His words sank in, each one tugging at my heart. He had to be talking about himself. This was as close to a confession from him as I could hope.

"You call me anytime you need something, Lana. I'll

always show up for you." He dropped my wrist, looking away.

Before I could overthink it, I hugged him, circling my arms around his waist. Dylan's arms wrapped around me, squeezing gently. He rested his chin on my head, tucking me in closer.

"Good night, Dylan," I whispered into his chest, not wanting to let go.

"Good night, Lana," he murmured into my hair.

Slowly, I rose up on my toes and kissed his cheek. "Thank you, for everything tonight."

He turned his head toward me, his cheek touching mine. I wondered if he could feel my heart beating wildly in my chest. We stood for a moment, neither of us moving.

I breathed him in deeply, burning his scent into my memory before forcing myself to step back. Finally, he released his hold.

Walk away before you do something stupid, Lana.

11

LANA

Over the next couple days, I thought about what Dylan said. That I deserved to be with someone that made me happy.

But mostly I couldn't stop thinking about what he'd said at the end of the night.

You call me anytime you need something, Lana. I'll always show up for you.

It ran through my mind several times a day. Sometimes several times an hour.

I hadn't seen Todd after the night he blew me off. He'd called the next day, apologizing, saying he thought I'd be ok with the change of venue. It was complete bullshit.

I was meeting him tonight. I wanted to have a heart-to-heart with him in person. I wanted to be there for him. If not as a girlfriend, then at least as a friend. I knew he was going through a hard time, and I didn't want him to go through it alone.

But I needed to take care of myself too.

I had my mind made up that if Todd didn't show any remorse, it would be the last time I'd see him.

Honestly, I wasn't sure where our relationship was going

Falling For My Ex's Brother 95

to be by the end of the conversation. I wondered if he even had a clue as to how I was feeling. Or if he even cared. Todd probably thought he loved me. I knew he believed it, but I was starting to think Todd's one true love was himself. I had just started getting ready to go out when Todd called.

"What's up?" I asked.

"Hey, I'm just not feeling very well. I'm sure I'm coming down with something." Todd sniffed, and he did sound a little congested.

"Oh," I said. "There's been a really bad bug going around… Want me to bring you some chicken soup?"

Todd chuckled. "Thanks, but that's ok. I don't want to get you sick. I'm just going to rest and hopefully, we can get talk in a few days when I'm past it."

"Okay. Feel better." I stared at my phone after we hung up.

In my gut, I knew he was lying to me. But if there was a slim chance that he was actually sick, I wanted to be there for him. Either way, I had to see him and find out.

I decided it would be a nice gesture to take him some chicken soup.

I put on jeans and a T-shirt and went to the kitchen to see if I needed to make a grocery run.

A few hours later, I stood in front of Todd's door and knocked, holding the insulated thermos full of soup and orange slices against my chest.

Dylan answered the door. "Hey, Lana." His smile faded when he saw my glum expression. "Everything ok?"

"Just dropping off a care package for Todd." My mind was so wrapped up in what I was going to say to Todd, I hadn't even thought about Dylan being there.

"Care package?" Dylan said, his eyes narrowing.

"Todd said he's coming down with something. I made

him some chicken soup." I tried to look over Dylan's shoulder to see if he was on the couch. "Can I come in?" I asked, realizing he hadn't moved out of the doorway. "How sick is he?"

Dylan sighed and stepped back so I could come in. Then he put his hands on his hips. "Lana . . . he's not here."

I stared at Dylan, not surprised at all. "Did he go to the drugstore?"

Dylan looked frozen in place for a moment. Then he dropped his head. "No. He didn't go to the drugstore."

I glanced around the living room, knowing exactly where he went.

"Do you want to come in and sit down?" Dylan motioned toward the couch.

I put the container on the coffee table and sat on the couch. I had expected it, but somewhere inside, I'd hoped that I was wrong. A sinking feeling, a cold ball of steel, felt like it was running from my head down my body.

Dylan sat next to me. His T-shirt showed off the winding serpent tattoo on one bicep.

God, why did he have to be so sexy? I forced myself to focus on why I'd come there in the first place.

"If he's not here, where the hell did he go?" I looked up into Dylan's eyes with a glimmer of hope that Todd wasn't really lying. That there was a misunderstanding, or a mistake. That Todd hadn't called and lied about being sick to go somewhere else. Even if we were breaking up, I didn't want to end it this way.

Dylan sighed heavily and laced his fingers together, his arms resting on his thighs as he leaned forward. "I think he went to the club he goes to all the time. You probably know the one."

I tried to hold my head high as I nodded. "I do."

I knew it before I even asked, but hearing it from Dylan somehow made the reality sink in.

My eyes stung, so I tried to blink away the urge to cry. I was *not* going to cry, not there, not with Dylan.

"Lana, I'm sorry he lied to—"

"It's not your problem to be sorry about, Dylan. But thanks." I put my hands on my thighs, about to get up and leave. But the way Dylan was looking at me kept me in place. "What I can't really figure out is why he didn't just tell me he wanted to go out. Why he had to lie to me."

Dylan looked like he wanted to say a lot of things and didn't know how to do it.

"It's okay, Dylan. I'm not asking for an answer. Just thinking out loud." Then I cleared my throat. "I do have a question for you, though."

"Okay." He inhaled through his nostrils and leaned a little closer. "I'll answer it, if I can."

"I'm really sorry to put you on the spot, Dylan. It's not fair, but I have to know." I watched Dylan's face carefully as he nodded, his lips pressed tightly together. I swallowed hard and said, "Do you think he's cheating on me?"

Before the entire sentence was out, Dylan's face fell.

And I knew. I felt myself start to crumble. I put my hand over my face.

"Lana—"

"That's ok," I said, already in tears. "I'm not all that surprised. Do you know for how long?"

Dylan just looked down and shook his head.

I'd been so foolish to keep giving him chances when he clearly didn't give a shit. I felt humiliated. How long had it been going on?

I should have gone with my gut and ended things when

it started to go downhill. I should have ended it the night he didn't show up at the diner.

Maybe if I'd had the guts to break up with Todd earlier, things could at least be different between me and Dylan.

What kind of person are you? You'd just jump from one brother to another?

That thought pushed me over the edge. I started sobbing into my hands.

"Hey, Lana. *Hey.*" Dylan pulled me into his arms and rocked slowly from side to side. "I'm sorry. I'm sorry for everything," he said, as if he had any hand in this.

I pressed myself against him and wrapped my arms around his waist. I let myself cry into his shirt like a little girl.

"He's an asshole," Dylan said.

"He is," I agreed.

"A real butthead," he added.

"A bug—crumb—" I was trying to call him too many names at once and they got jumbled. "A big crumb pickle," is what came out.

Dylan snorted. "Okay. A big crumb pickle. With a side of slime."

I laughed, despite being so upset.

Dylan stroked my hair. "A damn stupid idiot," he whispered.

Being in Dylan's arms, even while I was crying over my own messed up guilt and regret, felt so right, I almost forgot myself.

I lifted my face, letting my cheek brush against his chin, to look into his eyes.

His warm brown eyes stared back at mine. His lips parted. It would have been so easy to lean forward, just a little, and press my mouth against his.

And God, I wanted that so much.

But I couldn't. He was Todd's brother. Even if the bastard was lying and cheating on me.

"Thanks, Dylan. Thanks for coming to my rescue again. But I've got—" I leaned back, trying to stand up. Dylan's big hands wrapped around mine, holding me in place.

"Lana, you don't have to leave," he said softly.

His eyes dropped to my lips for just a second before meeting my gaze again.

My breath caught at his words. Heat rushed straight down my body, settling between my legs.

I wasn't imagining the look in his eyes.

Dylan leaned closer, just an inch, his eyes darkening. I struggled to keep my breathing even.

"Dylan..." I whispered nervously.

I knew I should pull away, shut this down. But I felt frozen in place. I couldn't bring myself to stop him.

Dylan slowly lowered his face, his eyes flicking over my features, until his lips barely brushed mine.

He stayed like that, his breath shallow.

He was waiting.

Waiting for me to meet him the rest of the way. He wasn't going to push his way onto me. He needed me to be ok with this.

I squeezed my eyes shut, wanting to give in, but the guilt came flooding in.

Even if Todd was cheating, wasn't it shitty of me to have any kind of feelings for his brother?

"Dylan, we- we can't," I stammered as I leaned back. "Forget this happened."

Dylan held my gaze, emotion swirling in his eyes.

"What if I don't want to?" He finally said. "What if that was just a taste of what I really want with you?"

Pulling out of Dylan's arms, I stood abruptly. "I have to go."

Dylan stood at the same time and caught my wrist to keep me from walking away. "You don't, Lana. You don't *have* to go anywhere."

"I-I do have to go," I stuttered. "I really do."

"Lana...," his voice was asking me to stay, but his hand released me as I pulled away.

I ran out and drove away without looking back, feeling embarrassed and foolish. And wanting nothing more than to run back and throw myself into Dylan's arms.

12

DYLAN

I didn't sleep worth a shit that night. I had to keep fighting the urge to call Lana. And I kept thinking about how she'd felt in my arms.

How I didn't want to let her go. I knew their relationship was done at that point.

I woke up to see Todd passed out, still sitting on the couch, a half-empty bottle of bourbon on the coffee table and a glass spilled everywhere. That combined with being tired made me lose my cool.

"Wake the fuck up," I growled, shaking him, hoping he didn't puke on me.

One eye cracked open. "It's not time," he said, his voice raw.

"It's time to get up."

"I just fell asleep," he complained.

"I don't give a fuck." I put my hands on my hips. "It's morning. Don't you have to go to work?"

"I'll call in sick." He felt around for his phone. After watching him struggle for a couple of minutes, I produced it from between the cushions. And I threw it into a chair out of his reach.

"What the fuck, Dylan?" He stumbled up and fished the phone out of the chair.

I waited while he called the dealership, claiming to be sick. After he hung up, I crossed my arms.

"Won't they know you're just hungover? You *were* out with some of them last night, right?"

"Some." He grinned at me, and I wanted to slap his face.

"Some of them. And whoever you're fucking around on Lana with?" I picked up the glass and bottle, then I put them back down. He could clean up his own fucking mess.

"I didn't say that," Todd said, but his tone was so smug, I knew I was right.

"No, but Lana did," I said, waiting while that sank in.

Todd slowly blinked at me. "What?"

"She came here yesterday evening. Brought you some chicken soup since you told her you were sick and needed to rest."

Todd jumped up. "And you fucking told her I was cheating?"

"I didn't have to. She figured it out on her own." I wiped my hands down my face, tired of Todd's bullshit. "Damn it, Todd. We've been through this. Get your shit together. Lay off the drinking and partying. Figure out what the hell you want in life."

He plopped down on the couch again and reached for the bottle. Before he could take a drink, I snatched it out of his hands. He grabbed for it, and when I stepped away, he threw his hands up.

"I *had* figured out what I wanted. Lana. But she said no, remember?" He let his head drop back onto the couch.

I went into the kitchen to dump out the bottle into the sink.

Todd followed me in. "Do you have any idea how embarrassing that was? How humiliating?"

I sighed and leaned against the counter, staring into Todd's eyes. "No, brother. I don't. I'm sorry that you were embarrassed. But do you think it's been a fucking cakewalk for her?"

Todd blinked like he'd never considered how Lana felt before. Only a few seconds passed before he pointed at me.

"Don't turn this around on me. I'm the one who got humiliated, not her."

"And you've been making her sorry for it ever since, huh?" I slammed the empty bottle on the counter. "Drinking, drugging, fucking around. While she's feeling bad about everything and cooking for you while you're sick. Hope you're proud of yourself."

"God damn it," Todd growled. For a minute, I thought he was going to launch himself at me to tackle me. If he hadn't been so hungover, he might have. "You fucking told her. I *know* you did."

"Todd, I didn't. But Lana's not stupid."

"I don't believe you," he said through his teeth.

While I was putting things in my bag, he followed me from place to place.

Finally, he cleared his throat. "What did she say?"

"That she's not surprised." I shoved a light jacket into my backpack.

"She knew? And you didn't deny it?" He was like a puppy on my heels, so I spun.

"I wouldn't have denied it, and I didn't get the chance to. Before I could say anything, she broke down, crying about your sorry ass." I pushed past him to get some ibuprofen out of my bedroom.

"You might have well as told her then!" he accused.

"Todd, if she saw it in my face, maybe it's because I was in the kitchen when a woman tried to sneak out of here yesterday morning with bed hair and her shirt on backwards. I can't help *knowing* the truth when you did such a shitty job of hiding it!"

I stopped in the kitchen doorway, wanting to punch a wall because I was so frustrated at the entire conversation. The whole fucking situation.

I should want them to be happy together. To work their shit out.

But I didn't. I wanted them to break up.

That was the truth, as messed up as it was.

"I'm going to take that soup with me. I knew you wouldn't be in soon enough, so I put it away after she left. Tasted it first."

Todd's eyes went wild. "You tasted her soup? *My* soup?"

I opened the fridge door, and he slammed it shut.

"Yeah, I did. It was fucking delicious." He was lucky that was the only thing I tasted.

"She made it for me," he growled through his gritted teeth. "I'm going to have it for lunch."

"You don't even like chicken soup." I opened the fridge again, and he slammed it hard enough that two magnets jumped off the door.

"I don't. But you're sure as hell not getting it." He glared and held the door shut.

"Do you have any idea how stupid you sound right now?" I asked. I yanked the door open, which pushed Todd back a couple of feet, and pulled the container out. "There's no point in it going to waste."

Todd grabbed the container, but I held on. So he slapped down on it, causing it to crash to the floor. "She made it for me. Not. You."

I slammed the fridge door shut. "Fine. Waste it. Just like you wasted your chance with her by being a fuck-up."

"Maybe I am a fuck-up," he shouted. "But at least I never tried to ruin any of your relationships."

"Todd, for the last God damn time," I said, pausing at the kitchen door. "I didn't try to ruin your relationship. You did that all yourself."

If only he knew how hard I'd had to fight to keep myself from ruining it. My efforts to stay away from Lana had been painful and difficult.

It was almost damned heroic as far as I was concerned. Because I'd never wanted any woman the way I wanted her.

I couldn't say any of that to him. And if I could, he probably wouldn't believe me anyway.

"We were trying so hard to make things work," Todd practically wailed. "And you couldn't have my back this one time."

That was it. I couldn't listen to any more of his bullshit.

"She was trying to make it work. You were drinking and fucking around. And I had your back, Todd. More than you will ever fucking know or appreciate. Believe it or not. Right now, I couldn't care less."

"Misery loves company, Dylan. I know it sucks getting divorced, but you didn't have to ruin my—"

"Shut the fuck up right now before you say something you can't take back." I stormed out and threw my backpack into the car.

Todd followed me. "You ruin everything, Dylan. Everything."

I got into the car and spoke to him through my open window. "You're still drunk. Go back to fucking bed."

I drove away, trying hard not to take it personally. He probably did still have alcohol coursing through his system. But that was no excuse. He was just lashing out because he knew Lana was probably going to be done with him.

But we weren't going to be able to deal with it until he was sober and rested.

I called Brent and told him I was running a few minutes late, but I was on my way. Then I slammed my hands onto the steering wheel a few times until my palms ached.

I wanted to go back, pack my shit, and leave. But knowing Todd as I did, that would have been the worst thing I could do. I knew I had to stay for him.

I took a deep breath and tried to focus on the work ahead of me at the brewery. Whatever was going to be said and done would have to wait until that night.

I only hoped that Todd didn't say anything stupid to Lana to make her feel worse than she already did.

13

LANA

I pulled into the Crystal Fountains parking lot and looked at my buzzing phone.

Todd. Again. A text immediately came through.

> Please call me, Lana. Please let me explain.

I thought for the fiftieth time that maybe I should just block his number.

I'd broken up with him the day after I took him soup, thinking he was sick, while he was out partying.

That had been over a month ago, and he still kept calling and leaving messages, texting me, apologizing. Begging me to take him back.

Even though I felt things for Dylan and wanted things I knew I shouldn't, couldn't have, it had been hard to call it quits with Todd.

It hurt even more than I'd expected to say the words, but I couldn't be with him anymore.

Still, I thought I'd always have a special place in my heart for him and what might have been.

I hadn't blocked him, because deep down I did still care. And there was always the chance I'd see him at the senior home anyway.

That was about to change. Maybe it was time.

I went in to see my grandpa. I'd been nervous about this visit since I made the decision, so I already felt like I was on the verge of tears. When I'd told him what I planned to do, he'd been so excited for me. Supportive as always.

But I felt like I was abandoning him. No matter how I looked at it, I thought that my grandpa probably didn't have all that many years left. How could I leave him and live so far away?

I guess how upset I was showed all over my face. The minute I walked into his room, he said, "Aww, honey."

I knelt next to his armchair and hugged him.

"It doesn't feel right, Grandpa. I don't want to leave you behind." I was trying not to sob and doing a poor job of it. "I still think we can find a senior home in New York where you can live, so I'll be close by and can come see you all the time."

He stroked my hair. "Lana, children are supposed to grow up and leave their elders. Make a life for themselves. Do you know how bad I'd feel if I thought you were putting off your life just to stay behind for your grandfather? No," he said, cupping my cheek. "I want you to go to New York, do a great job in that exciting new position you've been offered, and make us all proud."

"But what if you need me? What if I miss you?" I asked, almost embarrassed at how childlike I sounded. But this was my grandpa. I was having a hard time imagining not being able to see him anytime I wanted.

"You know, there are wonderful new inventions to help

with that. Maybe you've heard of them. Airplanes and telephones." He chuckled and patted my hand.

"I guess I never have to wonder where I get my sarcasm from, huh?" I smiled through my tears. Then he pointed at his bed and pulled a phone out of the pocket of his sweater.

"Go over there. Let's make sure I know what I'm doing with this fancy gadget." He squinted at it and touched the screen.

I sat on the bed and held my phone, waiting for him to call me. It rang in a video call, which I answered. I smiled at how proud he looked. "You've got it."

"Let me practice the regular call now." A minute later, my phone was ringing with a call. Then he texted and replied to mine.

"You see, sweetie. You're always just seconds away."

I sniffed and wished I could sit in his lap like I did when I was a little girl. "The offer of assisted living in New York is still on the table."

"Too expensive," he said, shaking his head. "After my Social Security, too much would be leftover to pay every month. We couldn't afford it."

I knew he was right. And whatever he had left in his savings wasn't going to last him very long. It was partly why I took the job in New York.

The living expenses were higher there, but I'd also be making a lot more than I would be at an agency here. It would more than make up for the cost. I'd be able to repay my student loans faster and help out Grandpa with his finances too.

As difficult as it would be to leave Grandpa, I knew it was the best decision for now. It also didn't hurt that I could start over in a new city, to start fresh after Todd. And Dylan.

How was it that I missed Dylan more than I did Todd?

He took my hand again. "Besides, I don't want to leave Dave here without me. We'd miss each other too much."

I knew he didn't want to leave his best friend. And I didn't want him to, either.

We talked for a while, and soon it was his dinnertime. And time for me to do my final packing and make sure I was prepared to leave for New York the following day.

I hugged him one last time. I had a hard time letting go.

"I love you, Paw-Paw," I said, loving how his face lit up at the name.

"I love you too, sweet pea."

"I'll call you as soon as I land," I promised, wiping my eyes. Then I hurried away before I bawled like a baby right in the hall.

DYLAN

I hurried into the senior home with the low-sugar cupcakes I'd bought for James and Grandpa and nearly ran into a woman rushing out at the same—

"Lana," I said, caught off guard to see her. Especially with her eyes so puffy and red, like she'd been crying. My chest constricted at the sight. I took a step toward her, wanting to pull her into my arms. "Is everything okay? Is James—"

"Oh, yes," she said with a laugh and a deep sniff. "He's okay. It's just been a day. They're about to go to dinner."

Her red-rimmed eyes made me think it was more than a trying day.

I hadn't seen her since the day she brought soup for Todd a month ago. Since the day I almost kissed her.

"Are you sure you're okay?" I asked, reaching for her.

She took a step back before I could touch her arm. I pulled my hand back, curling my fingers, and dropped it to my side. She didn't want me near her.

She looked away and bit her lower lip. "Really, I'm fine. Just in a hurry. Tell Dave I said hi."

Before I could say anything else, she ran for her car, leaving me standing there to watch her go. I heaved out a deep breath. I was always watching her leave.

I'd waited to call or text her, even though I'd wanted to the minute Todd told me she'd ended things between them and ordered me out of his house.

I'd told myself it wasn't right to swoop in on your brother's ex-girlfriend. Not when he was still hung up on her. I couldn't do it. Especially with Todd still angry and not speaking to me.

I went inside and found Grandpa and James at their dinner table together. I pulled up a chair and talked while they ate, both of them eyeing the chocolate cupcakes I'd brought.

"I saw Lana as I was coming in," I said to James. "She looked upset. Is everything okay?"

"She's just sad that I'll be here, and she'll be in New York, that's all." He paused mid-bite, staring at me.

Probably because I was in shock, and it showed. "New York?"

"Got a job at a big fancy marketing agency in the city." He cleared his throat. "She leaves tomorrow, you know."

Fucking hell. I didn't know.

I'd waited, trying to do the right thing. Trying not to hurt Todd more than he was already hurting.

And just like the day I'd met Lana, my hesitance had cost me my chance with her. Maybe it wouldn't have made a difference and she'd still be moving away.

There was almost no chance of anything happening between us, not with her in New York and me in Oregon.

What was the point in saying anything to her now? She clearly wasn't happy to see me just minutes ago.

Even knowing that, I had to go. I had to see her before

she left. Even if I never even got to kiss Lana, I wanted to spend time with her while I could.

"I'm going to leave these cupcakes," I said, and James put his hand up.

"I think we can handle it. Go see your girl," He winked at me, and he and Grandpa shared a look.

I should have called her before showing up on her doorstep. I should have at least texted. But I was in such a rush to get to her house, I was knocking before I'd even thought about how it would look.

Her eyes widened in surprise.

"Dylan," she said breathily.

"I'm sorry for showing up like this. But James told me about New York. And I . . . I had to see you before you left. To congratulate you on the job."

I couldn't help glancing down her body, at the way her short skirt gave such a great view of her shapely thighs.

Her full lips curved into a soft smile.

"Thanks," she said, her voice barely above a whisper.

Just when I thought that this was it, she'd say goodbye and close the door, she looked over her shoulder. "I was just about to have dinner. Do you want to come in?"

I followed her inside the small apartment. The walls were mostly bare now, boxes stacked everywhere, and a few remaining items were left out on the table next to empty bins, waiting to be packed up. The realization that she was going to be gone sunk in deeper.

"Are you hungry? I have plenty of pasta." Lana said, leading me to the kitchen area.

"Starving," I admitted with a grin.

She gave us each a plate to fill, then we sat in her dining nook and ate. Tension hung in the air between us. "How have you been?" Lana asked after a moment, her voice soft. "How are things with Todd?"

"That's a good question." At her frown, I added, "I'm sure he's fine. I know he's still working at the dealership, still has friends. I think he might have even slowed down on the drinking since you broke it off. I moved out and crashed in Brent's basement until I found a place to rent. He insisted since he decided to stop speaking to me."

Lana's face fell. "Dylan. I'm so sorry. I feel so bad about that. I tried to explain that you didn't say anything to me."

I waved her off. "I told him too. He'll get over himself eventually and realize that the only person who did Todd wrong was Todd."

The last thing I wanted to talk about with Lana was Todd. I leaned back and took a drink of water.

"Anyway, enough about that. Tell me about this job. James said it was at a fancy marketing agency in the city."

Her pretty face lit up. "Riggs and Boone PR. They do promotions for a lot of celebrities' perfume and fashion lines, write ads for a lot of Procter & Gamble products, that kind of thing. I found a cracker box apartment that's still way too expensive, but my salary's pretty good. I can make a real dent in my student loans, and once those are gone, find something a lot nicer."

"That sounds really fantastic, Lana. I'm so happy for you."

I was genuinely happy for her, even as my heart ached knowing she would soon be far away building her new life. Away from me.

"I'm just so scared that I'll go, and something will happen to Grandpa. I'll be three thousand miles away, and—"

"I'm here, Lana. When I go to check on my grandpa, I'll

check on James." "They're together most of the time anyway. Won't be hard."

"I'd appreciate that so much," she said, her voice tight.

Lana fidgeted, eyes flickering, like she was hesitating. She finally stood, biting her lip nervously.

"I, uh, have something for you. Just one sec."

Lana returned with a wrapped parcel from one of the boxes in the corner. "I wanted to give this to you sooner but things kind of..." she trailed off. "Anyway, I was thinking of mailing it once I got to New York, but I can give it to you now."

Gingerly, I peeled back the paper to reveal a beautiful wooden picture frame.

My breath caught at the image of myself, Todd and Grandpa from his birthday party, smiling and carefree.

Then my eyes trailed down to the bottom where my fingers traced the familiar markings. I looked up at Lana, torn between laughing and crying. "Is this...?"

Lana nodded, biting her lip.

My name was etched alongside Todd's, Grandpa's, and Dad's. We had carved our names into one of the tables at the bar years ago. I'd completely forgotten about it. A lump formed in my throat at the memory.

"I saw it on the night of your party and thought it deserved to be with the rightful owner rather than forgotten," Lana continued softly. "So I went back to the bar a week later and asked the new owners if I could take it."

"You went and asked for the table? How did you even manage to transport it?" I shook my head in disbelief. It was the most thoughtful thing anyone did for me.

"I can be pretty resourceful," she replied smiling.

"I don't even know what to say. I love it..." I trailed off, looking back down at the frame.

"I wanted you to have something to remember the good times. I know how hard losing the bar was for you," she said softly.

Setting the frame gently on the table, I took Lana's hands in mine. "It's the best gift anyone's ever given me. Thank you."

She squeezed my hand and smiled before pulling away. She stood, gathering the food and trash from the table.

She was leaving tomorrow. It was now or never, wasn't it?

"I'm going to miss running into you at Crystal Fountains." I stood and started helping her clean off the table. "Ever since we met, and especially for the last couple months, I'd hoped to see you every time I went."

Lana nodded, licking her lips. She blinked fast and took a deep breath.

"Me too," she admitted. Then she turned to the sink to wash some of the dishes. "And I've been finally feeling less guilty every time I've hoped for that," she said softly.

My blood pounded through my veins. I'd wanted to hear her say something like that for months.

"There's no need for guilt. Not anymore," I said softly as I stepped close behind her.

Her whole body tensed and her movements slowed as she seemed to sense my closeness.

I fought the urge to wrap my arms around her. I reached for the counter instead, bracketing her body between my arms.

Her hands shook as she put a dish in the drainer. I leaned closer, softly resting my forehead against the crown of her head.

"Lana," I murmured in her hair. "I can't stop thinking about you. I've wanted you since the moment I saw you."

She sighed and shook her head slowly.

I moved my hands from the counter and gently rested them on her hips. "Tell me you don't want this. Tell me I'm crazy and I've imagined this thing between us."

"I feel it too, but...," she paused. "What kind of a woman does that? Dates one brother, then jumps into the arms of the other brother after they break up."

"One that ended up with the wrong brother because the other one let her slip away."

She inhaled, her body shuddering.

I breathed in deeply, letting the light floral scent of her hair soak into me.

"Tell me to stop and I will." I leaned down enough that my lips brushed the shell of her ear as I whispered, "Just say the word, Lana. Or I won't be able to stop myself."

Slowly, I slid my hands up the sides of her body.

"Dylan..." she whispered.

My hands froze in place as I held my breath.

"I don't want you to stop," she continued. "I feel it every time I'm with you. From that first day we met. There's this connection between us I can't explain."

She leaned back against me, her body trembling lightly against mine.

Any doubts I'd ever had disappeared.

"Baby," I breathed as Lana ever so slowly turned to face me. I got lost in her beautiful blue eyes, wondering how the hell I'd ever let this woman slip through my fingers.

14

LANA

I turned and slid my hands up Dylan's chest. Looking into his eyes, I knew I was finally going to have what I'd wanted for so long.

It really wasn't fair. I was leaving tomorrow. The timing was terrible.

But there was no way I could resist. Not after the words he whispered in my ear.

"I can't fight this anymore," I said, my voice shaking.

My heartbeat pounded in my ears.

"Then don't," he whispered.

He brushed his lips against mine. The softness of his kiss and how careful he was being with me made my breath catch in my throat. And then he kissed me more forcefully, making my mouth yield against his.

Dylan let out a low groan that vibrated through me as he pulled me flush against him.

I moaned into the kiss as he bent me back, his hands sliding from my hips to grip my ass. Dylan licked his way into my mouth, his tongue twining with mine.

In that moment, nothing else mattered but the feeling of

Dylan's strong arms around me, his lips sealed over mine. I lost myself in the kiss, all the suppressed tension between us finally breaking free like a dam bursting.

There was only this moment, this connection neither of us could resist anymore. I didn't know what tomorrow held, but tonight, I was finally where I belonged.

Dylan gripped my ass and lifted me. He slid a couple of dishes into the sink and sat me on the countertop, parting my legs to pull me tight against him. I wrapped my legs around him and ground myself forward against the hard bulge in his jeans.

"*Lana*," he gasped into the kiss, as I cupped his face and curled myself forward, eager for more contact between my body and his.

He slid his hands up my thighs, inside my skirt, his warm grip on my hips making me eager for more.

Then he kissed down my jaw and throat to bury his face in my cleavage, popping my top button loose as he kissed my chest. He kissed across until he could mouth one of my hard nipples through my shirt and bra.

I arched my back and pressed my aching core against him.

"I've wanted you for so long," I admitted, my face heating up with both excitement and the shame that saying it made me feel.

But Dylan seemed to understand. He lifted his face, nodding, as he captured my mouth in another hungry kiss.

My back arched on its own. I wanted to lean back, let him kiss me anywhere he wanted, but the upper cabinets kept me from being able to move too much. Dylan must have sensed it, because he lifted me, sliding me from the counter into his arms to turn and set me on the table where we'd just had dinner.

"So fucking beautiful," Dylan growled as he started kissing his way down my throat again, this time sliding a hand inside my shirt and bra to cup my breast. He unbuttoned my shirt with his other hand while I squirmed on the hard table.

With my shirt open, he pulled my bra down and out of the way to lick my nipple and suck gently. I tossed my head back at the delicious pull, then I gasped when he pushed my skirt up and slid both hands slowly against my thighs.

As he kissed my breasts, teasing them, I leaned back on my hands and let him have free reign over me.

He licked his way down my stomach. I shuddered as his fingers caressed my inner thighs, pushing my legs open.

"Dylan, I need you," I said, reaching to undo the button of his jeans.

He captured my wrists, slowly pushing me back until I was lying on the table, and slid my hands above my head.

"Baby, I need you too. More than you know." He kissed up my chest, nuzzling my neck. "But I only get one night with you."

The need to feel him inside me was so overwhelming, I was shaking.

He gently kissed my lips, pinning one of his hands over my wrists.

"I'm going to take my time. I want this to last. I need this night to last," he said, brushing his thumb over my lower lip.

Then he slid his hand down my neck, his fingers softly wrapping around my throat. My breath hitched and his eyes flickered.

His hand continued to travel slowly down my body, making me shudder under his touch, until it reached my core. He cupped me between my legs before running his fingers up the center in a slow firm stroke.

"Ah!" I cried out as pleasure jolted through me from the sudden contact.

"I want to know what drives you wild," he murmured in my ear as his thumb circled my clit through my wet panties. "Where you like to be touched."

His face hovered inches above mine, his dark eyes fluttering over my features as he watched for my reactions to his touches. I whimpered as he continued to explore between my legs, moaning when he hit a spot of nerves.

"And when I find it," he whispered, pressing his thumb down on the spot, keeping his eyes on me as I came close to the edge.

"I'm going to make you feel so fucking good you're never going to forget me."

"Dylan," I shouted when an intense rush of pleasure overtook me.

I threw my head back and squeezed my eyes shut. He continued to stroke me through the wet fabric as I came down from my high. When I opened my eyes, he was watching me intensely, breathing heavily.

He sealed his lips over mine and kissed me slowly as he slipped his thumb under my panties, feeling my slick center. He groaned and deepened the kiss.

"So fucking wet for me," he murmured against my lips as he continued to stroke me. "I bet you taste as good as you feel."

I could barely stand the anticipation. I propped up onto my elbows, watching him kiss down until his face was between my legs.

He inhaled deeply and closed his eyes, groaning at the scent of my arousal. Oh God, I wasn't sure I could handle the intensity of this man. When he looked up at me, his eyes were primal, dark with lust as he pulled my panties to the side and his tongue slipped into my folds.

I hissed in pleasure at the feel of his tongue against me. He lifted my legs over his shoulders and wrapped his hands over my thighs, tugging me closer to his mouth.

Dylan moaned and sucked at me lightly, his long fingers spreading me open.

"So fucking good," he murmured before slipping his tongue into me in a few slow thrusts.

I cried out in pleasure and surprise.

He growled as he sealed his lips over my clit, sucking gently. Then he pushed his finger inside me, slowly massaging my front wall, and I started seeing stars.

Dylan's tongue sought out every part of me, bringing me closer and closer to orgasm. He cupped my breast with one hand, teasing my nipple with his thumb, while he finger-fucked me with his other hand.

I bit my bottom lip, feeling self-conscious at the sounds I was trying to hold back. Dylan noticed and kissed my inner thigh.

Then he hooked his fingers into my panties and pulled them down, letting them drop to the floor.

"I want to hear you, baby," he said, kissing my other thigh. "I want to hear you let go."

He worked me with his tongue and finger again. I usually didn't make much noise during sex, but I couldn't have held back any longer even if I'd wanted to. Dylan sucked my clit and pushed a second finger inside me, triggering the pleasure he'd been building.

I shouted as the orgasm rippled through me. He sucked and licked me all throughout, and I could feel his hot breath against me as he growled when I cried out a second time.

I arched my back and pressed myself against his mouth,

riding out the pleasure and squeezing around his thick fingers inside me.

Dylan had me worked into a frenzy I hadn't felt with any other man. No orgasm had ever been more exciting or satisfying. Yet I wanted more. I needed more.

I wasn't going to settle for his tongue and fingers inside me.

I sank my fingers into his short hair as the last wave of pleasure left my thighs trembling. He lifted his face, licking his bottom lip, then he rose and pressed his mouth against mine so fast I gasped.

He gathered me into his arms as easily as if I was a rag doll. I wrapped my legs around him and hung on while he carried me to my bedroom.

He had his shirt off and tossed aside by the time I unfastened his fly and helped him push his jeans down. I dragged his briefs down his thighs, and when his thick cock was free, I caught the head in my mouth.

"Lana," he gasped in shock, instantly tangling his fingers in my hair and rocking his hips forward for more.

He was thick in my mouth, bigger than I could comfortably take in, but I did my best. I swirled my tongue around the shaft and licked beneath the head, trying to give him as much pleasure as he'd given me.

His fist closed in my hair and he tugged gently to get me to look up at him. I'd never seen more than a peek of his tattoo before—it was a few wild horses running, their manes blown back, in a scene that spread across his chest. A growling wolf with narrowed eyes covered the shoulder and bicep of one arm.

Dylan was muscular and fit, things I'd always known, but seeing him naked made it obvious just how head-to-toe gorgeous he was.

I ran my hands up his incredible abs that tensed as I took him deeper in my mouth.

"Fuck," he growled as he pulled back, as if he couldn't contain himself if I continued.

He lifted me to my feet and kissed me. "I can't wait to have you."

My core throbbed in need, eager to know what his cock felt like buried inside me. I could imagine it. I'd thought about it enough times, after all. But I really didn't want to wait anymore either.

I cupped his face in my hands, then his neck. He lifted my leg and pressed against me, so I put an arm over his shoulder for leverage. Then he kissed my neck and slowly pushed inside me while I arched up and met his thrust.

He groaned as he filled me completely and stayed there, his harsh breaths against my neck. I hissed at the fullness of him inside me.

Dylan lifted his head, eyes searching my face. "You okay?" He asked, his voice straining to get out the words.

I nodded, rolling my hips to urge him to continue. He kissed up my jaw to take my mouth again as he started to move in slow, easy thrusts. He trembled like he was holding back.

I wrapped my arms around his body, my hands pressed against his back, and pulled him into me again and again with my legs around his hips. He panted against my mouth as he sped up, driving into me in his need.

"You feel so good," he breathed against my lips.

I held him tighter and squeezed around his cock, seconds away from coming again. He thrust deep, pulling a moan from me as I got close to the edge.

I shuddered, clinging to him. "Dylan, please."

Falling For My Ex's Brother

"I've got you." He rocked against me, sliding through my wetness and nudging my clit with every pass.

I met him thrust for thrust, nails biting into his shoulders, his cock hitting my sweet spot on every stroke, rocketing me higher and higher.

"That's it, baby," Dylan rumbled low, sensing my closeness. "Come for me."

His next thrust sent me over, my second orgasm jolting through me even more intensely than the first. When my inner muscles clamped around him, Dylan shouted and snapped his hips, holding himself deep inside me as he came.

Dylan didn't roll away as soon as he was finished. He cupped my cheek and kissed me deeply, with such care, bringing us both down as our heartbeats slowed together. Then he slid onto his side and pulled me into his arms.

I think neither of us knew what to say, or we didn't want to break the spell by speaking. We lay there quietly for a long time with Dylan stroking my hair and me stroking the skin at his waist.

I was suddenly nervous at the thought that Dylan might leave soon.

"Stay?" I asked.

"I'm not going anywhere. There's nowhere else in the world I'd rather be than right next to you." He wrapped his arms around me and kissed my forehead. "I want to keep you here, in my arms, as long as I can."

My heart twisted, knowing it would only be for that night.

After a moment, he rolled onto his elbow and pulled back to look at me, eyes lidded with a different emotion than before.

His gaze moved down my body as I laid there. I suddenly

felt self-conscious with him openly perusing me. I reached for the sheets, trying to pull it over my body.

"Stop," he said softly, tugging it to keep me from covering up. "Let me look at you."

"Dylan...," I laughed, feeling a little nervous as he reached for my arm that was now covering my chest.

"I've seen it all already if that's what you're worried about." He chuckled. "Lana, you're beautiful," he said, his face becoming serious. "I want to remember you."

I slowly lowered my arms, letting his eyes devour me.

"So damn gorgeous," he said, through hooded eyes.

He pulled me to him, cradling my cheek in his hand, and kissed me softly.

"How tired are you?" He asked.

I glanced up at him with a smile, understanding his meaning. "I can probably be convinced to stay awake."

He kissed me again, and sleep couldn't have been further from my mind.

Sunrise couldn't have been far off by the time we both started to fade.

"I wish this could be the beginning for us," I murmured, my eyelids heavy.

The last thing I remembered thinking before I fell asleep was again how it really wasn't fair that this happened the night before I had to leave. And that I was grateful it had. After wanting Dylan for so long, I would have that one amazing night to remember for the rest of my life.

As much as it killed me, I knew I had to let him go.

15

DYLAN

THREE YEARS LATER

Brent and I sat in the sleek conference room of Berman Agency, waiting for our meeting with the new marketing team.

Deft Rock Brewery has been thriving since we opened our doors more than two years ago. Our customers loved our beer selection, and it had become a hotspot for locals to hang out.

We grew it into what it was, but we knew there were still areas for expansion and needed help taking it to the next level. We hoped partnering with a marketing agency would do just that.

Brent looked at some of the framed ads hung around the meeting room, hands on his hips. He leaned close to one, reading the fine print.

"I don't know, Dylan. Are you sure about this place?"

He'd asked me that five times since I'd mentioned getting some outside help with marketing and event planning, and I'd answered the same every time.

"No, but I'm more sold on this place than any of the others. They put the Clayton Winery on the map and seem to know their stuff when it comes to wineries and breweries."

Brent was about to say something else when people started filing in, folders and laptops in their hands.

The last person to come through the door stopped and stared at me, her mouth falling open, then she hurried to her seat at the opposite end of the long table from me.

Lana.

I breath caught in my throat. She was even more beautiful than I remembered. She looked more professional now, in her slim knee length skirt and a crisp white shirt. Her hair was pulled back in a sleek ponytail. My cock throbbed at the thought of wrapping it around my hand, and then I had to remind myself we were in a meeting room full of people.

She glanced up at me again, and I smiled at her. She smiled back a little shyly, then looked down at her papers again. Her cheeks were pink, getting pinker by the second.

Alexander McCain, one of the partners of the firm, started talking about Deft Rock and some potential campaigns he thought could really take the brewery to the next level.

I hoped like hell Brent was paying close attention, because I couldn't really focus on what he was saying.

I was too busy looking at Lana, just taking her in after not seeing her for so long. And after spending all those years unable to stop thinking about her or the night we spent together before she left.

Her eyes kept meeting mine and darting away throughout the meeting.

Brent elbowed me and nodded in Lana's direction with a grin like he'd just realized it was her.

I nodded and tried to stop staring. Maybe I'd catch something that Alexander was proposing for our business.

"... and that's why I'm confident that Lana Murphy and Beth Curtis will be a great team to be in charge of your account," he said.

Lana looked surprised as he touched her shoulder. "She cut her teeth at one of the top New York agencies before coming here six months ago and has done nothing but outstanding work for businesses in Everbrook and the surrounding areas. And Beth has been with the agency for four years and has been instrumental in handling our top accounts," he said.

Lana opened her mouth like she was going to say something, but Brent spoke instead.

"I'm sure they'll do a great job." He winked at her, and her sweet little smile made me want to dive over the conference table and kiss her again.

So many nights after she'd moved away, I'd been awake in the middle of the night and nearly called her.

But I knew her life was in New York.

She had a new job, probably a new group of friends, a new boyfriend maybe. I had no right to try to hang on and hold her back.

All I could do was hope that maybe she'd call me. Text. Give me any excuse to go visit her and hold her in my arms again.

That never happened, so I'd tried to move on.

And I was left with the duty of helping Todd get back on his feet. I had to be there for him even though he hadn't wanted the help. He had wanted nothing to do with me after our blow up.

It took a long time for us to get to a place where we were able to speak openly about what had happened. But I couldn't get myself to tell him about my night with Lana. I knew it would negate all the progress we'd made.

And she was gone. I didn't expect to see her again. Telling him would've only made things worse between us.

But here she was, back in Everbrook. And being in the same room with her had my body instantly on edge, almost ready to pounce.

Alexander talked to Lana for a few minutes, and it hit me. I really didn't know if it'd be a relief to finally be near her after so long, or if it'd be torture because she'd moved on and had no interest in reliving anything we had together.

"I didn't know you were back," Brent said warmly. "I wasn't sure about this place, but now that I know you're a part of the team, I'm not worried."

They talked pleasantly for a bit, and Lana immediately started brainstorming some promotions and marketing opportunities she thought would work well for a brewery and for Deft Rock in particular. She promised to have more ideas to run past us within a few days.

When the meeting was over, I made my way to Lana when Beth approached me.

"Hi, I wanted to come introduce myself officially." Beth held out her hand. "I'm looking forward to working with you and Brent. I'm excited to see what we can do for your business."

"Likewise," I replied. "I hope we can come up with some great things together."

I watched as Lana spoke to Brent, but she seemed in a hurry to leave.

"Will you excuse me?" I said to Beth, not taking my eyes off Lana.

I reached her before she could make it out the door.

"Lana, hang on a sec," I said, then I said to Brent over my shoulder, "I'll catch up with you in a little bit."

When he and Beth left, Lana and I stared at each other for a second. Then we both smiled, stepping closer, and I carefully pulled her into a hug.

"It's so good to see you, Lana. How have you been?"

She hugged me, tentatively at first, then more tightly, before letting go and stepping back.

"I should have told you I'd moved back. I-I've just been so busy," she said awkwardly. "What about you? The brewery seems to really be taking off."

"Yeah, it's going great," I said.

An uneasy silence stretched between us. The time apart hadn't changed my pull towards her. I still felt magnetically drawn to Lana.

Being so close to her again made my blood pound through my body. I still wanted her so much. The urge to kiss her was fucking unbearable, but I knew better than to do anything at her workplace.

"What are you doing tonight?" I asked. I'd missed being near her for three years. I didn't want to add another day to that tally. "Have dinner with me." I brushed my knuckles against her forearm, wanting to make my meaning clear. "Let's catch up."

Her big blue eyes met mine. I thought I saw want in them. Something that matched the way I felt.

But I could also tell that something was wrong.

16

LANA

Alexander and my direct boss, Chelsea, had a habit of springing things on me and the other managers.

I had no idea I was going to work on the Deft Rock account until Alex announced it in front of the whole room.

I was surprised not at the job or the work, but at being so unprepared to see Dylan Easton again. I was sure I gaped like a fish trying to breathe the second I saw him.

He was wearing a dark grey suit that fit him perfectly, accentuating his broad shoulders and tall frame. He looked so damn good. Even after three years, my knees went weak at the sight of this man.

And the look in his eyes... they were the same as I remembered from our night together. Filled with raw need.

I'd thought about that night almost every day while I was in New York. And seeing him again sent those memories flooding back in. I was barely able to focus on the meeting.

His hug was as warm and firm as I remembered. His body felt just as good as it had back then. My thighs clenched at the way he smiled down at me.

The way he asked me to dinner. To catch up.

I stared into his eyes, knowing exactly what he meant. What he wanted.

But I had moved on.

"I'd like to catch up sometime, Dylan," I said. And though the words were hard to say, I made myself say them. "I've missed our friendship. But my boyfriend's coming over tonight, and I don't want to change our plans this late in the day. Maybe we can have you over for dinner sometime soon?"

His soft brown eyes hardened when I said *friendship* and *boyfriend*. He seemed to lean back, further away from me, and dropped his hand with a slight nod.

"Boyfriend," he said, not making it sound like a question.

If he was trying to hide his disappointment, he was doing a bad job of it.

"Austin and I have been together for a few months. He's a great guy." I said.

He nodded again, his jaw twitching. But after a moment, the corner of his lips turned up slightly.

"A few months isn't very long."

"No. I guess not," I admitted.

Was he going to try to convince me to have dinner with him anyway?

"How's Todd doing?" I asked, both to bring him to Dylan's mind, and because I really wanted to know.

"He's actually doing great. You'd be proud of him," he said with real pride in his voice. "Lana, I've thought about—"

"Sorry to interrupt." Chelsea, my boss, popped her head into the room. "Lana, we need you for a meeting with the Neighborhood Pharmacy people."

I could have kissed her for interrupting us when she did, because I didn't know how to handle the conversation I thought Dylan wanted us to have.

"Of course. Excuse me, Dylan. Really great seeing you again," I said quickly. "I'll call with ideas soon."

I got out of there before he could say anything else. Naturally, I kept thinking about him for the rest of the day, even after I arrived home.

I sighed and flopped back onto my bed. Seeing Dylan today had stirred up so many old feelings and memories.

The morning after our night together, Dylan had kissed me with a passion I'd never felt from anyone else.

He'd said, "I know you're heading for a new life. But you remember what I said, Lana. You call me anytime you need something. I'll always show up for you."

Then he'd kissed my forehead and left.

Living in a new city was tough at first. I missed Grandpa and my friends like crazy. And most of all, I missed Dylan.

I thought about him a lot those first few months. I wondered if he ever thought about me too. At first, I hoped that he'd call. Thought that he would. But he never did.

I'd pulled up his number countless times but never let it ring through. The thought of Todd always kept me from pressing that green button. He was Todd's brother. I should never have slept with him, even though I couldn't really bring myself to regret it.

Todd had still been calling and sending me texts when I first got to New York. Leaving everything in the past felt like the right thing to do.

In New York, I had the opportunity to do that by simply not calling Dylan, no matter how much I wanted to.

So I didn't. It was hard, but I decided to let Dylan go. Maybe Dylan felt the same way about me.

I did my best to focus on building my new life. I threw myself into work and getting to know my new friends.

I dated around and met some decent guys, but none compared to Dylan. Not even close. I began to wonder if I'd ever have that kind of connection again, if I'd always feel a void without Dylan.

I came back to Everbrook six months ago to be closer to Grandpa. His health was declining, and I could hear his voice getting weaker each time we talked on the phone. He'd told me he was doing fine, but I knew he just didn't want me to worry about him. I decided it was time to come home.

Luckily, I was able to secure a job at Berman Agency before I even left New York. They were the largest agency in Everbrook and my top choice of the few companies I applied to. I thought about Dylan when I returned. Considered calling him, but for what? It had been three years since we shared just one night.

Surely, he had moved on. Probably had a girlfriend. Maybe even remarried.

It would've been stupid of me to call him after all that time, right?

And now that I was with Austin and things have been going well, I didn't want to rehash the past.

I was just going to have to be strong and learn to leave the past where it belonged, no matter how much the old feelings came rushing back.

I was done with messy relationships. I wanted smooth sailing, no complications, or any more damn guilt. No more feeling like I was doing something wrong or feeling things I shouldn't be feeling.

My phone buzzed with a text. It was Austin, letting me

know he was on his way to pick me up for our date. I smiled thinking of him.

We had been dating for about three months, and he was really a great guy - smart, successful, sweet.

A bit of a control freak, but I thought it was kind of endearing. At least most of the time. I knew his intentions were good.

I started to get ready, trying not to obsess anymore about Dylan. Austin was the man in my life now. So what if he didn't make my stomach erupt in butterflies the way Dylan did?

I had just finished refreshing my makeup when the doorbell rang. I opened it to find Austin standing there looking crisp as ever in a button-down shirt and blazer. He was tall, lean, and handsome in a clean-cut way, a stark contrast to Dylan's rugged-

Stop it. Stop comparing him to Dylan.

"Hey babe, ready to go?" he asked, as he gave me a quick kiss before he looked me up and down. He didn't say anything, but I knew what he was thinking. If I was really going to wear the outfit I had on.

I glanced down at myself - a short black skirt and silky camisole. Maybe a little sexy for a casual date night, but nothing over the top.

"What? You don't like it?" I asked.

Austin frowned. "I do. Of course, I do. I mean, it's just a little revealing, that's all. I don't want other guys ogling my girlfriend all night."

Austin's jealous streak annoyed me sometimes. But I tried to brush it off as him being a caring boyfriend.

"It's not that bad," I said lightly. "Just thought I'd dress up a bit." I grabbed my jacket and bag. "Come on, let's go enjoy our night."

Falling For My Ex's Brother

Austin still looked bothered, but he dropped it as we drove to the restaurant. He knew arguing with me about my outfit would lead nowhere.

At dinner, Austin talked about his week at the office, his upcoming business trip, and his tennis match. I chimed in here and there, but my mind kept wandering.

"You seem distracted," Austin commented over our entrees. "Everything okay?"

"I'm sorry," I said, snapping back to attention. "Just tired, I guess. But tell me more about your meeting with the Caldwell Group."

Austin launched back into his story as I sipped my wine.

But I couldn't stop thinking about Dylan. His muscular arms, his warm smile, the heat in his eyes when he looked at me...

"Okay seriously, where are you right now?" Austin said, waving a hand in front of my face.

I shook myself out of my daze. "Sorry, really. Just a little out of it today." I reached across the table to squeeze his hand. Time to snap out of it.

After dinner, we came back to my place. As I poured us some wine, Austin came up behind me and wrapped his arms around my waist.

"Why don't we take this to the bedroom?" he murmured against my skin.

He started nuzzling my neck and turned me around to kiss him. I kissed him back a little more enthusiastically than I usually did.

And I quickly realized it was because I was trying to feel something. Trying to find a hint of the feelings Dylan had given me years ago. And the feelings that reared up when I saw him at the meeting.

But I felt nothing remotely close. I couldn't get into it

with Austin when I had Dylan on my mind. I pulled away and gently removed his hands from my waist.

"Actually, I should probably get some rest," I said.

Austin's face fell. "What? I didn't get to see you the whole week."

I avoided his hurt puppy dog eyes, feeling guilty. "I know, I'm sorry. It's just been a long day and I'm exhausted. Raincheck?"

Austin folded his arms across his chest.

"Is this because of what I said about your outfit earlier?" he asked.

"No, it has nothing to do with that," I said shortly.

It had actually bothered me a little. Dylan would've told me I looked hot and spun me around. It was suddenly, painfully obvious, that he wasn't Dylan.

"I'm just tired, that's all."

Austin's face softened and he cradled my face in his hands. "Are you feeling ok? Maybe you're coming down with something."

"I'm fine, just need some sleep I think."

"Okay, you must have had a long day. You get your beauty rest." He kissed me again. "Just call me if you need anything."

I kissed him softly. "Thanks. I promise to make it up to you this weekend, okay?"

After Austin left, I decided to call it an early night.

I laid in bed ready to sleep when a text buzzed on my phone. It was Dylan suggesting that he show me around Deft Rock later in the week so I could see the place and be better able to help promote it.

A dinner meeting and tour, he called it.

It made sense from a business standpoint. But I knew it was more than that.

I'd have to make sure it was a team meeting and not just the two of us. I quickly set up a formal invite with Beth, Chelsea, and Maddie.

Maddie was my partner in crime at the office. She and I became close after working on our first project together. She oversaw the visual side of the marketing campaigns. She was brilliant.

I wasn't looking forward to working on the Deft Rock account with Beth, another manager at the agency.

She was smart and good at what she did, and also my biggest competition. We didn't always see eye to eye and tried to stay out of each other's way. Working on a project together was going to make that hard.

We were the same age, twenty-seven, and had the same years of experience. Needless to say, we were both gunning for the upper management position that was opening up in a few months.

I had a feeling Alexander assigned both me and Beth to Deft Rock's account to see which one of us would take the lead. This was an opportunity for me to prove myself. I'd been waiting for this ever since I had started working at Berman.

Even as the highest paying company in the area, the salary wasn't near what I was making in New York. Between my student loans and Grandpa's bills, it didn't take long for me to start falling behind on my finances. The thought always weighed heavily on my shoulders.

This was my chance at getting that promotion and raise that I so desperately needed. I wanted it so badly I could taste it. I'd have to stay focused on the job and it was going to be hard with Dylan being the client.

One thing was clear. My feelings for Dylan would have to remain in the past.

17

DYLAN

I should have expected that Lana might bring someone else from the agency with her to the meeting. Brent was around, after all, because he was almost always there. But I'd hoped that once Lana showed up and we got the tour out of the way, she and I would be able to talk alone.

Lana brought Chelsea, Beth, and Maddie.

I let Brent take the lead on the tour, pointing out the features of the place and answering questions.

I stuck to Lana's side the whole time. I couldn't help it. I was like a magnet to metal, feeling the pull of her anytime she was near me.

Maybe I was an ass for feeling the way I did, but I wasn't about to let some boyfriend of just a few months discourage me. She'd dated Todd longer than that, after all, and that wasn't exactly great for her.

Lana probably had no clue as to how much I'd held back when she was with Todd. Only because he was my brother. This boyfriend of hers would be a different story.

I was going to make sure she knew how I felt. And what I wanted. This time, I wouldn't let her slip away.

Not if I was right about what I thought I saw in her eyes. That she still wanted me too.

"Over here we have our fermentation tanks," Brent explained, leading the group over to the towering metal vats.

"And this is our bottling and canning line," I chimed in, steering the group across the production floor.

"Impressive operation you guys have built," Lana said, giving me a look like she was proud. "Really Dylan. I knew you'd make it a success, but this is really something."

I smiled warmly. "Thanks. We've worked hard to get it to this point."

Our hands brushed as we walked, and Lana shifted away. I glanced down at her to see her blushing. I wanted to pull her into my arms and let her know exactly how much I missed her.

"And this is the taproom," Brent said once we'd reached it.

Dinner arrived then, so we set up there to eat. I maneuvered to sit by Lana on one of the barstools.

Beth asked why we didn't have a dinner menu at the brewery.

"That's something we've been considering," I said. "We do have snack foods available. We've experimented with things like wings and pizza on the weekends."

Lana spoke then. "Taprooms usually focus on beer, but it can be profitable to offer the right foods. I've done some research if you'd like a copy. If you're interested in expanding into more food service, of course."

I grinned at her. She really seemed to be throwing herself into learning our business.

"I'd like that. Thanks. We'll have to sit down and discuss it sometime."

Chelsea ran with that idea, and Brent and Lana discussed the types of foods usually served at breweries while we ate.

I couldn't take my eyes off her. She wore a soft shade of lipstick that seemed to make her skin look creamier and her eyes even more bright blue.

Everything she said demonstrated a knowledge of breweries and their customer base that she had to have gained in the previous few days with a lot of research. I was impressed, but I'd expected to be.

"You really know your stuff," I said when the conversation died down. "I'm more confident than ever that we're putting Deft Rock in the right hands."

Her sweet little blush made me want to touch her cheek. If we'd been alone, I would have.

Maddie said, "Lana tells me you two know each other. Or knew each other, before the other day."

She was clearly just trying to make friendly conversation, but I wished she hadn't brought that up in front of the other team members.

I wasn't even sure why it bothered me. It felt a little like putting our past relationship on display, even though Maddie probably didn't know the half of it.

"I dated his brother," Lana said quickly, glancing at Chelsea and then at me. "And his late grandfather was my grandpa's best friend."

I thought it was curious that she didn't mention our grandfathers first. Grandpa had passed a couple of years earlier, and his friendship with James had been what introduced us in the first place.

It seemed that she wanted to point out that she'd dated Todd to make sure I didn't say anything about us. As if I would tell her coworkers that we'd had one hot night together before she left.

"Thank you, by the way," I said to her. "For the card. I appreciated that."

She'd sent a card after my grandpa died, addressed to me and Todd. She'd written inside it about what a special man he was, and how lucky he'd been to have us as grandsons, and how happy it had made her that he'd been her grandpa's best friend.

After dinner, we toured the rest of the brewery. I was ready for the show to be over long before it was.

When it was clearly winding down, the group followed Brent into another room. Lana moved to follow, but I took her arm to stop her.

"It really is great to see you again. And I appreciate the work you're putting into this. But I'd like to see you outside of work one of these days," I said. "Maybe I can take you to dinner?"

I moved closer, encouraged by the way she stared at me with those pretty blue eyes. She still wanted me, even if she didn't intend to let herself have what she wanted because of some boyfriend.

I hoped I could change that.

She swallowed hard and stepped back but didn't pull free. "Dylan—"

"I'm sorry I never called," I said quickly. "I should have. But I didn't want to hold you back. Now that you're here again," I stepped closer and looked down at her. "I want to see you, Lana. And I hope you want that too," I whispered.

She stared long enough that I thought she was going to admit it. But instead, she stepped away, carefully pulling her arm out of my grip. She lowered her head, adverting my gaze.

"We can't, Dylan."

"Why not?" I asked, trying not to sound hurt.

Lana gave me an exasperated look. "You know why. You're a client, I'm working on your account. And I have a boyfriend."

"Right. Boyfriend," I said, clenching my jaw.

Maybe I had underestimated this boyfriend and things were more serious than I realized. The thought made my gut twist.

I had no right to sabotage a relationship that was going well. I had to know if I stood a chance. I decided to cut to the chase.

"Do you love him?"

She snapped her eyes back to me and inhaled sharply. She hesitated for a moment before answering.

"I care about him. But that's not the point."

She didn't love him.

I smiled as I nodded. "Okay."

"The point is you're my client now and I'm in a relationship," she said, sensing my skepticism.

"I could always fire the agency, if that helps," I said, only half teasing. "If I'm not your client, then that won't stand in the way."

She laughed softly, probably thinking I wasn't serious. "You wouldn't fire us just to—"

The group came back, interrupting us, so I simply raised my eyebrows as if to say that *maybe I would*.

LANA

I was pretty sure Dylan wasn't serious about firing us to eliminate the obstacle of him being my client. But the way he raised his eyebrows was so *Dylan*, it made me want him even more.

I didn't let him get me alone again, because I honestly wasn't sure how long I could hold out if he kept trying to get me to go out with him. He was the most tempting man I'd ever met, and I was starting to feel weak around him.

When the tour was officially over, I stuck with the group so we could walk out together, and I could avoid talking to Dylan again.

The next day, I went to visit Grandpa and stopped into the business office to talk to Cheryl, the admin at the senior home. I'd been bracing myself for the conversation for a while, and I figured it was best to get it over with.

I sat in the chair across from her desk.

"I can't pay everything that's owed today, but I can make another partial payment toward the balance," I said, pulling out my wallet and checkbook.

"No need," she said, waving me off. "The balance has

been covered by an anonymous donor. That doesn't solve the problem of future payments, but for right now, the balance is zero," she said happily.

"An anonymous donor?" My hands trembled with relief. I'd been dreading how long it would take me to catch up on the thousands of dollars it had been behind. That debt disappearing in a blink was such a gift. "It happens sometimes. People find hospital and nursing home bills to cover as a charitable donation. And it's usually the big bills that they figure people will have the most trouble paying. You got lucky!"

I almost cried, but I managed to keep myself together.

"There's no way to find them and thank them?" I asked.

"Technically, yes, but that would be an ethical misstep. If they wanted the recipient to know who they were, they wouldn't insist on doing it anonymously." She shook her head. "I won't violate that. When someone's that generous, I can't see going against their wishes."

"Of course not," I said. I took a few deep breaths, enjoying the relief, before pointing at the papers on her desk. "So, how does the billing look going forward?"

Grandpa's monthly balance had been building up ever since I moved back. I'd managed to cover both mine and Grandpa's expenses when I had my job in New York, but with the pay cut when I took the job at Berman Agency, I came up short every month.

I really needed that promotion. By my rough calculation, the salary at that level would be just enough to keep Grandpa at Crystal Fountains.

It was worth it to be near him during what I knew would be his last years. But the stress of it was starting to get to me.

And I didn't want to move him to a less expensive senior home because that meant he'd lose his friends all at once.

Losing Dave had nearly done him in, so if he left everyone at one time . . . no. I'd work three jobs to keep from putting him through that.

Once Cheryl and I were done, I went to see Grandpa. As usual, he talked about missing Dave at first, then switched to asking questions about my life.

"How's the new boyfriend treating you?" he asked like he did every time.

"Austin's fine."

"That's not really what I asked," he said, one eyebrow cocked.

"He treats me well, Grandpa. Brings wine and flowers, takes me out. He's a good guy."

"Does he know you don't really care for flowers?"

I shrugged. "It's the thought that counts."

"Your old boyfriend stops in to see me sometimes," Grandpa said. "Dave's grandson."

I had no idea Todd still visited my grandpa. "Why didn't you ever mention that before?"

He shrugged. "Forgetful, I guess." He opened his night table drawer to dig inside it. "I think he misses you an awful lot."

Todd had eventually stopped calling and texting after I went to New York. I guessed he'd gotten the hint that I wasn't taking him back. He'd texted only once more after I sent the card when Dave passed away to say thanks for thinking of them. I suspected Todd was well and truly over me.

"I'm sure he's moved on by now. We haven't really spoken since we broke up over three years ago. But it's nice that he comes to see you."

He grunted, then handed me a deck of cards. "Got time for a few hands?"

"Are you going to cheat?" I asked as I shuffled.

"I never cheat. Dirty, dirty lies," he said with a wink.

I laughed and dealt the cards, still wondering if Todd came to see him because he missed me, or because it made him feel the loss of his own grandpa a little less.

18

DYLAN

"I want to take you somewhere," I said to Lana on the phone.

"Dylan, we've discussed this," she answered, her voice shaking a little.

"Hear me out, Lana. Killer Luck Brewery. They do a booming business and serve food in their taproom. I figure we can go and check it out. For business reasons, of course."

"Business reasons," Lana said, her voice skeptical. "Well, let me see when Chelsea or Beth can fit it into their schedules and—"

"That's not going to work for me."

"Why not?" Lana cleared her throat. "Wouldn't you want the team there to soak up the atmosphere and take notes? Offer suggestions?"

"Not really." I knew my ploy risked being transparent, and I didn't care. "I think you're perfectly capable of handing it without help. And your input is really all I'm interested in."

"The more people helping, the better. Let me check with them," she said, sounding almost as if she was pleading.

"I'd like this meeting to be just us. I want to experience the place as a regular customer would. Not an agency analyzing every last detail. Know what I mean?" I held my breath and waited for her to answer.

"As old friends," I added when she didn't reply.

She sighed and finally said, "Fine. But it's a business meeting, even if it's at night at a brewery, Dylan."

"Of course. I'll pick you up so we can talk more in the car."

She started to protest, but I turned on my 'boss' voice and said, "I just need your address, and I'll be there tomorrow at five sharp."

She caught the change in my tone—that of a client to the account manager working for his company—and gave me the address.

Maybe she thought I really did mean it to be all business after that. As long as she came, I didn't care.

I just needed some time with her, just the two of us, so I could convince her to give us another try.

So I could remind her how *right* we were together.

She seemed different from the Lana I knew from three years ago. She had put up a wall between us, resolved to keep her distance from me. And I was determined to tear it down, to get a glimpse of what we once had.

The next day, I pulled up to Lana's place at five till. I was going to knock on her door, but she must have been watching for me. She came outside as soon as I pulled up.

My breath caught in my throat.

She looked gorgeous in dark skinny jeans that hugged every curve and a loose sweater that hung casually off one shoulder. I drank in the sight of her as she slid into my car, catching a whiff of her flowery perfume.

"Thanks for indulging me on this research outing," I

said, flashing her a grin. "I think you'll really like this place, Killer Luck Brewery. Super hip vibe with amazing beers."

Lana gave me a wry look. "Well, it is technically work related. And beneficial to check out the competition." But her lips twitched into a hint of a smile that gave me hope.

"Hands-on experience is best. And two heads are better than one." I was a filthy liar.

Sure, I thought it was a good idea to see how some other owners ran their business. But it was really just an excuse to spend time with Lana. If she didn't already know that, she would soon enough.

At the brewery, I led Lana inside the bustling taproom.

The space was crowded, forcing us to squeeze through crowds of drinkers to get to the bar. I'd picked the right one to research given how many people were there.

Maybe serving more food was a good idea after all. We walked around the place, then ended up back in the taproom.

Lana looked a little nervous, like she didn't quite know how to act around me. I hated it. I wished I could put her at ease.

We managed to order beers, although the noise made it hard to hear each other. I leaned down close to Lana's ear to ask if she wanted food too.

She looked over the menu and ordered a few things.

A big group moved past us, and Lana stepped back to get out of the way. She stumbled and caught herself against my chest. I steadied her with my hands on her hips, like I'd done the day we met.

"You okay?" I asked, wrapping my arm around her waist and turning her away from the crowd.

Even though she'd regained her balance, I still held her close. I wasn't letting her go this time. Not until she pushed me away. Her body was inches from mine, and I could feel her heat through her clothes.

It took all my willpower to keep from kissing her right then and there, when she looked up at me with those wide blue eyes.

She nodded, cheeks flushing. "Yeah, sorry. It's just so packed in here."

I couldn't help but lean in, my lips coming dangerously close to her ear. "It's alright. I don't mind a beautiful woman falling into my arms," I whispered.

She glanced up at me, stifling her laughter the same way she'd done before.

"Still using those lines, I see," she said under her breath.

"Only on you," I replied, laughing softly.

For a second, I saw her mask slip. She smiled at me playfully, her eyes sparkling, before she turned away.

She broke our eye contact, but she held on to me, even though she wasn't in any danger of getting knocked around between me and the bar.

And in that moment, I felt it. She clung to me in the same way I did to her. I knew there was a chance because she still obviously felt something for me too. The pull between us was undeniable.

I felt another group of people passing behind me, so I took another step forward closer to her. Lana let out a small gasp as my body pressed flush against hers. The sound made my cock throb.

"Just letting the group pass," I said, nodding my head toward the crowd when she looked up at me with a startled expression.

I smiled down at her pretty face, grateful that the place was a little crowded. I was enjoying this more than I wanted to admit.

As I held Lana, I could feel her heart racing, and I knew it wasn't just from the crowd.

Her lips parted as if she was about to say something, but then she hesitated.

Lana's hesitation only fueled my need to have her closer. I moved my hand to the small of her back, pulling her body tighter against mine. I couldn't help but inhale deeply. Lana's body shuddered in response.

I wanted her. Wanted her in a way that was all consuming.

As if coming out of a daze, she cleared her throat and shook her head lightly. She gently pushed against my chest and leaned back. I reluctantly eased my grip on her.

"I hope we can find a table," she said, looking around nervously.

We managed to find a small high-top table in the corner to claim. I hopped up on the tall stool, aware of Lana's knees between mine as she situated herself.

"So what do you think so far?" I asked. "Living up to the hype?"

Lana took a thoughtful sip of her beer. "It's really nice. Trendy space, quality beers. Definitely some tough competition."

"But no one can beat Deft Rock," I said with a wink.

Lana laughed. "Obviously I'm partial, but yes your brewery has its own unique charm and personality." Her eyes softened. "You and Brent have really built something special there."

"And we're excited to see where it goes with your brilliant marketing plans," I said sincerely.

The loud music and energetic crowd seemed to fade away as we lost ourselves in conversation about the brewery.

Lana's knees remained between mine, our faces close together.

The server arrived with our order of food Lana had ordered for us. She flushed when she saw the heaping pile of appetizers.

"Sorry, I think I got carried away ordering," she said with an embarrassed laugh. "When I'm anxious I tend to overdo it on the food."

"I think it's adorable," I said sincerely. "Besides, it's great for research. And I'm very happy to help you eat all this. I'm starving."

Lana rolled her eyes and laughed. "I'm sure Austin would not be thrilled if he saw me stress-eating like this. He doesn't say it, but I know he must be thinking I don't need any more junk in my trunk."

I stopped mid sip and put my beer glass back down. She glanced up at me as she noticed me staring at her, probably looking like I was about to lose it. Because I sure felt like I was about to. Who was this idiot she was dating?

Her smile faded. "Dylan, I didn't mean that you stress me out. It's just that your brewery account is really important to me. I want to do a good job."

I didn't know she was stressed over our account, but that topic would be tabled for later. I needed to address her asshole boyfriend first.

"Austin sounds like a fucking idiot," I said, not meaning to sound as angry as it came out.

Lana's mouth dropped open, and her cheeks turned pink.

"You're gorgeous, Lana. Trust me, I'd know. I remember you. Vividly."

Her blush deepened and she busied herself arranging the plates between us. I could tell she was uncomfortable with my blunt comment, but she had to hear it. She had to know she was fucking beautiful.

"You're too much sometimes, you know that?" But she smiled and shook her head in amusement, so I knew she meant it in a good way "I appreciate it, but you don't have to worry about that. It doesn't bother me what Austin thinks. Or what anyone thinks, for that matter. I happen to think my body is perfect the way it is."

That had me sitting back in my seat. At that moment, I realized she carried herself differently than she did three years ago. More confident and sure of herself.

I simply grinned and nodded in agreement.

She laughed softly so I decided to press my luck.

"You didn't really answer my question when I asked you if you loved him," I said, taking a sip of my beer. "So I know you don't."

She gave me an exasperated look.

"Does he make you happy at least?" I asked.

A thoughtful look spread across her face.

"Of course, he does." She nodded, frowning like she was trying to convince herself more than me. "He's great, really. He's sweet and very caring."

It didn't sound like he made her all that happy either.

She told me everything I needed to know.

"You sure about that?" I asked with a smirk.

She shot me a look. "Yes, I'm sure. Now stop trying to poke holes in my relationship and let's discuss what we're here for."

I held my hands up in surrender and decided I'd better change the topic. Her comment earlier about being anxious gnawed at me. Was the agency overloading her with work?

"I didn't realize you were so stressed over our account. I hope you're not overworking yourself."

She waved me off. "I'm not. But I really want to do a good job. Obviously, because it's your business and I want to help make it an even bigger success. And it'll be a good opportunity for me to prove myself to Alexander and the other partners."

Lana started talking about the food Killer Luck was serving, the things Brent and I could adapt for Deft Rock that seemed to be working well for them, the ROI on various types of promotions.

She was all business even though she kept glancing up through her lashes at me. And I hadn't missed the way her cheeks pinked up right before she pushed away from me earlier.

I let her do her job, and when she didn't have anything business-like left to say, I put my hand over hers.

I didn't want to waste any more time than the years we'd already been apart.

"I've wished so many times that I'd called you after you went to New York," I said. "If I had it to do over again, I would."

Lana shook her head. "You wouldn't, Dylan. Not when Todd needed you. And we can't do it over again anyway. That's the thing." She put her other hand over mine and squeezed. "I should have called when Dave passed. I—"

"It's ok, I know why you didn't. You sent a card. That let us know you were thinking of him, and us."

"No, it wasn't enough. I was so afraid . . ." She looked down and blinked fast.

"Afraid of what, baby?"

"Don't, Dylan." Her gaze turned cool as she met mine. "Don't call me that. We're not doing that. I told you. I have a boyfriend. You're my client. I'm not going to break up with Austin, and you're not going to fire me."

"It doesn't have to be that way," I said.

She pulled her hands away and leaned back.

"It does, Dylan. Too much has already happened. Todd asked me to marry him, for God's sake. What happened between you and me later, that should never have happened."

I often felt the stirrings of guilt about that too. But Todd and I had mostly mended our relationship. At least, we'd been on speaking terms for a while. And it wasn't like he was still pining for Lana.

I didn't feel like what happened between us was that big of a deal anymore, but apparently Lana still did.

"Todd's okay, Lana. He still thinks fondly of you, but he's not hung up on you anymore. And *he* cheated on *you*, remember? Nothing happened between us when you were still together," I pointed out.

"I know that," she said. "But jumping from one brother to another—"

"You didn't. You know it wasn't like that." I leaned closer. "If anything, I think you jumped from me to him when you saw my wedding ring."

She looked stunned that I'd brought that up. Her brows pulled together as she swallowed.

Shit. Why did I say that? Like it was her fault for how things played out that day. I knew she already felt guilty for everything that had happened, and I didn't need to add to it.

"I didn't mean it like that," I said softly.

To my surprise, she nodded. "You know, you're right. I wish things had gone differently that day. That I didn't walk away from you, that I didn't end up with Todd. But Dylan, that's all in the past."

"It doesn't have to be," I whispered. "Haven't you

thought about me over the years? Did you think about me when you were in New York?"

Her beautiful blue eyes stared into mine. She let out a deep sigh as she said, "Yes, how could I not? And yet here we are. You're still Todd's brother. You're still my client. And I'm dating Austin."

I shook my head, frustrated at our situation.

"Our timing has just always been horrible. Haven't you ever noticed that? We're like some kind of star-crossed lovers, never quite getting to the same place at the same time."

I did notice it, but I also noticed how we always found our way back to each other.

I shook my head. "I don't believe that."

"Todd happened to show up right when I saw your ring. And I moved away after... after that night. Now you show up as my client, and I have a boyfriend."

"I don't believe in fate, Lana. I think we choose what we want and who we want to be with," I replied softly. "But if you do believe in fate, let's talk about the times it brought us together too. Haven't you thought about how we met? We happened to park next to each other and get out at the same time. How about the time I had a date at the same restaurant you were at? And how we ran into each other again the day before you moved. And we're here now... together."

Lana stared at me, processing all the times that we saw each other.

She bit her lower lip, brows drawn together like she was torn on what to believe.

"It still doesn't change our circumstances, Dylan." Lana sighed, eyes downcast. "I've moved on. I think we should just be friends."

Just friends? I shook my head, trying not to look wounded.

"I don't want to be friends," I replied bluntly.

Lana shifted in her seat, conflict plain on her lovely face.

"Dylan..." She sniffed, and I realized how emotional she suddenly was.

Lana put her hand over mine this time. "Dylan, it took me a long time to get past everything and move on. From you. From Todd. I don't want to go back to the past. I don't think we were meant to be."

It felt like someone took a battering ram to my chest. Was this what she really believed? I wondered if this was it for us. I'd have to let her go, no matter how much I wanted her.

She clearly wanted to leave things in the past.

I wasn't one to give up easily on something I wanted. But I also wasn't going to force my will on her. If this was happening, I wanted her to want it too. If she didn't, I'd respect her wishes. But not until she looked me in the eyes and told me she didn't feel anything between us.

I didn't think about how hard it might have been for Lana after she'd left. I always imagined that she moved on happily with her new life.

A server came to our table then, but Lana shook her head and said she was ready to leave.

She was quiet in the car, and I didn't feel like pushing the issue was going to help while she was still upset.

But I thought I'd see if I could get her to invite me in when I dropped her off so we could talk more in private. I wanted to get to the bottom of this *not meant to be* nonsense. A car I didn't recognize sat in the driveway. Obviously, her boyfriend was there waiting for her.

I'm still not giving up on you.

She thought we'd been star-crossed lovers, and maybe we were. But that didn't mean things couldn't change.

When I pulled up behind the car, a man got out. The Austin she'd spoken about. Before I could say anything, Lana got out and headed toward him after a quick goodbye.

I watched them walk in together, his arm around her waist. He glanced back at me, recognizing me seconds after I recognized him.

I couldn't believe my eyes. Of all people, she was dating that asshole.

I hadn't given up on having Lana in my arms again. But I knew that even if she never looked at me again and I didn't stand a chance, there was no way in hell that bastard was ever going to win her heart.

Not if I had anything to say about it.

∽

The restaurant wasn't too packed for a Saturday, which was a relief. I spotted Todd as soon as I walked in, so I brushed past the hostess and sat down. Todd and I did the usual catch-ups and chatted about the sales he'd made over the last few weeks. He asked about Brent and the brewery, and I told him about the ad agency.

I didn't mention Lana. I didn't think he knew she was back in Everbrook. If he did, he hadn't mentioned her, and I didn't want to be the one to bring it up.

Shortly after our food came, Todd handed me his phone. A pretty woman with a bright smile and incredible green eyes was on the screen.

"Lisa," he said. "We met at the dealership. I asked her out, and after a few dates, we realized we had something special."

"Lisa," I repeated. "She's gorgeous."

"Isn't she?" he said, beaming.

It was nice to see him so happy about it, but only a few dates . . . Todd tended to fall fast and hard, a lesson we learned from him being with Lana. He gushed about Lisa, telling me so much I almost felt like I knew her.

Lisa apparently had some issues with alcohol too, but she'd been sober for years. I was a little concerned, but I did my best to be a supportive big brother and offer as much encouragement as I could.

"But remember, you've got plenty of time. Time to go slow."

"I know, I know," he said, waving his fork at me.

The reason for my warning, his relationship with Lana, was behind his eyes, but he didn't bring her up. He had occasionally mentioned her since she went to New York, but it was usually in relation to our grandfathers or something casual.

After he gushed about Lisa some more, I almost told him that Lana was back, to warn him if nothing else. Something stopped me.

Maybe the fact that she was his ex, and I didn't know how he'd react if he ever found out we'd spent the night together.

Or that I was determined to have her again.

19

LANA

After talking to Dylan at the brewery, I'd been even more desperate to try to wring some kind of feeling out of myself when I was with Austin.

I was more affectionate, more hands-on, but nothing quite drummed up the excitement or passion I'd felt with Dylan.

Nothing matched how my heart thudded in my chest when I saw him again at the agency after so long.

"So, he's your client?" Austin had finally asked me the night Dylan dropped me off. He'd had an odd, skeptical look in his eyes.

"Yes, Dylan and Brent, his partner, own Deft Rock, and I've been assigned to run their campaigns," I'd explained.

Austin had been strangely quiet after that and a little reserved for the next couple of days.

Austin had wanted to take me out for dinner, so we sat enjoying our meal at a local place. We had mostly nice conversations, but he'd been on edge since the night Dylan dropped me off. It still showed.

I thought this dinner out was a sort of apology for him

being so standoffish since that night. It didn't take long to realize I was right.

Austin cleared his throat. "I'm sorry, Lana, about the way I've been acting for the last couple of days. Seeing you get out of that car—"

As I tried to focus on Austin, I caught someone staring at me in my periphery. I glanced up and froze.

Dylan had just been seated at a table across the restaurant, and he was staring right at me.

"Everything okay?" Austin asked, noticing my distraction.

Before I could respond, Dylan was making his way over to us, lips pressed in a flat line.

"Fancy running into you here," Dylan said, his eyes locked on mine before moving over to Austin. I frowned, confused by the hard tone of his voice.

Austin twisted around, surprised when he saw Dylan.

"What do you want?" He asked with a scowl.

Dylan looked Austin up and down dismissively and turned his attention back to me.

"So this is the infamous boyfriend?"

"Yes. Dylan, this is Austin."

"Oh, I know who he is," Dylan replied.

What the hell was happening?

Brent was behind Dylan, wide-eyed, staring at me, but I didn't know what his expression meant. I shifted uncomfortably in my seat.

"I think you should leave, right now," Austin said.

And the way they looked at each other made it clear that this wasn't the first time they'd met.

"I didn't see you come in, or I'd have left then. Fortunately, I already finished my dinner, or I'd have lost my appetite by now," Dylan said, his voice so tight and deep it was like he hated the man.

"Dylan!" I said in surprise.

Before Austin could explode, I quickly stood up.

"Okay, I think we're done here," I said, turning to Dylan. "I really do think you should go."

Dylan finally broke his stare down with Austin to look at me. His face softened when he saw my flustered expression.

"Sorry, I didn't mean to interrupt your...date," he said the last word like he was swallowing acid.

His gaze burned into me before he turned on his heels and left.

What the hell was going on between them? I was sure it wasn't just some sort of jealousy on Dylan's part, because Austin was clearly seething as he watched Dylan stomp away.

"What was that all about?" I demanded.

Austin sighed. "I'll explain, but can we finish our dinner first and talk later?" he asked. "I don't want to talk about it here."

I didn't have much of an appetite left, but I waited to ask any more questions.

Once we were back at my house, I let him sit on the couch while I stood, arms crossed. "Are you going to explain what that was all about?"

"I was about to tell you when he showed up. The reason I've been acting a little strange since he dropped you off... Dylan used to be my brother-in-law. And seeing you with him? I don't know. It did something to me."

Brother-in-law? My jaw dropped as I processed this information. Austin was the brother of Dylan's ex-wife. What were the chances...

"He was married to your sister? Your sister is his *ex*?" I

said, knowing I sounded dumb and repetitive but unable to help it.

"Yep," he said.

"Wait, were you your sister's lawyer? Because he said her lawyer raked him through the coals."

Could Austin have been the one to make Dylan so miserable?

"I advised her and sort of off-the-record consulted with her lawyer, but no, I wasn't in charge. Being the brother and brother-in-law made it a conflict for me. Not a good look, or I'd have represented her, of course." He threw his arm up on the back of the couch. "I made sure she got her fair share from the divorce."

"Then you're the one that insisted on splitting the bar," I accused.

My anger towards Austin started to grow. The thought of him taking Dylan's bar away from him downright pissed me off.

"That place meant a lot to him. To his grandfather. It was in his family for more than forty years!"

"He was a dick to my sister. He should've given her the whole damn thing if you ask me," Austin snapped.

"Wasn't she the one that cheated on him?" I argued.

Austin scoffed and frowned at me. "Yeah, but she had her reasons. It's not like he was a saint and she just cheated on him for no reason."

That made me stop. What did he mean by that? I knew there were two sides to every story, but I had always just believed she'd been the cause of the divorce.

"What's that supposed to mean?" I demanded.

"Dylan got what he needed from the relationship and moved on to other things when my sister didn't meet his needs anymore. He abandoned her. She found another man who would be there for her when her own husband wasn't."

I shook my head in disbelief, thinking back to Dylan's story about his divorce.

"Why are you defending him? What's your history with him exactly?" Austin asked, his eyes narrowing.

The question caught me off-guard. "History? I told you, he's my client at the agency."

Austin nodded and got a little smirk on his face, like he knew something I didn't.

"I know, but it's more than that. Dylan's not normally rude, not even to me when he sees me around town. He avoids me, of course, and I don't blame him. I took my sister's side, naturally. But seeing you with me seemed to send him over the edge. So, he has to be more than just a client to you."

I sat on the couch but didn't lean back against his arm. "We met about four years ago at Crystal Fountains. A birthday party for his grandfather, who was my grandfather's best friend. And..."

I looked into Austin's eyes, considered telling him the whole truth, but decided it would only make matters worse. Besides, nothing was happening between me and Dylan. I had made that clear to him.

"I dated his brother for a while before I moved to New York."

He narrowed his eyes and considered that. "Ask to be removed from his account. Let someone else handle the brewery campaign. I don't want you around him."

"Excuse me?" I scoffed. Austin liked to be in control of everything, but that was beyond the pale.

"I don't want you to have to spend time with him. Not

after the way he behaved at the restaurant. Tell them to reassign you."

I was suddenly so angry, I almost couldn't speak. There were so many things I wanted to say that I didn't know where to start.

"I told you how this campaign was my shot at a big promotion the day they assigned it to me," I said in disbelief that he'd ask me—no, *tell* me— to give it up just like that.

"I know. There'll be other chances at a promotion." He turned to me and put his hands on my shoulders, then tried to smile. "I don't want you around someone like him. Why don't you send your boss a message right now? Then we can put this behind us and enjoy the rest of the evening."

I pulled away from him and stood. "I think you should go."

"Are you serious?" He stood and reached for me. "Don't be so dramatic, Lana. I'm trying to look out for you."

"I said leave, Austin. I don't know who the hell you think you are that you can just tell me what to do, but I've had enough of it for one day. Go home."

I turned and walked away as if I fully expected him to go.

He did walk toward the door, but he stopped before he opened it.

"I don't want you around him, Lana. You don't know him like I do. I hope you come to your senses and get reassigned."

He left and closed the door before what I was thinking turned into the words I wanted to say. *Fuck off.*

DYLAN

"Fucking Austin," I growled as I slammed my clipboard down and sat, hoping I was nicer to the last two suppliers than I felt like I had been. "That fucking bastard."

Brent stopped checking boxes on his never-ending list of to-dos, and looked up from his own clipboard

I'd been a bear since we saw Austin and Lana in the restaurant a couple of days earlier. After we'd left, Brent had wisely not said a word about it, and had mostly walked softly around me since.

I couldn't believe it when I saw that Lana was dating Austin.

Of all people. That dipshit was the reason I lost the bar in my divorce settlement. He pulled every dirty trick in the book to make sure I got screwed over.

And now he was dating Lana?

Just the thought of his hands on her made me want to punch a hole through the wall. Brent laced his fingers together behind his head and stretched.

"Okay, I'm settling in to hear a story, because there's a lot more to this than *fucking Austin*. I'd like to know about it so I don't get caught in some cross-fire anger down the road because I say or do the wrong thing."

"What the hell are you talking about?" I said, but there wasn't much heat behind it.

"You've seen Austin around town for years and have never as much as given him a stink-eye. Well, maybe a few times, early on. But at the restaurant, I thought you were going to pick him up and body slam him or something. What was that about?" His eyebrows shot up. "And don't tell me stress or that you were in a bad mood. I know you better than that. You don't get your feathers ruffled that easily."

"Hey, I can be an asshole when I'm stressed and in a shitty mood."

"You can. But you almost never do it in public, and not because of a little nobody from your past like Austin."

When I didn't say anything right away, Brent asked, "It's Lana, isn't it?"

"He's her fucking *boyfriend*, Brent. Can you believe that shit?" I was close to shouting, so I took a deep breath. "She has no idea the kind of guy Austin is. He's no good for her."

His eyebrows went so high they were damn near on top of his head.

"And you are?"

"I didn't say that. This is about what a horrible little creep *he* is," I said, glancing at my clipboard. I was ready to change the subject.

"Nope. Come clean, Dylan. This is about you and Lana." He scratched his fingers into his beard. "You think I don't see how you look at her?"

I paused for a moment, trying to say the words right. Then I gave up and told Brent about Lana.

How I'd been more attracted to her when we met than any other woman in my life. How I didn't explain the wedding band when I should have. How Todd showed up, and how I backed off.

He was there when Todd proposed and knew all about their breakup already. I told him about my night with Lana before she went to New York.

And I told him how I wanted her back, more than anything.

Brent, being the good friend and business partner that he was, didn't try to guide me in one direction or another. He didn't condemn me for sleeping with my brother's ex or wanting her now.

He just listened, and after I'd said everything I had to say, he said, "Feel any better?"

I did.

"How's Todd lately?" he finally asked. "He was looking pretty good last time I saw him. Healthier. Looks like he's doing a good job staying clean, staying out of trouble."

"He is," I said with some pride I probably wasn't entitled to. "Got a new girlfriend, Lisa something, seems crazy about her. She's been sober for at least a few years, and I think that's probably a good influence on him. Seems like he's finally getting his life together."

"Glad to hear that," Brent said. "And glad you two made up so you get to see it."

Brent sucked his front teeth, then he sighed. "Does he know any of what you just told me?"

"He doesn't," I admitted, raking my fingers through my hair. "And I have no idea what he'd say about it."

Brent leaned on his elbows on the table. "If you get back with Lana, his reaction might not be good. You willing to risk that?"

It was a good question. An important one.

It took Todd a long time to get over Lana. Even after he

became sober. He really regretted how things ended, saying how he messed up the best thing he ever had.

I'd always done what I could to protect Todd and take care of him. Maybe I'd done too much at times and not enough at others.

But I was tired of giving up my happiness to keep him from being upset, either.

"I've thought about Lana for the last three years, and I don't think that's going to stop anytime soon, Brent. I'm going to have to risk it. I'll tell him everything when the time's right. And when I know that Lana's willing to make things work. There's no point in upsetting him if I don't have to."

If Lana couldn't be convinced that we belonged together, I guessed I'd never have to tell him. But that wasn't a possibility I was anywhere near ready to face.

20

LANA

I walked into the bustling taproom of Deft Rock Brewery with Maddie. We were there for an informal meeting to go over new marketing materials with Dylan and Brent.

We came a little early to scope out the customers and get a better feel of the regulars that frequented the place.

I glanced around, taking in the busy taproom. Groups of people laughed and chatted over pints of beer. Rock music played over the speakers, adding to the lively ambiance.

Dylan waved when he spotted us, but he was staying busy with other things, only glancing my way now and then. I tried not to let him catch me looking at him.

We hadn't spoken since the night out at the brewery. And after the incident at the restaurant with Austin, I wasn't sure what to say to him.

All I knew was that I didn't want to be alone with him, or even around him much at all. Because what he wanted, what *I* wanted, was too damn tempting. I didn't like the guilty feelings creeping back in. I was still with Austin and feeling this way about Dylan wasn't fair to him.

Carl, the general manager they'd hired, and Shayna and

Jason, the taproom servers, were all there and all busy. They had a bus of older people from some group doing a tour, so Dylan was talking to most of them and being friendly.

Maddie pushed some art mockups toward me so we could check the designs against the general ambiance of the place.

Shayna hustled by, and I waved her down. "What group is this?" I asked, motioning toward the throng of people surrounding Dylan.

"I can't remember their official name. It's kind of like Red Hats, you know, the group for older ladies, but it's for everybody. They pride themselves on getting out and doing cultural things. Museums, breweries, theater, that kind of thing. And that group," she said, pointing at some women walking into the taproom, "are just regulars. They come every couple of weeks."

Then she hurried away to serve the other guests.

We focused on the designs until Carl stopped at our table, curious to see what we were working on.

Laughter rang out from the other side of the room, so we all looked. Two women stood in front of Dylan, both laughing louder than they needed to.

It was instantly obvious that they were flirting their asses off. They seemed to be in some sort of competition to get his attention, one trying to out-laugh the other and flirt harder.

Carl's eyes flicked to the women as he chuckled. "I see Dylan's fan club is out in full force."

Fan club?

I glanced at Carl, confused. He just laughed good-naturedly.

"That's just what I call them. I think they come here more for him than the beer. And that one," he said, nodding in the direction of the one with the tightest pair of jeans, "is like the fan club president. She's been trying to get with Dylan for months. We have to pry them off so he can actually get any work done some nights."

I watched her step closer to him.

"Those jeans have to be cutting off circulation to *something*," I said, amazed that she could breathe at all.

Dylan seemed to be eating up all the attention.

He smiled and laughed, patted their shoulders and touched their arms. They touched him more, though, and a couple of times he seemed to lean into it when Miss Tight Pants stroked her hand down his arm.

I felt an odd pang in my stomach. I shook my head, slightly annoyed with myself.

None of my business if Dylan had admirers.

It shouldn't bother me at all.

I had a boyfriend.

"You should have seen her when she noticed Dylan's tattoo below his collar and insisted that he show it to her." Carl shook his head.

Jason was rushing by and caught what he said. He stopped and leaned down.

"I thought we were gonna need a mop," he said with a laugh before he hurried away.

Carl shook his head again and said, "I've got to get back to work, ladies."

I watched Miss Tight Pants flirting with my—with *Dylan* —for a few more minutes until she and her friend went elsewhere, and Dylan headed our way.

We were still waiting for Brent to join us before starting the meeting, so I tried to act normal and focused on the art, ready to show it to them as tentative designs to see which they liked best.

When Maddie excused herself to use the ladies' room, Dylan touched my shoulder.

"I'm sorry about the other night at the restaurant. I acted like an ass."

"You sure did," I said, but I couldn't help but smile at the end of it.

"Forgive me?" He made pleading eyes at me.

I narrowed my eyes playfully. "I'll think about it."

"Austin and I have a bit of history. I'm sure he told you about how he and I know each other."

"Yeah, he did," I replied softly, reminded of what Austin had said about Dylan not being faultless.

Miss Tight Pants appeared behind Dylan, saying she and her friend were leaving, making it obvious she wanted him.

I wondered how many of them he took home. My heart sank at the thought. Did he have a lot of casual relationships?

I realized I didn't know a whole lot about Dylan's history other than the fact that he was divorced. Maybe that's why his ex-wife cheated on him. She was tired of his flirty nature. Is that what Austin had meant? I shook away the thought, mentally kicking myself for getting caught up in Dylan again.

After the woman left, Dylan turned back to me.

I grinned and tried not to look like I was jealous. "Wow. The thirst is real."

Get it together, Lana. Stop being so weird.

"What?" he said a little cheekily because I'm sure he knew it was true. He leaned his elbows on the back of a chair. "I'm flattered you noticed."

"Hard not to. It was quite the spectacle." It came out a lot snippier than I had intended, so I shot him an apologetic smile.

"Don't worry about them," he said quietly. "It's just harmless fun. They keep things entertaining around here."

"Right, of course," I said quickly. "None of my business."

Harmless fun, sure. Sounded like code word for no-strings-attached-night-of-sex kind of fun.

Dylan held my gaze for a beat, his expression unreadable. I looked away, my face growing warm.

"They're just friendly," he added casually, like it was no big deal.

But it clearly was a regular thing for him to get hit on by hordes of horny women when he was just trying to work. I guess that hasn't changed since the last time I saw him.

Maddie reappeared then and scoffed, saving me from having to do it. "Friendly. *Right.* She was flirting like it was two a.m. and the bars were about to close."

Dylan laughed and waved her off.

"I'm not interested." He turned and looked into my eyes. "Not in her anyway."

"Hey, sorry I'm a little late," Brent interrupted. "Was just wrapping up a call with a supplier. Ready to start?"

"Yes, let's get started," I said, pulling out a folder of materials. "So I figured we could go over the new promo flyers and branding guidelines first. And then discuss any upcoming events or partnerships."

Dylan and Brent nodded, settling in to look everything over. We launched into a productive working discussion, going over the marketing timeline and strategies.

"Well, looks like we're all set for now," I said, trying to keep things professional. "We'll be in touch if anything else comes up. Thanks for your time."

Brent gave me a friendly handshake. "Of course, let us know if you need anything else."

Dylan held out his hand to me, giving me his sexy smile and a wink.

"Yeah, reach out any time," Dylan said. "Always happy to meet with you."

I cleared my throat, pulling my hand back.

I turned and headed for the exit, not looking back.

What was happening to me?

I prided myself on being professional and composed but a simple work meeting had turned into a mess of jealousy and guilt. Both of which I didn't want to feel.

I had to get my head on straight. Time to move forward, not backward.

At least, that's what I told myself. But a small voice inside wondered if moving on from Dylan was really what I wanted at all.

21

DYLAN

So I flirted back a little. I wanted to see if Lana cared. She did. Jealousy was good. I could work with that.

Especially if she was going to be so damn adamant that we keep our relationship as friends.

Fucking friends. Of all things.

I was starting to wonder if that was all we'd ever be.

"Man, I love this idea. Collaborations like this can really put a place on the map," Brent said, tapping his fingers on the shiny conference table at the Berman office. "And you didn't even need help to come up with the plan."

"The agency and some of the work they've done gave me the idea, though. And they're going to help make it a success," I replied.

I'd talked to the people at Emberox Spirits about a collab between them and the brewery after seeing some partnerships the agency had put together for other companies.

They wanted us to come in a couple weeks to pitch the idea.

I figured that's where the agency could work its magic.

Lana could go and help us through the pitch. She was better at that stuff than me or Brent.

And it didn't hurt that it was a two-day trip to Colorado.

Brent and I were meeting with Alexander to review the team's progress, so it was the perfect time to discuss our upcoming needs for the Emberox presentation.

"I think it would be great for Chelsea to accompany you on the trip. She spearheaded Clayton Wineries' campaign and really knows her stuff," Alexander suggested.

Chelsea was smart and professional, but she hadn't been as involved with the campaigns as Lana had been. She didn't know our brand as well. Besides, I wanted Lana to be there with me, not just for business reasons.

"How about Lana? She's been the one that's been the most involved and knows the brand. I'd feel much better if she worked the presentation and assisted with the pitch in Colorado," I countered.

Alexander considered it before he replied, "Great point. In fact, why don't we have Beth join too? I know the two ladies have been working hard on the brewery campaigns. It would be good to have more support with you, right?"

I tried to hide my frustration at his suggestion of Beth joining the trip. But it would've been a little too obvious if I insisted on just Lana.

"Perfect, it's settled then," I replied.

"Alex, sorry to interrupt, but you have a call on line one." Alexander's assistant gave him a look that said he needed to take it.

After a few minutes, Alexander stepped back into the conference room.

"Sorry about that, it was a call I couldn't miss. I ran into Lana on my way back from my office and told her about the trip. She's excited to go! She and Beth will work with you to prepare the presentation and can deliver it for you or with you, whichever you prefer."

We finished up and went to leave, but I made a detour by Lana's office first. She wasn't in it, and another person saw me looking and said she'd just left for lunch. I hurried out, hoping to catch her in the parking lot.

She was hurrying through the lot, and Brent was already gone since we'd driven separately. I rushed after her.

"Lana, wait up," I called.

She stopped and turned toward me.

"Hey, I just heard about the collab with the liquor company."

"Yeah, it's a really great opportunity for us," I said. "I know you'll do a bang-up job on the presentation, and we can relax afterwards. See some sights, if you want."

"You don't give up, do you?" she said, shaking her head.

She smiled so I knew she didn't hate the idea.

"I don't, Lana. Not when it comes to you."

As I stepped closer, a car pulled into an empty space next to us. My mood soured when I recognized it.

"Son of a bitch," I mumbled.

Lana put her hand up, an inch from my chest. "He's picking me up for lunch."

"Tell him to fuck off," I said angrily.

She looked shocked, and then almost like she was going to laugh from disbelief. By the time Austin was out of his car, she said, "Look, I get that you don't like him, but don't speak to me like that."

She said the last half of the sentence much louder than the first.

I closed my eyes and sighed.

"Sorry," I said, realizing I'd overstepped badly. It was

damn near impossible to keep my emotions in check these days. Especially when it involved Austin being near Lana.

"Dylan, I'm only going to tell you this once." Austin rushed up to me like he might be considering taking a swing. "Stay the fuck away from my girl," he shouted.

I straightened, coming face to face with him. Austin wasn't a small guy so I didn't tower over him like I did with most people. "Your girl?"

"You heard me," he said, trying to sound macho.

Lana got between us. "Both of you, knock it off."

I almost laughed. "Stay away or *what*, Austin? What are you going to do about it?"

"Just stay away from my girl," he said through clenched teeth.

Hearing that again, *my girl*, was too much.

"She was mine before she was yours," I snarled.

Lana gasped and held her forehead. "This isn't happening."

Austin shook his head. "What did you say?"

"You heard me, you little—"

Austin lurched toward me, and I stood my ground, unflinching. So he did nothing, like I expected.

"I *work* here!" Lana whisper-shouted, gesturing toward the building. "People are looking out the window!"

She was right. People were peeking through the windows, and some had stopped on their way to their cars to see what all the commotion was about. We were making a scene and it wouldn't be good for Lana.

It wasn't the time or the place.

I had to back off, so I held up my hands.

"You're right. I'm sorry, Lana. Have a nice lunch together," I said, through gritted teeth.

"We will," Austin said smugly, placing a hand on Lana's

lower back and pushing her in the direction of his car. "Get in the car, babe."

Lana shifted away from his grasp, clearly uncomfortable with his claiming gesture.

I knew I should just walk away, but I couldn't let it go.

"I'm sure Lana will get in the car when she's ready," I snapped, glaring at Austin.

Austin's head whipped around, his eyes blazing.

"You better watch yourself, man," Austin spat out. "Get in the car, Lana," he said, not taking his eyes off me.

I took a step closer. "Don't talk to her like that," I threatened.

He turned to Lana and grabbed her wrist. "Let's *go*. Now."

That's it.

Before I could push him back to release his grip on her, Lana wrenched her arm away.

I finally broke my stare down with Austin and looked at Lana. She was fuming like she was going to start shooting steam out of her ears.

"Get your hands off of me." Lana hissed in a low tone, but the fire in her eyes would have melted steel. "Austin, *you* get in the damn car. And the next time you speak to me like that, it'll be the last words you ever say to me."

My eyebrows shot up in surprise.

That's my girl.

I smirked in satisfaction, but then Lana leveled her hard gaze on me, quickly wiping away my smug expression.

"And *you*," she huffed, her lips pressing together. She paused, seemingly remembering I was still the client. "You go back to Deft Rock and prepare for the presentation."

"Yes Ma'am," I said quietly, then pressed my lips

together to suppress another smile threatening to break through.

She narrowed her eyes and I looked at my shoes to hide my smile.

She looked so damn hot when she was fired up. Even if that anger was directly partly toward me.

"Both of you need to leave. Now!" With that, Lana spun on her heels.

Austin tried to stop her with a quick apology and pleading, but she snatched her arm out of his grip again and stormed back toward the building.

I hadn't started this, but I was damn sure going to finish it.

I turned to Austin after she went inside the building, "You didn't seem to hear me clearly before. So let me repeat it for you. I said she was mine first. Save yourself the embarrassment and give up now. Because you don't have a chance in hell with her. Have a nice day."

I got into my car and texted Lana an apology before driving off.

22

LANA

I had just gotten home from work and slipped off my heels when there was a knock at my door. Austin stood on my front porch, a bouquet of flowers in his hand.

"These are a little wilted since I meant to give them to you at lunch to apologize for earlier" he said, his eyebrows raised. "But I managed to screw that up. And have even more to apologize for now."

I was still pissed about the way he'd acted, like he had some kind of ownership of me in front of Dylan. Going to lunch was supposed to be a sort of an apology for him telling me to get reassigned. He hadn't helped his case by acting like a damn fool.

"Come on in," I said, trying to smile as I took the flowers.

He followed me inside while I put them in a vase of water. Then we sat at the kitchen table.

"So I guess you didn't find the "my girl" thing romantic, huh?" he said sheepishly.

"I didn't." And the thing that bothered me the most about it was that if they'd been reversed, if Dylan had told

Austin to stay away from his girl . . . I might have liked it. At least a little.

I felt like that said things about our relationship.

"That thing he said to me, about how you were his first? What did he mean by that, Lana?"

Austin's entire presence changed. He'd been contrite, sad looking, apologetic at my door. With that question, his face went a little hard, and he sat a little straighter.

I didn't like the change. And just like that, I decided to tell him the whole truth.

"We slept together the night before I moved to New York. We didn't have any contact after that, not until he showed up at my workplace and I got assigned to his account."

Austin's face turned red with anger. For a moment he just sat there with his jaw clenched.

"You left that part out when you told me about your history," he pointed out, his voice sharp.

"Yes, I did. Because it's in the past. It just didn't seem important since there's nothing going on between me and Dylan now." I laced my fingers together on the table. "We had a thing once upon a time. But that's it. Nothing's going on now aside from me working on the brewery account."

He didn't say anything, so I forged ahead. "In fact, we're going to Colorado next week where I'll present a pitch I need to work on. If it's successful, the brewery will collab with Emberox Spirits. It's a really great opportunity for me to prove myself."

He almost choked. "You can't go on a trip with him!"

"You make it sound like I'm we're going on a weekender alone. We're going as a team, with Beth and Brent. The four of us. In separate rooms. On a business trip." I emphasized each point.

"I don't care if there are ten of you," he snapped. "You can't go. I'm not going to have you make a fool of me by going on a trip with your ex. I won't just ignore another man trying to stake some claim over you."

"No one is staking a claim on anybody. He's a client. We work together." I rubbed my palms on my eyelids. "And he's not my ex. We spent one night together. How exactly does this make a fool of you?"

"He knows, Lana. He knows exactly what he's doing, and he'd happily taunt me that you were with him states away while I was here alone. You have to cancel the trip," Austin spat.

"Absolutely not. This is a huge opportunity for me." I stared at him in disbelief.

"You're so ambitious you'd put your career above our relationship?"

His words stung. I had worked damn hard to get to where I was. I wasn't about to feel bad about it.

"There you go again, making me feel guilty for prioritizing my job," I shot back. "What if the tables were turned? Would you put your career on the back burner for me?"

He flinched and pressed his lips together. And I knew that he wouldn't.

He tapped the table with his pointed index finger. "You can't go, Lana. I won't be humiliated this way."

I couldn't believe how he was acting. I threw my hands up in exasperation.

"It's a business trip. If that humiliates you, I'm not sure what to say." I kept my voice firm.

Austin stood his ground. "There's no way in hell I'm letting you go on that trip," he said in a low voice. "If you go, we're through. I mean it."

My blood boiled at his tone. Not *let* me go? As if I needed his permission?

"It's not your damn call," I said, my voice rising with each word. "I sure as hell won't sit here and listen to you give me some kind of ultimatum."

"It's him or me, Lana," Austin said coldly.

I shook my head in disgust. "I won't be manipulated. I'm done talking about this. Get out."

After a few seconds of staring at me, he slowly stood and left without another word.

I was tempted to take the flowers he'd brought and run them out to him. Tell him I didn't want them. Tell him where he could put them.

I grabbed the bouquet and walked over to the trashcan instead, throwing them in with a huff.

I felt no desire to smooth things over or comfort him. Any feelings I had for Austin seemed to be rapidly disappearing.

As I cooled down, I could see why it wouldn't make a boyfriend happy to have his girlfriend going on a trip with someone she'd slept with. Even if it was for business. But we were going as a team. This was my career.

No, the trip was fine. Austin would just have to live with it.

After a long hot shower to wash away the tension in my muscles from my spat with Austin, I settled on the couch with a glass of wine when I heard another knock on my door. It had better not be Austin coming back for another round.

I put my remote down from scrolling through shows and opened the door.

Dylan stood there holding a paper bag in his hand. He

looked so damn good in his fitted shirt that showed off his muscular arms, a few strands of hair falling over his forehead.

"Hey, I thought about calling first, but I wasn't sure you'd respond. Thought I'd risk it and just come," he said, giving me his innocent boyish grin that probably worked like a charm on women. "I wanted to apologize again. In person."

After my argument with Austin, I was mentally exhausted. I really wasn't in the mood. I breathed out a deep sigh.

"Dylan, can we talk about this another time?"

His eyes glanced down my body and his lips turned up in a smile.

I looked down and realized I was wearing his burgundy hoodie. The one that he'd put around me when he picked me up at the diner years ago.

My cheeks heated at his recognition.

"I brought a peace offering," he said smugly, holding up the bag.

It had 'Marcella's' printed on the front. It was from the restaurant that he'd taken me to when Todd had canceled on me.

Brookie explosion.

I wanted to stay mad, but my resolve started to crumble.

"It's still warm," he said, cocking his head to one side and smiling hopefully.

I briefly considered grabbing the bag and shutting the door on his too-handsome face. Then I remembered he was still the client and we had to work together. And I was eager to find out more about this new partnership with the liquor company.

I sighed and stepped aside. "Come on in."

He smiled down at me as he walked past.

He set the bag on the table and took out its contents.

"I brought ice cream too." He winked.

"You're lucky I was craving chocolate tonight," I replied, fighting a smile.

"Lana, I'm really sorry about earlier today," Dylan began earnestly. "I know I was completely out of line. I shouldn't have encouraged him. Especially in front of your workplace."

He looked at me sincerely. I was still upset with him, but I was upset with Austin even more.

I nodded. "You were. Just don't let it happen again."

A look of relief spread across his face and then he quirked an eyebrow. "Absolutely not. I do *not* want to be on your bad side."

I suppressed a smile that threatened to break through. I plated the dessert and pulled two forks from the drawer as Dylan went to toss the bag into the garbage. He stopped for a moment, probably looking at the big, crumpled bouquet of flowers stuffed inside it.

He chuckled quietly, "Austin come by?"

"Yup," I sighed. "He did."

Dylan turned to me with a big grin but didn't say anything when I narrowed my eyes and shook my head.

He just smiled and nodded slowly in response.

I didn't feel like telling him about the big blowup. I really didn't feel like talking at all. Dylan must have sensed it because he didn't say another word.

He simply joined me on the couch, handing me one of the plates as I sat down.

I took a bite and sighed in satisfaction. Dylan always knew how to make me feel better.

He smiled, glancing at me. "Good?"

"Better than I remember," I replied honestly.

We ate in silence and the stress that had built up from my argument with Austin had started to melt away, replaced by the unexpected comfort that settled in my chest at having Dylan there.

Sitting next to him in my home, wearing his hoodie, eating our dessert. It just felt right.

"So tell me about the collab. It sounds exciting from what Alexander told me." Alexander had mentioned it in passing and hadn't given me much details. I was eager to hear more about it.

"It's with Emberox Spirits, in Colorado. Their brand aligns well with ours. I've researched other similar companies that have had successful partnerships at retail and I thought why not go for it. I think we've done pretty well at the brewery, but a partnership with them would take us to the next level."

"I love it!" I said excitedly. It really would be the perfect collaboration. My mind immediately started racing with marketing ideas. "That would really expand the reach of the brewery's current customer base."

"Exactly," he replied, pointing at me.

We sat side by side, our shoulders nearly touching, as we enjoyed our dessert and chatted about what we could include in the pitch.

Dylan glanced down at me with a smile, catching my eye.

"What?" I asked, smiling back at him despite myself.

"You kept it," he said, leaning in to nudge my shoulder with his. My traitorous heart skipped a beat at the contact. He stayed that way, his arm against mine.

I shrugged, knowing he meant his hoodie.

"Well, I wasn't sure what to do with it," I said, trying to

play it off. "I was planning to ship it back to you and then I forgot. So, I just kept it."

That was such a lie. I loved this hoodie, and there was no way I would've sent it back. It had served as my comfort blanket since I moved to New York. I slept with it practically every day for the entire first year. It was silly, but it made me feel better. On some days, when I let my mind drift, it almost felt like it was Dylan himself holding me.

"Is that the only reason?" He asked, side-eyeing me.

"It's warm and comfy." I glanced at him.

Dylan nodded, the corner of his mouth slightly turning up.

"You've had it for years," he pointed out.

I didn't reply, but I knew what he meant. I'd clung onto that hoodie all this time, a small reminder of him. It was an admission that I'd missed him and still hadn't let him go.

"Do you want it back?" I asked, knowing well that he'd say no. And if he did want it back, he'd have to pry it out of my fingers. It was mine now.

He looked down at me and leaned in closer, softly shaking his head. "I like it better on you."

He reached over and squeezed my hand. I instinctively squeezed back, but tried to pull away, realizing what a bad idea it was. His fingers tightened around my hand, not letting go.

I looked up at him, ready to say something cheeky, but he spoke first.

"I missed you. I thought about you every day," he said, his voice low and intense.

My heart thudded in my chest as I tried to ignore his words and the way his thumb traced circles on the back of my hand.

God, I still wanted him. I wanted him more than anything in the world.

"I thought about you every day too," I said quietly. There, it was out. I couldn't hide it anymore. But I had to remind myself that it still didn't change things. I still need to keep boundaries between us.

I pulled away and got up to put away the plates, trying to regain my composure.

Dylan helped and then settled back on the couch.

"What are we watching?" He asked, getting comfortable. He started scrolling where I had left off.

"*We* aren't watching anything," I replied, taking the remote from him.

"You're kicking me out after I brought you dessert?" He asked in disbelief, giving me sad puppy eyes.

I had to laugh at that. It was adorable. I was more than tempted to snuggle up with him on the couch, but I knew I wouldn't have the willpower to keep my hands off him.

"I appreciate you coming by, with dessert and all, but I kind of want to be alone tonight."

"Okay. I understand." He nodded and gave me a small smile. "We'll meet soon to prep for the presentation."

I got up to see him to the door. Before I could say anything, his fingers gripped the hoodie and slowly pulled me to him. I went willingly.

He wrapped his arms around me, crushing me into his broad chest. My arms circled his waist. I couldn't help but inhale deeply as I melted into his embrace.

My heart raced and all I could think of was how damn good it felt to be in his arms again.

When I tried to pull back, he didn't let go. He kept me pinned to his body, gazing down at me. He stroked my cheek with his knuckles, his eyes dropping down to my lips.

He leaned down slowly, like he was giving me a chance to push him away if I wanted to. I didn't. I tilted my head up to meet his gaze.

Then he ever so gently pressed his lips to mine, so softly and tenderly, his thumb brushing my cheek. He held the kiss for a long moment before whispering good night and leaving my heart in a puddle.

23

LANA

It was Monday morning and I was at the office early, eager to get a head start on the presentation for our Colorado trip.

The weekend passed with no word from Austin. And I didn't bother calling him either. I really didn't see our relationship working out after the fight. Especially after that kiss from Dylan.

Maddie stepped inside my office, closed the door, and asked gently, "How are you holding up? You were pretty upset on Friday."

I sighed, stirring my coffee. "My relationship is imploding, my work situation is awkward as hell, and I feel like a terrible person."

Maddie gave me a sympathetic look. "Just take a breath. Tell me what happened with Austin. I thought they were going to come to blows."

"So that was you looking out the window?" I still cringed at the image.

"Me and a few other people," she admitted.

"Ughh," I groaned, covering my face. "Did Chelsea or Alexander see?"

"No, but Beth was there," she replied, wincing. "What's with the two of them acting like they're having some sort of a duel?"

I hesitated, wondering if I should share my history with Dylan. I met Maddie when I started working at Berman so she didn't know all my history with Dylan. Only that I used to be in a relationship that had ended dramatically.

I leaned back in my chair and gave her a short version of everything that happened. From meeting Dylan first, my relationship with his brother, the unforgettable night that we'd shared, to finding out that Austin used to be his brother-in-law.

"Oh my God," Maddie said, her fists under her cheeks as she took it all in. "No wonder there's all that tension between them."

I slumped and pressed my forehead against my hand.

"Austin tried to get me to give up the account and cancel the Colorado trip. Didn't even ask. *Told* me to. He said we'd be over if I went on the trip."

"What!?" Maddie's eyes went wide, looking enraged. "That pisses me off, and I don't even know him."

"I know!" I huffed, my anger returning at the thought of our conversation. "The thing is, *I've* even thought maybe it would be best if I got reassigned and dropped the account."

I really didn't want to, but I couldn't help but wonder if it wouldn't make things easier on everyone. Especially me.

"Don't do that, Lana. You're nailing this account so far. And once you wow Emberox Spirits, you're on the fast track to top management here, for sure."

I knew I'd be shooting myself in the foot if I dropped the account now. I wouldn't. I'd worked my ass off on that account.

I was determined that no matter what happened, I was

going to make sure Deft Rock got that collab deal, and my career stayed on track.

"I need to break up with Austin," I said quietly.

Maddie patted my arm. "It's clear things aren't working with him. Don't stay with him if it doesn't feel right."

Hearing her say what I thought lifted a weight off my chest. I had been trying so hard to force this relationship into what I wanted it to be instead of what it was.

I realized in that moment, I didn't want Austin himself all that much. I wanted a partner.

"Do you still have feelings for Dylan?" Maddie asked gently.

I paused, the question forcing me to be honest with myself.

"I've been trying to deny it but... I do. Seeing him brings up all these old emotions, you know? I don't think they ever went away."

Maddie nodded understandingly.

"It just feels like the timing is never right with him. He comes back into my life right when I'm with someone else. I feel so guilty for wanting him," I said.

"Well, you won't have to worry about that anymore," Maddie replied. "Once Austin is out of the picture."

"Yeah, but it still doesn't feel right. He's a client of the agency. We do have a policy against fraternizing with the client," I said.

We'd need to maintain a professional relationship. At least for now.

"Yeah, you do have a point." Maddie scrunched her nose. "And this account is pretty important for you."

"Yeah, it is." I sighed softly before blurting out, "He kissed me."

Maddie gasped, grabbing my arm. "What? What else? Don't hold out on me, woman."

"Sorry to disappoint, but that was it. Just a really sweet, gentle kiss," I sighed, remembering how the softest, tamest kiss had turned my knees to jelly.

Maddie quirked her eyebrow. "And it sounds like it won't be the last. Dylan seems like a man that gets what he wants."

"That's what I'm afraid of. I don't think I have the willpower to resist him."

"So don't," she replied with a shrug. "You know my motto. You only live once. Don't deny yourself that fine ass man. Get what you need."

I laughed, shaking my head. I should've known better than to expect anything less from Maddie. Unlike me, she didn't overthink things.

"Just don't get caught," she added, wiggling her eyebrows.

"Thanks for letting me talk it out, Mads." I gave her a hug before she left my office.

"Glad my hunger for gossip could help," she said with a laugh.

I figured I'd hear from Austin before the trip, maybe with another ultimatum if not an actual apology.

I decided that it would be best for us to talk in person, to make a clean break.

When I called, his phone went to voicemail. I didn't leave one. He'd see that I called and return it or not.

An hour later, my phone buzzed with a text from Austin.

> I think it's best if we end things. This just isn't working.

"Wow..." I whispered as I stared at the screen in disbelief.

He was breaking up with me? Over *text?*

"Take care" were the last words of the message.

My first instinct was to call him and demand a real conversation.

But as I went to dial his number, my fingers froze over the screen. Was there really anything left to say at this point?

We'd both made our positions clear.

I should've been angry or sad. But I wasn't. Instead, I felt...relieved.

Relieved it was done. With that chapter over, I really didn't want to think about him anymore at all. I didn't even bother responding to him.

I pulled out my laptop and worked on the Emberox Spirits presentation instead. I wanted to win them over.

I wanted a promotion.

And I had to admit to myself, I really wanted to make Dylan proud.

24

DYLAN

The afternoon sun streamed through the windows of the Deft Rock taproom as our mixology session got underway.

We were making final adjustments to the beer cocktails before we left for Colorado the following day to present our concept to the Emberox team.

We didn't need the agency here for this, but I had invited Lana anyway. I was glad she decided to come. I wasn't sure how she felt after I kissed her the other night. It took all my willpower to stop when I did, but I knew her mind was still on Austin. They were still together, after all. To my surprise, she hadn't pushed me away. That was a good sign.

Seeing her again put me at ease. She seemed different today. Like something had shifted between us that night. I felt it and I knew she did too.

Or maybe it was the alcohol.

"Are you drunk?" I asked Lana with a laugh as she sipped the drink Jason had made for her.

"Who, me?" she said, her cheeks a little pinker than normal. "Noooo."

She wasn't actually drunk, but she was starting to get slightly tipsy. Even just one sip from several cocktails added up over the course of our meeting.

"What do you think?" Jason asked after she tasted the cocktail.

"Delish," she declared with a grin. "This might be the best one yet. What is it?"

"Our signature Deft Rock ale with their best tequila and a splash of lemon-lime soda to add to the tart citrus taste of the lime juice." Jason looked so proud as he said it.

He and Shayna had been brainstorming cocktails for days, testing out different recipes for this mixology meeting.

Brent tasted everything along with me and Lana.

"Deftrox Margarita!" she said, gleefully enough that I was sure that the hard liquor was getting to her, just a little.

"Water time," I said, pushing an icy glass in front of her. "Don't want you dancing on the tables before the night's over," I whispered, leaning in.

One of her perfectly groomed eyebrows cocked.

"You don't?" she asked, her half-grin almost too damn cute to take.

I smiled back and pushed the water into her hand. "Drink."

She rolled her eyes but took a few gulps.

Jason and Shayna had gone through all the drinks they'd worked out, so we all sat drinking water to get our equilibrium back.

"You might have missed your calling, Lana," I said, motioning at all the cocktail glasses.

"Should have been a bartender?"

"No, a barfly," I teased.

She slapped my arm and shook her head. I laughed as I caught her hand in mine.

"I'm serious. What if I paid you to sit in the taproom drinking all day, being friendly to people who came in? You'd be like the town welcoming committee." I leaned a little closer. "You'd certainly bring in the male clientele. Even the ones who don't drink a drop."

She smirked at me, but I could tell by the way her face reddened that she liked the compliment. Then she straightened and sipped more water.

"Maybe I should take you up on that. Between us, we'd have it covered. Because you certainly bring the female clientele in the door."

I scoffed, but she put her hand up. "Oh yes. I saw that loud woman when I was here the last time. She looked like she was about to climb you like a tree. Maybe if her pants were a little looser so that she could move her legs, she could have tried."

She laughed at her own joke, and I had to admit it was funny because it was true.

"Okay. You got me. My milkshake brings all the girls to the yard, I guess."

She snorted at my bad joke, and I found myself next to her, our shoulders pressed together while we laughed and chatted.

The more we talked, the more I realized it wasn't the alcohol that had changed Lana's attitude toward me. Enough time passed with us sitting and talking that we were both completely sober. But we were still flirting and laughing. It was the first time that things felt completely natural, at ease between us. With nothing hanging over us. Like the first day we'd met.

I finally started seeing glimpses of the Lana I knew. The woman who had stolen my heart. The reserved, distant version that had been so determined to maintain a wall between us was starting to fade away.

"I still feel like we need something to round it out," Jason said. "We've got frozen drinks and light alcohol drinks, but not really anything with whiskey or stout . . . nothing very dark. At least one drink like that would give the whole collection a better profile, don't you think?"

Shayna and Brent nodded, and I agreed. "Yeah, I think so. But you guys have worked so hard on this already. You should take off and let me handle that one."

As they packed up to head home, I stood and stretched. Carl had gone into the other room with Brent, so I turned to Lana.

"I'm going to go look in the storeroom to see if I get any inspiration." Before I walked by her, I made a quick decision. "Want to come and help?"

I wasn't ready for the evening to be over.

"Sure," she said, then she walked with me to the elevator that took us to the basement level.

We went into one of the stockrooms with a collection of dark liquors and a random assortment of lagers and stouts.

"Stout Embers," she said, holding up a bottle of stout and a bottle of single-malt whiskey, still as playful as she'd been all evening. "Stout, whiskey, tequila, and malt liquor! It puts hair on your chest and the soles of your feet or your money back!"

"That would be a hell of an ad campaign," I said with a laugh.

We continued bouncing flavor combinations off each other, unaware of how much time had passed.

Our bodies would touch as we joked about the drinks and sometimes looked at them seriously, trying to figure out what would be a good addition.

Then she turned to face me when we were between two shelves set close together.

Lana's back was against the shelf, her arms behind her.

"I think what we have so far is fantastic. Unless I screw something up, I'm sure they're going to go for it."

We were only a couple of inches apart, but she stood there, unflinching, when I moved closer. "You're not going to screw anything up, Lana. You're obviously very good at your job. I've had a front row seat for that over these last few weeks. I ought to know."

She smiled shyly at me and looked down. When I moved closer, she lifted her face again. Oh, those blue eyes. The way she stood there, staring up at me.

"I wasn't sure this was going to work. But Dylan, I'm glad you showed up at Berman. This is a really great opportunity for me, and I feel like I haven't really thanked you for that."

"You don't have to thank me, Lana."

"I know. I'll thank you by doing the best job I can. But still. Thanks."

I reached up and brushed my knuckles under her jaw.

"Lana," I said softly.

When she didn't move away, she just kept staring up at me, I leaned closer.

The stockroom lights went out. Lana gasped.

"Did the electricity go out?" she asked, looking around.

"I'll bet Carl just left and turned on the automatic shut-off. I'll go reset it."

The room was dimly lit by the moonlight through the small windows near the ceiling. Lana followed me to the door. I turned the handle, but it was stuck in place. I jiggled it, then I put all my might into twisting it before I realized what had happened.

Carl must've assumed we all left and locked up for the

night already. I banged on the door and called out to see if maybe he was still close by. There was no response.

I patted my pockets to call Carl, but my phone was on the table in the taproom. I'd had it out looking up liquor varieties.

"Can I use—"

Lana was already shaking her head. "My phone's on the table next to yours." She tried the handle herself. "We're really locked in here with no phones to call anyone for help? Maybe he'll see our cars and come back inside? He'll realize we're still in here?"

"I'm in my office a lot after he leaves. He's not going to know we're locked in."

"What are we supposed to do?" she asked, her voice sounding a little nervous.

She wrapped her arms around herself.

"Hey," I said, pulling her close. "Everything's okay. When the staff comes in the morning, somebody always comes through here to eyeball the stock. And we even have a bathroom, through there." I pointed to the back corner of the room. "Bottled water in the corner back there. We'll be fine."

"But it's pretty chilly in here, isn't it?" She sounded less flirtatious than before, maybe a little scared.

I pulled her even closer, wrapping my arms around her.

"I can take care of that, too," I whispered into her ear.

25

DYLAN

Lana shivered as I pulled her close, promising to dispel the chill in the room.

She really was nervous about being locked in there until morning. I couldn't blame her. But I also couldn't bring myself to regret that it had happened, because it meant more time with Lana. And since it was a little chilly, more time with Lana in my arms.

I held her tightly, sharing my body heat, and gestured toward the east wall.

"Come on. I know fifty-pound sacks of malt aren't exactly a soft bed, but they'll be more comfortable than the floor."

"We really do just have to wait it out, don't we?" she asked, looking up at me.

"We really do," I said, leading her to the pallets of supplies. "And in case you're unsure, I promise I didn't set this up."

She laughed. "I believe you. At least, I would hope that if you ever set something like this up, you'd at least find a way to get a blanket, maybe a nice picnic lunch, down here somehow."

"Damn it. I knew I'd forget something," I said, snapping my fingers.

Lana laughed softly, then we got as comfortable as we could on the sacks. We weren't lying completely flat, but more sitting up and reclined.

As soon as we were settled, I pulled her close again to stave off the chill. Even in a stockroom, trapped in the dark until morning, I felt more *right* than I had since she'd gone to New York.

Her body molded against mine, her arms around my waist. My arm was around her back, cradling her against me.

Before long, I found myself moving my hand up to gently knead her neck. Stroke her hair. It was so easy to do, and Lana wasn't stopping me.

She cleared her throat. "How's Todd? I know you said he was doing well, but you didn't give any details. What's he been up to since I left?"

I put my arm back around her and rubbed her arm with my other hand. I didn't think stroking her hair or touching her neck was going to lead to anything, not in a stockroom.

That wasn't where I wanted to make love to Lana for the first time in three years.

But I could feel the pull for more, being that close to her. I suspected she felt it too and wanted to talk to distract us.

"He had a hard time at first. I figured he texted and called you a lot back then."

"For a little while," she said.

"Everything he was already doing that was self-destructive, he doubled down on. Lost his job at the dealership, lost some friends, just couldn't seem to stay sober and responsible. He cut me out of his life for a while, until Grandpa took a turn for the worse. It took that for him to take a long, hard look at himself and make some changes."

"So you're getting along now?" Lana's voice was soft.

Maybe she hadn't realized how hard his life had been for a couple of years.

"We do. We have dinner and see each other on a regular basis. He got a job at another dealership, got off the booze and the drugs. He has a new girlfriend now, she's in recovery and might end up being good for him." I realized I was stroking her hair again. "We just had dinner the other day. He looked really happy when he talked about her."

"I'm so glad," Lana said, and she sounded completely sincere. "Todd deserves to be happy."

After a long pause, I asked, "So, how's Austin these days? I know things were messy after that blow up."

I knew Lana didn't like talking about Austin with me, but I was curious what had happened that day. It couldn't have gone well, judging by the flowers in her garbage.

She snorted. "He's probably trying to control everything and everyone around him. Aside from that, who knows."

"Trouble in paradise?" I teased, though I knew I was right.

"No, only because being with Austin, honestly, was never paradise." She took a deep breath. "He broke up with me."

"What?" I said with a laugh. "*He* broke up with *you*?"

"He did."

"Have we slipped into some kind of alternate reality where everything is the opposite of things that should happen?"

I couldn't understand how someone like Austin, with Lana as his girlfriend, could ever willingly let that go.

"Has he lost his mind?" I asked.

"You flatter me, but thanks. Want to hear something even worse?" she asked. "He did it over text."

I laughed and put my hand over my eyes. "Wow."

Lana laughed softly. "That's what I said."

"Smooth operator, that one. I can't imagine why he'd dump you in the first place, but not even in person?"

"Ew," she groaned. "Dumped. That word makes it seem so much worse than 'broke up with me.' Dumped over text. Truly a life highlight." She laughed, so I knew she wasn't too broken up about it.

"Sorry. Dumped *is* an ugly word, isn't it? How about he made a huge mistake by not doing everything possible to keep you in his life? He fucked up at a level ten on a five-level scale? He did the stupidest thing I can imagine a grown man doing by ending things with you? Any of those better?" I asked softly.

My teasing was turning serious without me meaning to.

Lana didn't have a boyfriend anymore. I didn't have to try to convince her to dump Austin. I felt suddenly light.

"Those are better. Mostly not true," she said with a laugh, "but they sound much less awful."

"Are you okay?" I asked.

I knew she would be, if she wasn't already. Having an asshole like Austin no longer in your life could only be a positive thing.

And it was sure as hell a lot better for me.

"You know," she said, sounding a little surprised, "I really am. I was actually going to break up with him anyway. It wasn't working out."

My chest thudded with excitement at hearing her say those words. She was planning to break up with him. She brushed her cheek up and down against my chest, getting more comfortable.

Curiosity got the best of me. How could someone like Austin give up someone like Lana?

"Did he lose his mind, literally, and think he could find someone better? Or did you leave too many wet towels on the floor?"

"You're such a good guesser. Both. Both of those," she said.

"I'm serious. What could have possibly made him break up with you? What dark secret are you hiding that would drive a man like him away?" I couldn't keep the laughter out of my voice. "Snoring? Chewing with your mouth open? *What?*"

When she stopped laughing, she shook her head.

"He thought he could tell me what to do, and when he found out he couldn't, he'd had enough." She paused, probably sensing that I was waiting for more detail I wasn't sure she would give.

Then she sighed. "When he found out I was working with you, he demanded that I drop the campaign. And when he found out about the Colorado trip, he gave me an ultimatum. Cancel it, or we were through."

I let that sink in. She'd chosen the trip over Austin.

"I'm glad you chose the trip. As long as you really are okay?"

"I really am. We obviously weren't meant to be."

I stroked her hair, relieved, then rubbed her shoulder.

"You said something like that to me once. That we weren't meant to be."

Lana tilted her face up toward mine. "That was different."

"So you don't think you and Austin were some kind of star-crossed lovers?" I smiled as I said it, but I held my breath while I waited for her answer.

"No. Not at all." Lana took a deep breath. "I wasn't upset at the thought of not seeing Austin again. But you..." she trailed off, seeming to search for the right words.

I touched her cheek, let my thumb slide down her jaw. "Different story?"

Lana nodded. "Very different." She inhaled a sharp breath and paused. "It nearly broke me, Dylan. Forcing myself to move on. Not being able to see you."

I dipped my head, bringing our faces close together.

"You leaving wasn't easy on me, either. I've thought about calling you, maybe going to New York to see you. Every day I've regretted not telling Todd to take a hike when he started talking to you. God, how I wished I'd explain the ring that day."

I felt her swallow hard. "You were still technically married," she whispered. "It might not have changed anything."

I tilted her face up to look at me and brushed my thumb on her lower lip.

"It would have, and you know it."

I couldn't resist anymore, so I closed the distance between our lips and kissed her, soft and slow.

The kiss was an apology for screwing up that moment years ago. And it was a promise that I wasn't going to make a mistake like that again.

My tongue slipped between her lips as she parted them, granting me entrance. I pulled her closer, pinning her body against mine as our tongues slid together. She tasted so fucking good. I pulled her chin down with my thumb, wanting to kiss her deeper. Needing to feel more of her. Like I had to make up for the time we'd been apart.

She let out a small sound that vibrated right down to my

cock. I felt the tension leave her body and her soft lips moved against mine as she relaxed in my arms.

As much as I wanted her right then, a dark stock room and sacks of malt weren't how I wanted anything like that to happen between us.

I pulled back, breathless, and rested my forehead against hers.

Lana obviously felt the same. She put a hand on my chest and leaned back slightly. But in the dim light, I could see her hooded eyes and softly parted lips.

"See, the universe does want us to be together. It even locked us in a room so we can't be apart," I said.

She laughed. "I'm starting to think you have a point."

She rested her cheek against my chest with a sigh, and we didn't need to talk about anything else. At least not for a while.

I watched the steady rise and fall of her breathing as she drifted off. She looked so peaceful and beautiful. I could almost imagine this was just a normal night together, being side by side like it was the most natural thing in the world.

Only it was going to be hell trying to fall asleep with Lana draped over me. My cock apparently hadn't gotten the message yet. I let out a deep breath and tried to think of our presentation to get my mind off how much I wanted Lana.

She nuzzled in closer with a contented sigh.

Sitting there with her curled up against me, it felt perfect and right. Being close to Lana just felt like home. I kept drifting in and out with those thoughts until I eventually fell asleep.

When morning rolled around, I woke, groaning softly. Lana blinked awake slowly, looking momentarily confused to find herself tucked against me. Then she quickly sat up, smoothing her hair self-consciously.

"Morning," I said softly. "Sleep okay?

"Yeah, uh, not too bad," she stammered adorably.

"You weren't cold?" I asked, rubbing her arms as if she might still be chilly.

"Not at all. You're like a furnace," she replied smiling. "Thanks for keeping me warm."

"Good." I kissed her forehead and got up to grab a couple of bottles of water from one of the pallets, stretching my stiff legs that were a little tingly from the position I'd been in.

"Thanks, I needed that," Lana said after downing a third of her water bottle. I drank greedily too and stretched again, my back popping.

"Not as comfortable as the last time we slept together," I said with another groan.

Lana laughed. "Not nearly."

I tried to smooth Lana's hair down with a laugh. It was mussed from rubbing against my shirt, and her makeup was smeared around her bright blue eyes.

She looked so damn sexy.

"You look like you slept a bit rough," I said, grinning.

"How is it that you look like you just finished getting ready for the day?" She laughed and tried to smooth her hair. "I'll bet I do look a mess."

"You look a little like you slept outside in a bush, yeah," I said, laughing with her. Then I cupped her cheek and brushed my thumb over her chin. "But you're still the most beautiful thing I've ever seen."

I stepped forward, thinking maybe making love on sacks of malt wouldn't be such a bad idea after all. Lana leaned close, so I dipped my head to kiss her.

26

LANA

The stockroom door creaked open. "You in here?" Brent said, his keys jingling.

I stepped back, wiping beneath my eyes, hoping I'd gotten most of the mascara smears off before Brent saw me.

Dylan glared at Brent, then he stared at me, a tiny smile on his face.

"I saw your cars in the lot and couldn't find you anywhere. I can't believe you got locked in here. We're going to have to talk to Carl about—"

"Wasn't Carl's fault," Dylan said, still looking at me. "He had no way of knowing we were down here."

"You all packed for the trip? We have to leave for the airport soon," Brent said.

Then I realized the time. "I've got to get home and gather my things, or I'll never make the flight."

"Anything I can help with?" Dylan asked. "To speed things up?"

I knew he was sincerely asking if I wanted help. But if he came with me, we'd be late for that flight. I had a feeling that we'd both felt the pull before Brent opened that door, and if he hadn't, we wouldn't be standing up and talking right then.

If I let him into my house, I wasn't sure I could resist him. I wasn't sure I even wanted to try.

"I think I can handle it, but thanks." I rushed out and upstairs to get my purse and phone so I could hurry home to pack.

I should have had everything ready and waiting to grab and walk out the door, but I was so caught up with preparing for the presentation. And I figured I'd finish packing after the mixology session. I didn't expect to be locked in a room all night with Dylan. I didn't have long to get the rest of my things into my bag if I had any hope of making the flight.

I quickly showered first, then I ran through the house, grabbing and shoving, and finally had everything I thought I needed. The whole time, I thought about the kiss with Dylan.

God, I wanted him so much.

I didn't know if we were right for each other or if we should be together. Only that I could no longer deny the rekindled fire that had been growing stronger between us since the day he came back in my life.

I raced through the airport terminal, hoping like hell that the flight didn't leave yet.

If I miss it, that's a sign, I told myself. *Maybe it really wasn't meant to be if that happens.*

I didn't miss it. I was the last one boarded, but I made it. I couldn't quite bring myself to believe that *that* was a sign, but at least it didn't rule anything out.

Out of breath, I stepped onto the plane and hurriedly made my way to my seat. I spotted Brent several rows back and waved at him. Dylan was a row behind him, sitting next to Beth. He nodded at me, looking relieved I'd made it.

As I went to stow my carry-on in the overhead bin, the man sitting next to my aisle seat stood up.

"Here, let me help you with that," he offered with a smile. He reached to grab my bag from me.

Before he could take it, I felt a hand on my waist. I turned to see Dylan smiling at me.

"I've got it," Dylan said to the man, gently moving me aside and easily lifting my suitcase into the compartment.

The man gave Dylan an uncertain look but sat back down without argument.

"You just made it," Dylan said. "I was getting worried when they started boarding that you wouldn't make the flight."

"Me too, I hit every red light on the way here," I said. "Good thing traffic cleared up just in time."

Dylan smiled, looking genuinely relieved I'd made it. That warm grin still made my heart skip a beat.

"You should get back to your seat. The flight attendant is giving me a look," I said, moving to slip past Dylan to my aisle spot.

But Dylan gently stopped me with a hand on my arm.

"Actually, do you mind if we trade spots?" he asked the man in the seat next to mine. The man hesitated to answer so Dylan added, "I'd love to sit with my girlfriend for the flight."

My eyes widened in surprise. Girlfriend? But I didn't correct him.

The man glanced between us and obligingly stood up again.

"No problem, enjoy the flight together," he said politely before heading back to Dylan's vacated seat.

I raised an eyebrow at Dylan.

Dylan just winked and gestured for me to take the window seat. I felt a flutter in my stomach as I slid in next to him.

"Playing my fake boyfriend again?" I asked cheekily.

Dylan chuckled as we settled in our seats.

"Hope that wasn't too presumptuous," he said. "Just wanted an excuse to be close to you." His eyes were soft, unsure.

I felt my cheeks warm. "It's okay with me," I said.

Dylan reached over and laced his fingers through mine, stroking his thumb over my knuckles absently. When I didn't pull away, Dylan's grip tightened gently, our hands resting together on my thigh.

I liked that he wanted to be near me, even if we didn't talk. Then Dylan leaned close.

"I'm glad Brent came when he did, so we didn't miss this flight," he whispered. "But I also want to punch him for interrupting us."

I glanced down at my lap and he squeezed my hand tighter. I looked at him sideways. "I'll admit he has terrible timing."

"He also has terrible ideas," Dylan said, still whispering conspiratorially. "He thought he and I should share a room to save on business expenses. But I vetoed that."

"I have a separate room anyway," I pointed out, realizing he'd brought that up to hear my reaction.

To verify that I was already thinking along the lines of spending time with Dylan alone, in a hotel room. I didn't even realize I had already made that decision until I said the words out loud.

I rolled my lips. "You could have doubled up to save cash."

Dylan's mouth turned in a half-grin, seeming to like my answer.

Then he shook his head. "Brent snores like a buzzsaw, so it's worth the extra expense."

We had to stop talking then, to listen to the safety procedures, but Dylan didn't let go of my hand. He rubbed his thumb over my knuckles again and again.

After we were in the air, my hand still in his, I felt him staring at me. So I turned to face him, and he smiled broadly.

"You're so beautiful," he said. "Bed hair, or freshly showered and ready for business. You're amazing, Lana."

I felt my cheeks warm up at the compliments. And the rest of me warmed up at the way Dylan was looking at me, lust obvious in his gaze.

"I know it's a cliche," I said, "but you're not so bad yourself."

He grinned at that, and in a few minutes, he whispered, "You know, if Brent hadn't shown up when he did, I think we'd have both looked pretty rough when he finally came. Because I was definitely going to mess your hair up even more."

My whole body went hot at how much I'd wanted that.

27

DYLAN

When we landed, I let go of Lana's hand and got her bag out of the overhead compartment. The four of us rode together from the airport to the hotel.

Brent kept looking at both of us on the drive, but he didn't say anything. Beth kept going on about doing a last run through of the presentation.

Lana and Beth's rooms were on a lower floor than ours, so Brent and I said goodbye to them in the elevator. When we stepped into the hall, he said, "Things are going well between the two of you."

It hadn't been a question, but I said, "Yes, they are."

He nodded and headed for his room further down the hall.

"In that case, I'll see you fine people tonight at dinner for one more run-through. Then tomorrow, we can meet in the lobby at two? Give us enough time to have lunch first, get organized, and get to the meeting without rushing?"

"See you then."

I appreciated Brent's friendship all the time but never more than at times like that. He knew when to say things, and when not. He'd been a rock through my divorce for the same reasons.

I only stopped in my room long enough to leave my bag. Then I went down a few floors, already feeling myself get hard on the way.

I needed her. Now.

I arrived on her floor as my phone buzzed with her text.

508

I smiled and I knocked on Lana's door.

"Room service," I said.

The door opened instantly. Lana was already wearing a short, silky robe.

I stepped inside and closed my fists around the thin fabric, pulling her flush against me.

She smiled, leaning into me. "Funny, I didn't order anything. What did you bring me?"

I cupped her ass, grinding her against my erection while I shut the door behind me. "This."

My cock throbbed against her, the tightness in the fly quickly becoming uncomfortable.

"Feels delicious," she said with a wicked smile.

I lifted her off her feet, kissing her as I walked us to the bed.

"Fuck, you're naked under this?" I groaned when I realized. "Ma'am, are you trying to seduce me?"

"Yes," she said with a laugh. "Is it working?"

"You tell me." I ground myself into her again. "I haven't thought of much else but you naked since last night." I pushed her back on the bed and lay above her, nuzzling her jaw and her neck. "I was tempted to convince you to become part of the Mile-High Club in that airplane bathroom."

Lana pushed against my chest to roll me onto my back.

She unfastened my fly and squeezed the mound in my pants while I tried to push them down my hips.

"I wouldn't have done it. I'd be afraid I couldn't stay quiet enough to get away with it. Wouldn't want to ground the plane because someone's screaming in the bathroom."

She looked so happy in that moment, so carefree. We pulled my clothes off then Lana straddled my hips.

She leaned down and kissed me as she rolled her hips, sliding herself against the underside of my cock. She was already wet and slick against me.

"I want to look at you," I whispered.

She sat up and I pulled her robe open to reveal her full breasts, her nipples tightened to hard, pink peaks.

I ran my hands down her gorgeous body, relearning her curves.

I pushed the robe off her shoulders and stroked my hands down her breasts. I thumbed her nipples and she gasped as she tossed her head back. Her pussy pulsed against me.

As much as I wanted to take her fast and hard, I wanted to take my time and make it last. I'd waited three years. A few more minutes was nothing, despite the way my cock ached for her.

I rolled her over, pinning her body beneath me and kissed her deeply, tasting her tongue against mine.

My cock throbbed as I licked down to her neck, the taste of her skin intoxicating me. I traced my tongue along the line of her collarbone.

"I want to taste every inch of you," I murmured against her, my fingers moving lightly over her exposed skin.

I moved down to kiss her breasts, letting my tongue trace circles around her nipple, feeling it hardened beneath my teasing touches.

Tracing my fingers up Lana's thigh, I relished her sharp intake of breath. I grinned against her skin, feeling her body shudder beneath me as I kissed every inch of her. I loved that I had this effect on her, that I could drive her wild.

She gasped when I grazed my knuckles over her center.

"Dylan," she hissed, squirming against the bed, hips lifting in silent plea. "Don't tease me."

With a low chuckle, I pressed my palm between her legs, giving her the contact she desperately needed.

Her breath caught in her throat, a strangled moan escaping her lips.

"Is that what you wanted?" I asked, as my fingers slid through her slick folds.

"Yes," she hissed.

I lifted my fingers to my mouth, tasting her arousal with a groan.

"Dylan," she pleaded, her voice desperate and needy. "Please."

"Tell me what you need, Lana," I growled, my own need clawing at my insides. It was a delicious torture, watching her squirm beneath me, her body begging for release.

"You," she panted, her fingers digging into my back. "I need you."

"You already have me," I replied, my voice low and husky. "Tell me what you really need."

"I need you to make me come," she whispered, her eyes pleading with me.

"Good girl," I murmured approvingly before I pushed two fingers into her wet heat, pumping into her tightness, as my thumb rubbed her clit.

She cried out, her hips rolling desperately as I kissed my way down her stomach, hooking her legs over my shoulders when I reached her throbbing pussy. I licked tight circles around her clit, and then sucked lightly as she tightened around my fingers.

"Ah!" She cried out as her fingers ran through my hair, gripping lightly.

"That's it, baby," I murmured against her, curling my fingers just right. "Let go."

Her back arched off the bed as she came undone, crying out my name.

I continued kissing her gently through her orgasm, slowing my strokes to ease her down as she trembled through the aftershocks.

I settled over her, pinning her wrists above her head and claiming her mouth in a searing kiss.

Our tongues tangled as I ground against her, the hard length of my cock nestled against her heat.

She moaned into my mouth, rocking her hips to meet me.

"I need you now," I rasped against her skin.

With her slick heat against me, I didn't have the patience anymore. All I felt was need. I needed to be inside her right then. I rubbed my cock against her entrance and slid home in one slow thrust. She moaned as her fingers raked through my hair.

I cupped her ass and ground myself deep into her, letting her feel how much I wanted her. How much I needed her.

"Do you have any idea how tempting you are?" I asked, kissing her deeply and panting against her mouth. "How often I think about fucking you?"

I didn't move but kept myself deep inside her. I needed a second to compose myself before I took her, or I was going to lose myself far too fast.

"As much as I think about it," she whispered.

Then she took my face in her hands and kissed me deeper than before, her tongue twisting around mine as she moaned.

I rolled my hips back and bucked forward as her legs wrapped around me.

Her gorgeous blue eyes stared up at me, her pink lips parting in a sweet, high-pitched gasp as I drove into her, pinning her to the bed with my body.

I wrapped one arm around her waist, tangling the other in her hair. She cried out, nails digging into my shoulders as I fucked her deep and hard. Pleasure spiraled through me, intensifying with each stroke.

"You, baby," I said, my words almost lost between our mouths. "You're what I need."

I pushed up on my arms, so I could watch her coming undone.

"Look at me," I demanded, my voice rough with need.

Her eyes fluttered open, hazy with desire. I groaned at the sight, snapping my hips up to drive into her.

I felt the first tremors of her release around me and I couldn't hold back anymore. I needed to feel her come around me as soon as possible.

I slipped a hand between us and stroke her clit, groaning at how hard and hot it was throbbing beneath my thumb.

"Dylan!" she cried out as I filled her, again and again, her hips moving to meet my thrusts.

"Come for me," I growled, pushing her over the edge.

Her body arched as she came with a shout. I pressed my mouth against her throat and sucked, my muscles trembling as I fought to hold back just a little longer.

Her inner walls clamped down as she shattered apart with a moan, and I let go, spilling into her with a growl.

While we rode out the pleasure, I kissed my way up her

neck to her jaw. She was impatient as she cupped my face and pulled me into a breath-stealing kiss.

Afterward, our hearts slowing, I held Lana close and took slow, deep breaths. I tried not to sigh with each one, but I felt so content, it was hard not to.

"That was some room service," she said softly, chuckling against my chest. "I'm going to have to order that again."

I laughed and kissed her. "It's available seven days a week, twenty-four hours a day. Rain or shine, and you'll always get service with a smile." I kissed the tip of her nose. "And I don't accept cash tips."

"No?" She was already smiling at biting her lip in anticipation.

"No." I covered her mouth with mine and pulled her tight against me, gripping her ass with both hands. "This is the only currency I accept."

She rolled on top of me with a laugh.

Once wouldn't be enough. We had until dinner with Brent and Beth, and after that, until the next afternoon. Unless she decided to run me out of her room later, I was going to take advantage of every minute we were together.

28

LANA

I woke to the warmth of his breath on my neck and a heavy arm draped over my waist.

Memories of last night flashed through my mind, Dylan's hands and mouth exploring every inch of my body, the delicious ache he left between my thighs.

I couldn't help the smile that crept across my face.

His arm tightened around me, pulling me flush against his chest. "Morning," he mumbled, his voice rough with sleep.

"Morning." I rolled over to face him, tracing a finger down the sharp line of his jaw. "Did you sleep okay?"

A slow, sleepy grin spread across his face. "Never better."

He rolled on top of me, nuzzling my neck. "But I need a wake-up call."

I laughed, the sound turning into a gasp as his hands found my hips, gripping tight.

Yes, it was definitely going to be a good morning.

His lips traced a path down my neck to my collarbone. My hands clutched at his shoulders, nails digging in.

"Dylan," I moaned, desire pooling low in my belly.

"I know, baby." His voice was rough with need as his hands slid up to cup my breasts.

He rolled one nipple between his fingers and I gasped, back bowing. His mouth closed over the other nipple, tongue teasing until I squirmed beneath him.

Dylan groaned against my skin before lifting his head. His eyes were nearly black with lust as they met mine.

His hips rocked against me, the hard length of him sliding through my folds.

I caught my lower lip between my teeth, pleasure spiking through me.

Then he was sliding into me, inch by inch, and I gasped into his mouth. So full, so perfect.

Dylan stilled above me, his whole body trembling.

I tilted my hips up, taking him deeper. "Move, Dylan. Please, I need you."

He didn't need to be told twice.

His hips snapped forward, setting a rhythm that had me clinging to him, soft cries falling from my lips. So good, so right.

Dylan braced himself on one arm, his free hand sliding between us. His fingers found my clit, rubbing in time with his thrusts.

"Fuck, you feel so good," he growled, circling my clit. "I want to feel you come around me."

His words sent me tumbling over the edge with a cry of his name. My inner walls tightened around him as I came apart beneath him.

Dylan thrust deep once, twice more before he followed, groaning my name against my neck.

For a long moment we lay there, breathless and sated, still joined.

Dylan lifted his head, brushing a kiss over my lips. "Round two after breakfast?"

I laughed, the sound turning into a moan as he shifted inside me. "We're going to be late for our meeting."

~

As we walked into the conference room at Emberox Spirits, I could feel the slight and pleasant ache in my inner muscles with every step. I glanced over my shoulder to give Dylan a smile before we sat at the table.

We met Shane and Vera, the brother-sister team that owned the company, and the rest of the Emberox Spirits team.

Shane was built a lot like Brent but didn't have an impressive beard.

Vera looked like she'd stepped off a corporate runway or out of a fashion magazine. She was all business in her sleek black dress. Her flaming red hair probably came out of a bottle, but it didn't matter. It looked amazing with her Patrician features and olive skin.

"Lovely to meet you all," she finally said after all the introductions. "We're eager to hear what you've put together. Are we ready to begin?"

Dylan and Brent gave a short presentation on their background and about the brewery. Then they handed it off to me and Beth, giving us encouraging smiles. I knew how much getting this collab would mean for their brewery. Beth and I couldn't let them down.

We had gone over our talking points so many times I could probably recite them in my sleep. But I glanced over my notes one last time just to be safe.

I took a deep breath, stood, and started the presentation, clicking through to the first slide.

If Vera's smile hadn't seemed so genuine and warm, I'd have been intimidated as hell. And I was nervous, but more so because Dylan was there, witnessing the whole thing.

I was good at my job, but the thought of possibly failing in his eyes made my stomach flutter.

After my part of the presentation, Beth started her slides about our client case studies and success stories. But instead of elaborating on them, she froze.

"As you can see on this slide..." Beth's voice trailed off uncertainly as she squinted at the screen.

I tensed. Something was wrong. Beth tried clicking forward again, then backward through the slides. Her eyes widened slightly in alarm as she looked at me. I tried giving her a reassuring smile.

Had she forgotten a section of the presentation?

My pulse kicked up a notch. The Emberox team was glancing at each other in confusion as Beth stood there fumbling. Dylan and Brent both sat forward in their seats, their shoulders tensing.

"I'm so sorry," Beth stammered. "If I could just have a moment to get my notes in order..."

Before she could finish, I jumped in to summarize a case study from memory. Beth shot me a look that was more angry than grateful. But I kept talking smoothly.

After a minute, she took a deep breath and jumped back in, having found her place in the slides again.

When we finished the presentation, the Emberox team applauded politely. Vera and Shane glanced at each other with a smile and the rest of the team exchanged approving glances.

I finally glanced at Dylan and Brent. Dylan gave me a

wink and a subtle thumbs up and Brent was grinning widely. I exhaled slowly, my shoulders relaxing, but Beth looked far from relieved.

"I have to say," Shane said, "I'm really liking what I'm seeing."

Vera nodded and crossed her shapely arms.

"And I have to agree. Let Shane and I give you a tour of Emberox Spirits. Why don't we all go to dinner so we can discuss this further? A little more informally." She said it more to Dylan than anyone, and then I noticed the way she narrowed her eyes at him, sizing him up.

She'd watched him a lot during the pitch, but I'd had to focus on the details and block that out. I couldn't help but notice, now that it was over, how invitingly she kept glancing at him.

"I need to ask legal a few questions, and then we'll meet you downstairs?" Again, she asked Dylan rather than the group. He agreed.

Business dinner and talking to legal meant the deal was as good as done.

There might be some compromises on the backend, but there was almost certainly going to be a collab between Emberox Spirits and Deft Rock.

Dylan put his hand on my shoulder and gave it a squeeze as we filed out of the conference room. As soon as we were in the elevator, Dylan and Brent fist bumped. Brent patted my shoulder. Beth and I congratulated each other on the successful co-presentation, even though her expression remained tight.

"You guys did great," Dylan said, beaming at me. "This could change everything."

Brent chimed in, agreeing, and they talked excitedly

about the deal that was probably going to be sealed over dinner.

The tour took a long time because Dylan and Brent had a lot of technical questions about their processes. I made some notes for the campaign and tried not to notice how close Vera stayed by Dylan's side.

As soon as they were out of earshot, Beth turned to me.

"Did you have to swoop in like that?" she snapped in a hushed tone. "Now I'm going to look like an idiot who can't present my own work."

I blinked in surprise. "I was just trying to make sure the presentation went smoothly. You looked at me like you needed help."

I thought I was helping, but clearly, she thought I'd shown her up.

"Dylan and Brent think I'm useless now."

"That's not true at all," I assured her. "They know we both worked on this together. And they were ecstatic at how it went."

She crossed her arms and shook her head. "No one asked you to jump in."

"Seriously?" I asked in disbelief. "I saved your ass in there."

"I had it under control," she retorted.

Beth turned on her heel and stormed off as I stood there stunned. I didn't think I'd overstepped. I tried not to let her resentment taint our victory.

After the tour, we went together to the restaurant. Vera quickly sat next to Dylan, and Brent sat with Shane next to him. Beth and I ended up next to each other, across the table from them, with a few of the members from the Emberox team.

Warren, the marketing director, slid into the open seat on my other side.

"Mind if I join you?" he asked with an easy smile. He was tall and broad-shouldered, with deep blue eyes and dimples when he grinned.

"Not at all," I said politely.

Warren had been very complimentary about the presentation and sounded excited about the collab. He asked thoughtful questions about the case studies we presented and seemed genuinely interested in the details. But I did notice he focused solely on me rather than speaking to anyone else at the table.

Brent and Shane got involved in a conversation about brewing temperatures and oak-barrel aging and Beth spoke to one of the designers about possible color directions.

I tried to focus on my conversation with Warren, but I couldn't help but try to listen in on what Vera and Dylan were saying. I watched Vera smile and lean in, touching Dylan's arm, clearly flirting.

And him obviously enjoying it as he laughed back. Something twisted sharply in my chest at the thought.

Vera kept complimenting Dylan on his business savvy. She even turned and complimented me and Beth on the pitch at one point, and she wasn't being insincere.

I wanted to hate her, but she seemed genuinely nice and thoughtful. Just thirsty as hell for my—for Dylan.

What I did hate was how Dylan loved the attention she was giving him. After last night, it hurt to see him so engaged with another woman, being so attentive. Especially one as gorgeous as Vera. He hadn't said a word to me all night.

His flirting reminded me of Todd cheating, and I couldn't help but wonder if the brothers shared the same habits. I didn't think Dylan was the type, but I couldn't completely shake away the doubt.

Not that it would even be considered cheating because it wasn't like we were actually together. Not after one night. Was that the point he was trying to get across? That we weren't exclusive?

I tore my gaze away, trying to focus on my conversation with Warren instead of the irrational jealousy creeping through me. Warren lightly touched my arm as he continued to ask about the collab.

At one point, I glanced up to find Dylan's gaze fixed on me, his brows furrowed. Our eyes locked and his jaw was clenched, his hand gripped tightly around his drink.

Was he bothered by seeing me with Warren? He couldn't be serious. He was the one shamelessly flirting with Vera all night.

I must have been making a face because Beth leaned over discreetly and asked, "Do you think he'll take her to his room later?" under her breath.

I dragged my eyes away from Dylan and Vera. "What?" I asked in shock.

"I mean, she's been eyeing him like a juicy steak all day. I'd be surprised if they don't end up banging each other at the end of the night." Beth eyed me, taking in my reaction. "Are you going to be okay?"

"Of course, why wouldn't I be?" I replied, quickly.

Too quickly apparently because Beth shot me a knowing look.

"I might have noticed him stopping by someone's hotel room after dinner last night," she said, eyebrows raised.

I nearly choked on my wine.

"What? That was just...a work thing," I stammered,

clearing my throat. I was doing a horrible job of playing it off. She smelled blood because she didn't let it go.

"Mm hm, must have been some important business to discuss that it couldn't wait," Beth said with a smirk. "I sensed something was going on between you guys, and I wasn't sure until just now," she said as she eyed me. "I'm sure Alexander or Chelsea wouldn't like an employee screwing around with a client."

My eyes went wide. Before I could respond, Beth continued, "But clearly he's moved on to the next pretty girl already. Men, right?"

I glanced back over at Dylan, who seemed completely engrossed in his cozy conversation with Vera. Laughing at her jokes, refilling her wine glass...

"They're talking business," I said, trying to convince myself more than Beth.

Beth just shook her head doubtfully. "Don't be so naive, Lana. What man in his right mind would pass up on an opportunity to be with a woman like Vera. Talk about sealing a business deal."

I knew Beth was just trying to get under my skin, but as much as I hated to admit it, she had a point. Dylan slipped easily back into flirt mode with a beautiful, interested woman. Especially a smart and successful one like Vera. Meanwhile, I sat here like a flustered schoolgirl, pining pathetically.

I felt sick to my stomach at the sight of Vera hanging off Dylan and the thought of people at the office finding out about our night together. The exact thing I had feared was coming true.

I could already see how this would play out. I'd fall for him and somehow, I'd end up getting my heart broken.

Maybe even fired from my job. I couldn't sit there any

longer. I decided to excuse myself for the night and head back to the hotel early.

Warren leaned in closely with a grin, asking if I wanted a drink from the bar.

Dylan's penetrating gaze turned back to us. His body was angled slightly toward us, like he was about to pounce.

"I'm sorry, Warren. I think I should get going soon. I'm feeling a little jet lagged," I said apologetically. "But thank you." I smiled weakly, avoiding Dylan's searing stare.

Warren looked disappointed but nodded graciously.

"Of course. I understand it's been a long day." He met my eyes.

I smiled, my gaze drifting back to Dylan. He had an inscrutable look on his face, his stare still locked on Warren.

I stood and said my goodbyes to everyone, explaining I was still feeling a little jet-lagged and wanted to go back to the hotel. Beth raised her eyebrows but didn't comment.

"Are you sure?" Dylan asked, starting to rise from his seat, concern etched on his face. "Let me help you get back."

"That's ok, I'll be fine. I'm sure you two still have a lot to discuss," I said, smiling tightly.

For a moment, I thought he was going to walk over, but he hesitated. Then he slowly sat back down, his jaw tight.

Warren stood at the same time. "Please, let me walk you out," he insisted.

Out of the corner of my eye, I saw Dylan with an irritated expression on his face, but turn away as Vera started speaking again, touching his arm.

I turned and headed to the exit, feeling the jealousy bubbling up again. Warren held the door open for me as we stepped outside into the cool night air.

"I'm looking forward to working with you, Lana," he said, handing me his card. "Give me a call anytime."

"Thank you, I appreciate that." I smiled tightly.

Once inside the cab, angry tears stung my eyes, but I held them back.

My feelings for Dylan had already deepened past the point of no return. But clearly, I needed to be smarter about this.

29

DYLAN

I almost rushed after Lana when Warren walked her out, but Vera touched my arm. "She's got a right to be tired."

"What?" I'm sure my eyes went wide, because how could she possibly know that we didn't get much sleep?

"She clearly worked very hard on that pitch. Let the girl get her rest," she said with a smile.

Brent was fighting a smile and couldn't even look at me. I must have been tired too to think anyone could possibly know how we'd spent the night before.

I watched the direction of the entrance, waiting for Warren to return. It had been a few minutes. What was taking him so long?

Damn it, I should've walked her out.

Without thinking, I stood up to make my way outside when I saw Warren heading back to the table. He commented that Lana really did seem tired after a long day she'd had.

I wanted to tell him she was tired because I'd kept her up all night and to keep his damn paws off her. If it hadn't been a business dinner, I would've lunged over the table the moment I saw him lean in close to Lana.

Shane, Brent, and the rest of the group headed to the bar, leaving me and Vera alone at the table.

When I sat again, Vera suggested that she and her team come to Everbrook to tour Deft Rock.

"I want to get a better sense of the people I get into bed with," she said, beaming.

I knew she was using a common phrase for getting into business with someone, but she'd emphasized the word bed just enough to give it a double meaning.

She'd been flirting with me all through the dinner. I suspected she was warm and friendly as a rule, but I knew world-class flirting when I saw it.

I tried not to flirt back, but years of dealing with customers and other businesspeople made it easy to be friendly and engaging.

I hoped I hadn't led her on. When she grinned at me, I realized I hadn't. She just went after the things she wanted, and probably got them most of the time. That was probably part of the reason Emberox Spirits was so successful.

Then Vera clasped her hands together and leaned close. "I realize this is forward of me, Dylan. And I want you to know that I keep my personal pleasures separate from business, so if anything happens between us, or doesn't, it won't affect our decision one way or another. But I'm hoping like hell you'll tell me that you're single."

I actually felt my face heat up. I'd never been propositioned quite so boldly before. Especially by a woman like Vera.

"Technically, I am."

She leaned closer, her smile growing.

"But . . . it's complicated. Because deep down, whether she knows it or not, I don't think of myself as single."

Vera pulled the corners of her mouth down. "I'm disappointed. And I'm also intrigued. She must be one special lady." She held up her glass. "Let's drink to her, and then you can tell me the whole story. If you want to, of course."

We toasted and drank. The group was still over at the bar, engaged in conversation. Shane appeared to be buying a round of drinks. I had a little time, at least.

And even though I'd have told any businessman to never tell such personal things to a business partner, the story poured out of me. I didn't tell her the woman was Lana or give a name, but I told her the important parts.

"She thinks we're not meant to be. Or she did. That might have changed, but I'm not sure. I just need more time to convince her that we belong together." I took another drink. "Because I'm in love with her."

Vera had listened carefully to my story, hanging on every word. She put her palms on the table. "Have you told her that? That might be the last encouragement she needs!"

"I'm getting there. Like I said, it's complicated."

"It is indeed." She took a deep breath and shrugged her shoulders quickly, like she was stretching her muscles. "Well, Dylan, you seem like the type of man who doesn't give up on someone he cares about. I suspect you'll make her understand. And if she realizes the type of man you are, I'm sure things will work out for you."

She toasted again. "My best wishes for you both."

"I'll drink to that."

She sipped her drink. "I have to know, though. If you were single..."

I laughed softly. Vera was a gorgeous woman. Any man would be so lucky to be with her.

"If I hadn't met the woman I told you about? We'd be ditching them." I shook my thumb toward the group still at the bar. "And halfway to my hotel."

Vera liked that answer.

Brent and Shane returned to the table a few minutes later.

"Shane here has invited us back to his place for a celebratory drink," Brent said, clapping my back. "He's got a bottle of Macallan Reserve he's been waiting to crack open."

"I'm definitely in," Vera said, turning to me. "How about you?"

I hesitated, my thoughts drifting back to Lana, but Brent looked at me expectantly.

I forced a smile. "Wouldn't miss it."

Brent went to make sure Beth would be ok getting back to the hotel and to let her know we were heading out with Shane and Vera.

After a couple rounds of drinks at Shane's place and discussions about them coming to tour our brewery, we decided to call it a night.

At the hotel, I paused when the elevator stopped on Lana's floor. Then I decided I should call her first before showing up after she left early as she had. Maybe she really didn't feel well.

In fact, it was late. She was probably already asleep.

I rode the elevator up and went to my own room, prepared to call Lana first thing in the morning. Or maybe I'd show up at her door with breakfast and see if I could find a few ways to make her feel better.

30

LANA

Like a fool, I'd stayed awake far too long waiting to see if Dylan would call or come to my room after dinner. But he hadn't even texted me.

I hadn't left early for sympathy or attention, but after our night together, I thought maybe he'd have reached out. He'd clearly been far too busy with Vera to worry about that.

Stop it. It was just a business dinner.

At least that's what I kept telling myself. That they probably had a lot of details to discuss.

I wasn't expected back at the office until the next day, so Dylan and I had planned on spending the day together. That plan suddenly felt like a very bad idea.

Especially after my conversation with Beth. She'd made it very clear she knew what was going on between me and Dylan. I couldn't risk her thinking I was sneaking around with him after the presentation.

It made me anxious knowing that she could jeopardize my career at Berman. Possibly get me fired. I couldn't afford to lose my job.

Knowing Beth, she'd probably be back in the office first thing in the morning.

It was still early enough that I could catch the first flight back. I'd return to the office before Beth, avoiding any suspicion about my day with Dylan. It was the best option.

I fired off a quick text to Dylan, letting him know I had to return early.

By the time the plane took off, Dylan still hadn't called or texted. With it on airplane mode, I wouldn't hear from anyone until we landed. I tried to watch a movie but couldn't stop thinking about Dylan.

Get out before your heart gets broken, Lana.

I tried to focus on the stupid comedy I'd picked. But I knew my heart was already cracking and about to shatter. If I wanted to avoid heartbreak, I'd have to go back nearly four years and start over.

I didn't turn my phone on right away after I landed. I suspected he'd at least texted, maybe wondering where I was by that point. And I just wasn't ready to deal with it.

From the airport, I went straight to the office.

I settled in at my desk, anxious at the thought of Beth saying something to anyone at the office about me and Dylan.

I figured I might as well fill Chelsea in on the presentation. As I headed to her office, someone shouted. "There she is! Kicking ass and taking names!" Maddie ran up to me and pulled me into a tight hug.

"You heard already?"

"Heard you guys killed it! Brent called this morning and gave us the good news. I mean, they want to see Deft Rock before any legal documents are signed, but they made a handshake deal. It's all but in the bag!"

I chuckled. "Yeah, they were pretty impressed."

I went into Chelsea's office to give her a quick recap, leaving out the part where Beth had fumbled on her section.

"You and Beth did a great job," she said.

Alexander stopped by to pat me on the back.

I should have been as giddy with excitement as Maddie was. Instead, I felt miserable.

Beth strolled in and looked at me in surprise.

"Lana. Thought you were taking the day off," she said, eyebrow raised. "Weren't you supposed to be...out of town today?"

I tensed, feeling Chelsea and Alexander's curious gazes shift to me. Beth was clearly fishing for information about Dylan.

"Change of plans," I said breezily, hoping my cheeks weren't flushing. I avoided meeting their eyes.

"Right," Beth said slowly, her tone suggesting that I was hiding something. "Well, maybe Dylan will be in to give us a recap. You know, of what he and Vera discussed after they left the restaurant."

After they left the restaurant? What did she mean by that?

I struggled to keep my cool while Beth smiled at me innocently. I knew Beth was just trying to get me to react so that Chelsea and Alexander would see for themselves that I had something going on with Dylan.

Chelsea glanced between us, a slight furrow in her brow. I scrambled for a distraction.

"Hey, did you all see the email from Emberox?" I asked. "We should probably start prepping for their visit."

"Oh yes, we definitely should coordinate," Chelsea said. She started discussing possible events we could put on while they were here.

Beth gave me a look but didn't press the issue further.

After our discussion, I headed to Alexander's office. I needed to put some distance between me and Dylan. Most of the work for Deft Rock was done anyway.

"Now that Emberox Spirits is pretty clearly on board, can I be assigned to a different account? Maybe let Beth handle the next steps?"

Alex blinked slowly at me like I'd lost my mind. Then he shook his head.

"I'd really prefer you stay on it. You've done such a fine job already, Lana. And I'm sure Dylan would be disappointed to— wait, has something happened that I should know about? Something that makes you want to drop the account?"

Sometimes, agency managers, especially women, got harassed by male clients.

It had never personally happened to me, but it sounded like that was what he was trying to find out.

"No, nothing like that," I assured him.

He sighed in relief. "Then can I ask why you want to be reassigned?"

I thought of the promotion and how dropping an account like this wouldn't be a good look for it.

"It's not really that I want to be reassigned. I just feel like I need something else too. Maybe if—"

Alex snapped his fingers. "I've got you. I don't want you to focus on one thing so much that you burn out, either. Let me see what I can do."

He was gone before I could try to explain further. I knew he'd give me another account, probably just something minor for the time being. But maybe that would help.

Back at my desk, I finally took my phone off airplane mode. Several buzzes and beeps later, I put it down again.

The messages could wait. But then it rang, a new call, so I took a deep breath and answered it.

"Are you ok? Why did you leave?" Dylan asked, sounding hurt and confused.

"I just felt the need to get back," I said. "I hope you still went and saw the things you wanted to."

"I spent a lot of time wondering what happened. Is everything ok?" He asked, his voice filled with concern.

"Yes, everything's fine," I sighed.

"Then what's going on?"

"Nothing, I just—"

"Lana," he said firmly. "Tell me what's happening here. You just *left*, and I don't understand why."

"I think we should just keep what happened as a one-time thing."

"What?" Dylan asked quietly, his voice filled with disbelief.

"I realize what's happened hasn't been entirely professional, but—"

"*Fuck* professional, Lana," he exploded.

Geez, he was upset. I sighed wearily, pressing my fingers to my throbbing temple.

I took a deep breath. I knew I owed him an explanation, but I couldn't do it at work. I needed to get off the phone before I did something stupid like fucking cry. My emotions felt chaotic after what Beth had said.

"Dylan, I'm at work. I can't really talk about this right now."

"Fine. Meet me when you get off. Or better yet, I'll come to you. I'm coming over when you get home tonight."

Our professional relationship, even if he didn't care about that at the moment, really was at the heart of my decision-making. It had to be.

How things ended between us would affect the account and my ability to represent Deft Rock. I couldn't just run away and hide from this like a little girl.

"Come over at seven, and we can talk."

"I'll see you then."

I somehow managed to focus on work for the rest of the day, maybe because I knew I didn't need to think about Dylan until seven o'clock. I could put it off that long, at least.

Dylan pulled into my driveway fifteen minutes early.

31

LANA

I didn't really believe Beth when she said Dylan had left with Vera. At least not in the way she implied. I knew she was just trying to get a rise out of me, but it worked. It fueled my anger that brewed at the memory of him and Vera that night.

I opened the door when Dylan was getting out of his car, waiting with my arms crossed. He didn't bring dessert or look at me with sad puppy-dog eyes, either. If anything, he looked pretty angry.

"Talk to me, Lana. Tell me what's happened," he said, before he even reached me.

As soon as he'd stepped through the door, he turned and looked at me with an irritated expression on his face, waiting for me to answer.

I went into the living room to sit on the couch with Dylan following close behind. When I sat, he sat next to me, his knee touching mine.

And despite the way I'd felt all day, like I should end things before I got in any deeper, I wanted to feel his arms around me again. I lost all my common sense the minute he got near me.

I knew how the conversation would end if I started off with Vera. I decided to keep it centered on the possibility of losing my job at Berman, instead of demanding explanations I likely didn't want to hear.

"I just think it's for the best if we kept our relationship professional going forward," I stated.

I couldn't even look him in the eyes when I said it. Dylan put his fingers under my chin and lifted my face, so I'd look at him.

"Bullshit, Lana," he said, looking at me fiercely.

"I'm serious," I countered firmly. "We had a wonderful night together," I added softly.

"Night and morning," he added pointedly.

"Night and morning. And I think we should keep it as that. A one-time thing," I responded as calmly as I could, suppressing the anger that was brewing at the thought of him with Vera.

"Two times," he pointed out, frustration evident in his tense jaw. "Two nights, Lana. And I definitely need a lot more than that with you."

"It was a fun night, but I think we got carried away with—"

"Stop it. You know it was more than that."

"Dylan, I need to focus on my job, and I can't do that when I'm sleeping with the client. We should keep our relationship strictly at the office. It's best for both of us," I said again.

Dylan raked a hand through his hair, looking far from convinced.

"It's not. It's a terrible idea," Dylan said shaking his head. "I don't think it's that big of a deal."

"It is to me, Dylan! You might get a pat on the back and be called a stud, but it's different for me. I won't be taken seriously at work after a scandal involving a client. Alexander and the other partners are very serious about client relationships."

He frowned and pressed his lips together as he reflected on what I said.

"Where's this coming from? I can't believe the night we had, and that becoming this. Did something happen?"

He stared intently, as if he was trying to figure out what I was thinking.

I hesitated, biting my lip. I didn't want to drag him into my messy drama with Beth. That was my problem to handle, but I knew he wasn't leaving without an explanation.

"Beth saw you that night. Coming to my room," I said. "I can't do my job being involved with you like this. Having Beth watch me like a hawk, just waiting for me to make a mistake."

His brows furrowed. "What did she say?"

"She threatened to tell Alexander and Chelsea. She's right, I shouldn't be messing around with a client." I explained. "I tried to deny it, but she saw you with Vera during dinner and said you'd probably take her to your room. I reacted and she knew," I said, then added with a huff. "She said you left with her, too."

Dylan studied me for a long moment, his eyes searching mine.

"This isn't just about Beth, is it? Clearly, you're mad about something, so let's hear it," he demanded.

I crossed my arms, holding back a swelling tide of hurt and irritation.

Dylan pressed on. "You're pissed about Vera."

It wasn't a question, but more of an observation. It finally broke my resolve.

"Yes! Damn it, Dylan." I shook my head angrily. "I didn't leave just because of Beth. Seeing you fawn all over Vera last night really upset me, okay? Excuse me if it ruined the idea of a cozy day alone together."

"Vera was flirting. Openly flirting. I was trying to be friendly, and if it seemed like I was flirting back—Lana, it really was unintentional."

"Anyone with eyes could see that you were all over her," I continued.

"I was *not* all over her. We only discussed business, Lana. I didn't flirt or make come-ons or imply that I would give in to any of hers. Just. Business." His eyes darkened, and he let out a huff of breath. "And that gives you a free pass to flirt with Warren then?"

My eyes widened. How dare he use that to turn this conversation on me.

"I was *not* flirting, and you know it. I was just being polite," I snapped. "And he was a perfect gentleman."

"Didn't look like a damn gentleman from where I was sitting," Dylan growled. "You couldn't just tell him you're taken?"

Was I taken? I wasn't so sure. It wasn't like Warren had made a pass at me where I could've even said that.

"No, because I'm not," I replied. "I'm not taken."

He looked at me with fire in his eyes, his jaw clenching. "You really mean that?"

"*My man* wouldn't do that to me. He wouldn't welcome advances from another woman." He flinched at my retort. It must have struck a nerve because I thought he looked a little guilty. "And at least I didn't leave with Warren," I added.

Dylan looked at me incredulously.

"You actually think I left with Vera that night?" He asked, raking his fingers through his hair. "You honestly believe that?"

Of course, I didn't believe that. I sighed and shook my head.

"We went to Shane's place afterward. With Shane and Brent. I wasn't alone with her. And I didn't welcome her advances," he gritted out.

I raised my eyebrows in challenge and he stood his ground, not breaking eye contact.

"You know how important that dinner was in closing the deal," he added.

We glared at each other, the air between us crackling with tension.

He suddenly leaned back, like he realized something. "You don't trust me," he stated, his eyes still locked on mine.

I broke the stare down first, looking away as I blinked back the tears as it dawned on me that I didn't fully trust him. Or at least I was afraid to.

"I don't know," I said, turning away from him. I was running high on emotions and I knew I'd say a lot of things I'd regret later. "I don't think we should do this right now."

Dylan let out a deep sigh and grabbed my arm, tugging gently so I'd look at him. "Fine. But we're going to talk this out when we've both cooled off."

He tried to pull me into a hug but I stepped back, crossing my arms in front of my chest. I needed to put some distance between us at that moment. Or I'd breakdown and cry like a baby in his arms.

He turned and walked slowly toward the door, pausing before opening it.

"Until then, I suggest you figure out if you want to be with me."

Dylan walked out, pulling the door firmly shut behind him.

32

DYLAN

I felt like shit after my blowup with Lana. How did I let it get out of hand so quickly?

Lana leaving without an explanation had really pissed me off, but I didn't realize my talking to Vera had bothered her so much. I had tossed and turned all night, our fight replaying in my mind.

I was tired of the bullshit constantly getting in our way. Like keeping a damn professional relationship. Ending our partnership with the Berman agency was the obvious solution. Her reluctance at trusting me would need to be resolved over time.

I knew convincing Brent to end our partnership with Berman would take some work. Sure enough, when I told him my plan, Brent balked.

"Are you kidding? We just had an amazing presentation with Emberox thanks to Berman," he argued. "Why would we sever that partnership now?"

I hesitated. I couldn't exactly tell him this was all because Lana didn't want to be involved with a client.

"The agency can stay on board until the event. After that, they really won't be a part of the process anyway. Emberox already has a team of experts so I'm sure we will be leveraging their resources for the most part."

Most of the agency's work was done already. And Emberox did seem to have an impressive marketing team already in place. Brent had to know Berman Agency would be taking a step back regardless.

Brent crossed his arms. "Level with me, Dylan. What's really going on here?"

I sighed, realizing there was no way around the truth. "It's a personal issue between me and Lana, alright? We can't work together anymore."

He looked at me for a long moment. I could see him processing what had happened on the trip, finally nodding when he understood the situation. I was glad he knew me well enough that I didn't need to explain.

"Alright," he shrugged. "I think you have a point. After the event, most of the work really is done for them."

I exhaled in relief. "We'll make it work, even if it's messy for a bit."

Brent chuckled and clapped my shoulder. "You've got it bad, man."

I raked a hand through my hair. "Yeah, tell me about it. I'm completely fucked."

After getting Brent on board, I felt much lighter. I went to Berman Agency to speak to Alexander in private.

"Your team has been an invaluable asset so far," I started.

"Well, we're thrilled to be working with you."

I cleared my throat. "I wanted to discuss plans moving forward."

"Of course, we're happy to support however we can," Alexander said amiably.

"I appreciate that. You've been a great partner," I said. "However...Brent and I decided to conclude our arrangement after Emberox's visit. I'd like to still have the agency help with the tasting event."

There was a brief pause. "I see. May I ask what drove you to that decision?" His tone was neutral and mostly curious. "It's not due to lack of performance on our part, I hope."

"Not at all, it's more about evolving needs on our side," I explained. "Lana and the team have done an amazing job."

"Well, that's good to hear this isn't based on any dissatisfaction," Alexander said.

We talked a little more about the event and then I walked out of Alexander's office and straight to Beth's.

We needed to have a chat.

I knocked and opened her door. She glanced up from her computer, surprise flashing across her face.

"Dylan. What brings you by?"

I closed the door behind me and smiled at her. "I think you know why I'm here."

Beth's eyes widened slightly but she kept her expression neutral.

"To let you know what a fantastic job you've done, Beth."

Beth's cheeks flushed and she smiled like she was surprised. "Thank you–"

"I just spoke to Alexander, and we'll be wrapping up our partnership with Berman."

She nodded, her smile fading. "Oh, I'm sorry to hear that."

"It would be awful if Alexander found out why." I paused, narrowing my eyes at her. "Someone at the agency has been spreading rumors about me and my new business partner."

Beth paled but quickly composed herself.

I raised my eyebrows and looked at her to see if I was getting my point across. She looked away, unable to hold my gaze.

"But don't worry, I told him it's because our business needs have changed." I continued.

"Right," she nodded, swallowing.

"It would be a shame if I had to tell him that one of his top managers said I took Vera to my hotel room after a business dinner." I continued.

Beth's mouth dropped open in shock.

"Or that she threatened a client."

She frowned in confusion and stammered, "I didn't. I don't know what you mean."

"I take threats to Lana very, very personally," I continued in a low, serious tone.

Beth's eyes flashed with anger and what looked like fear. After a tense moment, she gave a curt nod.

"Of course." She nodded, darting her eyes away. "I understand."

"Good, I'm glad we're on the same page."

She continued to nod as I walked to the door.

I stopped and turned. "Oh, and Beth?"

She looked up at me.

"Since this is our little secret, it's your job from now on to make sure it stays that way. Make sure no one else in the agency finds out."

I held her gaze a moment longer for emphasis. Then I turned and walked out, letting the door shut firmly behind me.

I returned to the brewery and sat in my office, trying to look over our forecast for this quarter. I couldn't focus. I had to talk to Lana and finish our conversation. Leaving it unresolved was eating at me. She had to know I was serious about us.

I sent an email to Chelsea, suggesting Lana come to the brewery to pick up some materials in preparation for the event with Emberox. Then I hoped like hell that Lana's decision was to be with me.

33

LANA

My email pinged with a message from Chelsea, asking me to stop by Deft Rock to pick up some materials. Great, I'd have to see Dylan alone after all.

I wasn't ready to see him yet after our argument yesterday. I was still processing our conversation and how to deal with the whole messed up situation.

I believed him when he said that everything that happened with Vera was all unintentional, but that still didn't change the fact that Beth knew about us and the looming threat of being fired from my job. I felt like there was a time bomb just waiting to go off at any second.

After pulling into the parking lot, I made my way to the taproom where Shayna was serving customers. She directed me to the back where Dylan's office was located.

I knocked and opened the door to find it empty.

I was about to head back to the taproom, but I wanted to see his office. I'd never been in it before. It was cozy yet professional, just like him. I breathed in deeply, taking in his familiar scent that filled the space.

A large mahogany desk sat on one side of the room, files

neatly organized on top. A black leather couch was on the other side next to a large window that lit the room with natural light. The pillow that I'd given to Dave for his birthday was propped up on it. He'd kept it.

My gaze wandered, taking in the surrounding, until it landed on a familiar frame hanging on the wall behind his desk.

I smiled at the memory until I noticed something was off. The picture inside now was a group photo from the party that included me and Grandpa. The photo was never meant to be taken out. I'd had it designed that way, where it was encased and sealed between the glass and the wood.

I walked over to it. My throat tightened at the memory of the note I had scribbled on the back at the last second before taking it to the frame shop. Realization dawned on me that Dylan must have seen it.

Why had I written that silly note? Maybe I'd wanted to leave a part of me with him.

Lost in thought, I didn't hear Dylan approach.

"Interesting story. Do you want to hear it?" I startled as Dylan asked from behind.

I slowly turned back to the frame and cleared my throat.

"Sure," I replied, but it came out as a squeak.

"I had that hanging in the taproom when we first opened. And then it fell one day. The drywall gave out and the screw came loose," he said as he walked closer. "I was so upset when I found the wood had split in the corner, so I took it to a woodworker to have it fixed. He asked if I wanted to keep the same photo, but I told him I had a better one."

I felt the heat from his chest against my back.

"Do you remember what you wrote?" He asked quietly, his breath in my ear.

"Of course, I do," I whispered.

I'm yours in our next life.

"It always gave me hope that we'd see each other again someday. Did you mean it?" His hands rested on my hips, squeezing gently. "Are you mine, Lana?"

I exhaled a shaky breath as his hands brushed up my arms.

"I meant it at the time," I admitted honestly. I had just broken up with Todd when I had written it. I wanted to be his, but I knew I couldn't then. "I wrote it at the spur of the moment. And besides, it's not our next life yet, is it?" I tried to play it off like it wasn't a big deal.

I turned to face him, but he was standing so close, so I took a step back, meeting the wall behind me.

He smirked, "You're really going to make me wait that long?"

"We agreed to keep our relationship professional." My voice was barely above a whisper.

Slowly, he stepped toward me and leaned his hands against the wall, trapping me between his arms.

He met my eyes steadily. Neither of us moved, just stood there gazing at each other, his face inches from mine. I swallowed and licked my lips. Heat flooded my center at his closeness.

He finally broke the silence. "No, I didn't agree," he said, raising his eyebrows. "I said it was a terrible idea. Besides, I think we're past that point, Lana." He leaned closer, breathing me in, and my thighs clenched.

"I know how you taste." His lips hovered above my neck, his hot breath hitting my skin. "I know the little sounds you make when I'm deep inside you. And what you look like spread out underneath me, begging me to make you come."

I held my breath, waiting for him to continue.

"I know what you feel like around my cock, hot and

tight," he whispered in my ear. "And I know you're wet for me right now."

I was. I could feel my panties were soaked. And he hadn't laid a finger on me yet. I trembled, torn between pushing him away and pulling him close.

"So I don't think we can be professional," he murmured against my lips. "Do you?"

I didn't. I really didn't. Damn it, why was he so tempting? It was like all my self-control went out the window when he was this close.

Dylan pressed his lips against mine, and I opened for him, letting him kiss me deeply. His mouth claimed mine, and I was lost.

I grabbed his shirt, pulling him forward as I ground myself into him, eager to release the throbbing intensity between my legs. His thick erection pressed against my stomach.

His fingertips traced up my thighs, pushing my skirt up around my waist. He cupped me between my legs and let out a low growl as his fingers dipped inside me.

"So wet," he rasped, fingers gliding through my slick folds. "So ready for me."

I couldn't wait any longer. I needed to feel him inside.

He was right. Fuck professional.

At that moment, the thoughts of my job, the promotion, how I was going to pay next month's bills, all of it went out the window along with any rational thought. All I knew was that I wanted him.

I quickly undid his pants, tugging it down, desperate to feel him. He let out a deep groan when I fisted his cock.

"Lana." My name was a ragged groan. "I'm so fucking hard for you, baby."

His hands gripped my behind, lifting and pinning me

against the wall as my legs wrapped around his waist. I felt his erection nudging at my entrance. He slid inside me in one smooth thrust, and stilled when he was fully seated, his hip bones hitting my thighs.

"Fuck," he growled, waiting as if he was trying to compose himself.

He pulled back and slammed back inside me, the sudden contact taking me closer to the edge.

"Please," I whispered.

I didn't even know what I was begging for, just that I needed more. He moved in and out of me and I stifled my screams against his shoulder as pleasure exploded.

My hands curled into his shirt, holding on for dear life, as my thighs clenched around his waist. He ground into me as I rode out my orgasm, mumbling incoherently. My limbs went slack as I tried to catch my breath.

He pushed off the wall and walked us over to his desk, putting me down on my back.

"I'm not done with you. I want you to come for me again," he rasped.

I wasn't sure if I could. My limbs felt like jelly, and I was still lightheaded from the intense orgasm he'd just given me.

His hand slowly slid up from my stomach to my chest. He cupped my breast and thumbed my nipple before softly pinching it. He leaned over, taking the other one in his mouth, licking and teasing.

He moved in and out of me slowly, building my pleasure back up.

His arm circled my waist, pulling me closer to him as he pushed himself deeper inside me.

"You're mine, Lana," he murmured against my skin.

"Yes," I whispered as I nodded against his shoulder. There was no denying it.

I was his. Completely. His.

His other hand fisted in my hair, tugging it back. I hissed at the sharp pull, enjoying the way his grip felt against my scalp.

"Say it," he growled low and husky, demanding submission from me. "Tell me you're mine."

"I'm yours, Dylan," I gasped. "Only yours."

His lips covered mine as he groaned deeply, his vibration rumbling through me.

I moaned in pleasure as he continued to thrust into me, my fingers sinking into his short hair.

He pulled back and slammed in again. Once, twice, again and again, pounding into me just the way I needed. The slap of skin and the wet sounds of our joining echoed obscenely in the office. I didn't care. I was too far gone for shame, lost in the frenzy of Dylan fucking me, hard and deep on his desk.

"Dylan," I moaned. "Oh god, I'm gonna come."

"That's it, baby." He increased the pace, muscles straining. "Let go for me. Let me feel it."

Dylan tore another orgasm from me with a sound I didn't know I could make. My back snapped into an arch as the second wave of pleasure hit. I shouted his name again, my fingers tightening in his hair.

I shook in Dylan's arms, inner walls clamping down on his cock. Dylan shouted at the sudden squeeze around him. Then he growled and started rocking into me with abandon, fucking me hard and fast.

He held himself deep as he came, his cock pulsing as he spilled inside me. We stayed joined as we caught our breath. I clutched him close, heart pounding against his chest.

For a long moment neither of us spoke. I didn't want to

move, to break the spell that had fallen over us. To face what came after.

After what felt like forever, he said, "I know you weren't flirting with Warren."

He lifted his head, his eyes meeting mine. They were soft and filled with what looked like regret. I'd regretted a lot of things I'd said too.

"It pissed me off he was trying to talk to you all night. And you just left, so I was mad. I'm sorry."

I nodded, immediately flooded with relief as I heard his words. The knot that had formed in my chest since our fight started to melt away. "I'm sorry too. I should've talked to you before leaving," I admitted. "And I know nothing happened with you and Vera. I know that."

He let out a soft breath and rested his forehead against mine, nodding in understanding.

His lips covered mine, kissing me slowly and thoroughly. I realized he was still inside me when his cock pulsed.

I laughed softly and pushed against his chest, "You're insatiable."

He grinned, holding my hands against his chest. "You love it."

"As much as I do, I should get back to the office."

I didn't need any rumors about us at work. I was already nervous that Alexander would find out. Dylan reluctantly pulled out of me with a grumble and we got cleaned up in his office bathroom.

When we were done, Dylan pulled me in his arms again and kissed me.

"You know, I'm kind of glad we had a fight," he said against my lips. "I might have to pick a fight with you now and then."

I leaned back to look at him, my brows pulling together in confusion.

He looked at me as a playful smile forming on his lips. "Because if our makeup sex is going to be that good, it might just be worth it."

I scoffed and burst into laughter. He was right. It was the best makeup sex ever.

"Go out with me. Tonight," he said, smiling down at me.

"You're supposed to take me out before we have sex," I said laughing softly.

"I'm serious. I never took you out on a date."

"You did. Marcella's."

He made a face. "That doesn't count."

I wrapped my arms around his neck and kissed him softly. "It was the best date I'd ever been on."

He gazed into my eyes, tucking a stray strand behind my ear.

"I want to do it right. I'm not bedding you without courting you properly," he said with a smirk.

I snorted, "Who even talks like that? You really need to work on your lines."

He laughed and tickled me as I squirmed to get away.

"We still need to talk," I said quietly, as our playfulness faded.

"I know." He nodded and sighed. "Do you have some time before you need to get back? There's something I need to tell you."

"Yeah, I have a few minutes. What is it?"

He led me to the couch on the other side of his office.

"I spoke to Alexander this morning. We're ending the contract with Berman after the event with Emberox."

My eyes widened. "What? How did Alexander take it?"

"He took it well," he replied. "The Emberox presentation

wasn't even a part of the contract initially, so it was really a bonus for the agency to work on a high-profile pitch. Alexander already knows the agency's reputation will grow from it. He was just worried that we were ending it based on performance."

"What about after the event? You and Brent will still need a lot of support."

"I've already spoken with Brent. We'll be working closely with Emberox's team, so we'll have most of our needs covered," he explained. "So, problem solved. You don't have to worry about being involved with a client anymore," Dylan said, pulling me close. "And you killed the presentation, so this would be the perfect way to wrap up the account."

He did have a point, even though I thought it would be beneficial for Deft Rock to have their own marketing team to make sure they would be equally represented in the partnership. I'd see to it that they did even if the agency was out of the picture.

"As long as you really feel you and Brent will be ok without the agency."

"And I spoke to Beth," Dylan said. "So you don't have to worry about her anymore."

I frowned, not sure how to feel about him talking to Beth about me without telling me about it first. "You didn't have to do that, Dylan," I replied. "I was going to speak to her myself. I don't need you to fight my battles. She's going to think I'm hiding behind you like a coward."

"It wasn't just for you, Lana. You were obviously part of the discussion, but I would've said something to her even if you and I weren't involved. What she said about me and Vera was unacceptable. It's offensive and damaging to me and my business." he said with an edge to his voice. "She had to know I don't tolerate that kind of bullshit."

I hadn't considered how Dylan might have felt about being the center of gossip at the office. He was right, it wasn't just about me. He had his reputation at stake too. It made sense that Dylan wouldn't take a comment that might affect his business so lightly. Especially with the event coming up.

"You're right. She shouldn't have said that about you. Sorry, I didn't consider your side."

He wrapped his arms around me and kissed my forehead, then he gently tipped my chin up with his fingers to look into my eyes.

"I don't want anything getting in our way, Lana. There has been too much keeping us apart. I'm done with all the reasons why we can't be together."

"So am I," I replied softly.

I really was. I wanted to be with him without anything hanging over us.

We may not have a working relationship in a couple weeks and he'd set Beth straight, but it still didn't quite put my mind at ease.

"Can I ask you something? It's really none of my business-"

"Lana, stop. You can ask me anything," he assured me.

I paused, trying to come up with a delicate way to bring it up.

"Tell me what's bothering you," he encouraged.

I couldn't think of any other way to put it, so I just blurted it out. "What happened between you and your ex-wife?"

Dylan narrowed his eyes, assessing my expression, like he was trying to figure out why I would bring that up all of a sudden.

"It's just that Austin said his sister had a reason for cheating and it's been bugging me ever since. I just..." He clenched his jaw and he shook his head, but let me continue. "I just want to hear your story."

His chest rose and he let out a deep sigh, like the memory weighed heavily on him. "We just wanted different things and it made us grow apart. I think I already told you before that we'd gotten married too young. Our relationship revolved around going out and partying together. Eventually, I wanted to settle down and start a family. She didn't."

I listened and waited for him to continue. He leaned forward, resting his elbows on his knees.

"So I stopped going out with her and started spending more time working at the bar. I think she felt like I was neglecting her, and she started acting out, trying to get me to go back to our old ways. I didn't cater to her like she thought I would. And then we just drifted apart even more."

He sighed and shook his head as he ran his hand through his hair.

"At first I thought she'd change, so I kept waiting for her to. But she didn't. I can't tell you what drove her to cheat because I don't know. Maybe she wanted to hurt me for hurting her. Or she was done with me by then too. All I know is that I came home one day and found her with a guy."

"I'm sorry that happened," I said quietly.

Hearing his side of the story helped me finally see the whole picture. I understood why Austin had said the things he said. I would never fully grasp what really happened, but I could see why it didn't work out for Dylan and his ex-wife.

He sat up and reached for my hand. "I'm not. We weren't right for each other and I'm glad we found out sooner than later."

"Still, I'm sure it wasn't easy," I replied, squeezing his hand.

"It wasn't," he agreed. "But it was nothing compared to letting you go." He brought my hand up to his lips, kissing my knuckles.

I gave him a small smile.

"Did that have something to do with you not trusting me? What Austin had said about my marriage?"

"Yes, it did," I replied with a sigh. "Thank you for telling me what happened."

"So… then do you trust me now?" He asked.

"I want to," I said slowly, recalling the times that I'd seen him with other women. I really did want to trust him, but I couldn't deny how I really felt.

"That's not a yes," he replied, looking down.

I needed some distance between us to get through this conversation. He released me as I stood. I walked over to the window and sat on the edge of the sill, crossing my arms.

"I want to, Dylan. And I think I do for the most part," I said, my shoulders tensing up. "I guess seeing you with other women and Austin's comment just made me doubt a little. I'm still processing what happened in the past couple days."

"Just tell me one thing, Lana," he asked, his expression serious. "Do you want this? Do you want us?"

"I do. You know I do," I replied. "More than anything. I have from the day I've met you. But I can't help but wonder if it'll work out between us. You have to admit it hasn't been exactly easy. I'm just afraid I'll fall in love with you and everything will fall apart. I barely managed to get over you before. My heart couldn't take it if we ended like every other relationship in my past."

A frown formed on his face, like he was deep in thought.

He heaved out a deep breath and nodded slowly. "I know you've been burned in the past. Todd hurt you. Your past boyfriends have hurt you. I get it." He sighed, his face softening a little. "But I'm not Todd, or any other man you've been with. I would never do anything to hurt you, you know that."

"I'm not sure that I do," I replied, the impulsive response slipping out before I could stop it.

He flinched back like he couldn't believe I'd think that about him. He just sat there looking down at his hands, not saying anything. I held my forehead in my hand.

Finally, he said, "Have a seat because I have a lot to say. Please." He gestured to the spot next to him.

His face was devoid of any emotion. I nodded, feeling nervous at the lack of his response as I slowly sat back down next to him. He reached for my hand and turned me to face him.

"Let me make it real clear because I don't want there to be any misunderstandings or you have any doubt about us. About me. I've always been honest with you, and I always will be. I give you my word. I'm not ok with you thinking I'd do something to hurt you. That actually pisses me off that you'd think that. I only want what's best for you. I'm going to take care of you. Your heart. And you have mine. You always have. You're it for me, baby. You always have been."

I opened my mouth to say something, but he held up a finger. I snapped my mouth closed.

"And before you get all freaked out, no, this is not some sort of proposal. Not yet anyway. This is me just telling you I only want you. Only. You. And if you ever have any doubts, you come straight to me and tell me before jumping to any conclusions. Because I have absolutely no problem repeating this to you until you get it."

He brushed his thumb along my jaw.

I stared and blinked at him, taken back by how forward and honest he was. It felt a little like I was scolded, but I'd be a liar if I said I didn't like it.

Dylan stared back at me intently, waiting for a response. "We good?"

He raised his eyebrows at me when I didn't answer.

"Mm hmm," I replied.

What else could I say? I believed him.

"Good." He gave me a sharp nod.

We sat next to each other in silence for a moment as I processed everything he'd just said. I believed everything. Yes, there was still a chance that we might not work out. But at least I knew where he stood, and what he wanted.

"Actually, I take that back. The honesty part," Dylan said, breaking the silence.

"What? What is it?" I asked, suddenly a little nervous.

He looked at me tentatively, his hand rubbing the back of his neck.

"I knew you were back in town," he said. "About three months ago. I went to see your grandpa and he told me you moved back."

"Grandpa told me Todd had been coming to see him." I thought back to my conversation with Grandpa. No, he'd said ex-boyfriend, not Todd. Could he have meant Dylan? "He meant you, didn't he?"

Dylan nodded. "I don't think Todd has been back to see him since Grandpa passed."

"You've come to see him all these years," I said softly.

"Grandpa would have wanted that too. And I always liked James. I promised you I'd keep an eye on him, didn't I? Besides, it didn't hurt that he liked to talk about you." he said.

He paused momentarily before continuing, "And I knew you were working at Berman."

"So... you came to Berman for me?" I asked, letting it sink in.

"We were looking at several agencies, Berman being one of our top choices, and when James told me you were working there, it was a no brainer which one to go with. The real reason I hired them is because you worked there."

I glanced up at him with wide eyes. I could hardly believe that had never occurred to me.

"I wanted to tell you earlier, but there was never a good time," Dylan said. "I wasn't sure how you'd feel about it. Especially when I found out you were with Austin."

He then paused, pressing his lips together. "Lana, I know it may take some time for you to realize it, but I meant every word of what I said."

"I know, Dylan. I know you did. And I don't need more time to realize it. I believe you. I trust you." I cradled his face in my hands and kissed him.

He smiled and kissed me back softly.

"Dylan?"

"Yeah, baby."

"Everything you said. Say it again for me later when you make love to me."

He burst out into laughter, grabbing me and pulling me to him. "Good idea, I'll whisper it in your ear every day so you don't forget."

I giggled as he nuzzled my neck.

34

DYLAN

We met with the agency team to go over the plans for Emberox's visit. It was hard to stay away from Lana, knowing that we'd worked out our differences and things were finally looking hopeful. She could barely look at me during the entire meeting, probably because we'd be grinning at each other like fools.

"Not only will you be able to serve the signature drinks in the taproom, but you'll also be able to sell them in stores. Regionally at first. And if that does well, the plan is national distribution." Lana clicked the screen to another slide. "All this is contingent on how impressed Vera and Shane are at the tasting event, of course. But I'd be surprised if they're not thrilled by the end of it."

Lana sat, and Alexander tapped the file in front of him.

"I've spoken to Shane. They've tried the drinks and they're impressed so far. If they're a hit with customers at the tasting event, I don't think there's anything standing between Deft Rock and full retail distribution. Nationally. Possibly by this time next year," he said with a huge smile.

I looked at Brent and wondered if he could see dollar signs in my eyes the way I could see them in his.

It was more than the money, of course, but you couldn't run a successful business poised for steady growth without it.

You couldn't put food on the table with a sense of accomplishment alone. But that was a big part of what had me feeling great.

That and Lana in my arms again.

I'd spent the night at her house a couple of nights earlier, making love to her well into the morning hours. Happy that we'd finally put to rest any doubts about us.

She smiled at me, clearly thinking about what I'd done to her that morning before we came into the Berman office.

Thinking about what I was going to do to her after she got home from work that night, if I was lucky.

All I wanted was to sweep her off her feet right into my arms.

I'd missed the last several things that people were saying around the conference table. When the meeting broke up, I followed Lana to her office and shut the door behind me. I sat with my hip on the corner of her desk.

"Well?" she asked. "Is it everything you were hoping for? A collaboration, even retail distribution of the prepared drinks. Anything left on your list to tick off?"

I pulled her close so that she stood between my legs, leaning against me. She glanced toward her door to be sure no one was coming through it.

"Any unfinished business?"

I kissed her quickly. I wanted more, but I also didn't want her to be caught in a compromising position.

"So much unfinished business," I said.

"Yeah?" she asked. "Like what?"

I ran my hand down the curve of her ass. "This." I dared to slip my hand inside her skirt to press my knuckles against the heat of her. "And this. Needs some work, doesn't it? Got to give this problem a lot of attention."

"Oh," she said with a laugh. "It's a problem now?"

"Mm hmm. A major problem." I kissed her cheek. "That needs to be resolved immediately."

She shuddered but pushed my arm playfully so that I'd put my hand somewhere else.

"I still have to be here for a few hours," she said, giggling. "It's not fair to turn me on too much."

"Hmm. You could lock your door and let me fuck you on your desk."

She scoffed, but she kissed me again.

"I like the way you think. But I'd also like to keep my job." She pointed to one of the chairs in front of her desk. "Behave."

I groaned and moved to sit in one. "I can't believe Vera and Shane are talking about retail distribution already. National, at that. You're a miracle worker, Lana."

Lana sitting in her desk chair and me on the other side of her desk was just too much space between us. But then someone knocked, and Chelsea and Brent stepped in, making me glad she'd had the sense to separate us first.

They gushed about the pending tasting event and all the good things that could come from it. I felt as happy as Brent sounded. And it was even better because I knew how instrumental Lana had been to this success.

It's the kind of break we'd been waiting and hoping for since we started Deft Rock.

"I have plans I can't get out of tonight," Brent said. "But tomorrow, I'm taking us all out for dinner. We have to celebrate!"

It was great to see Brent so happy. It was great to feel so happy about the business myself.

When Brent and Chelsea left, leaving me and Lana alone in her office again, I stood and pulled her from her chair into my arms.

"Offer to fuck you on your desk still stands, you know."

Lana giggled. "Raincheck?"

"You got it." I cupped her cheek. "You have plans tonight?"

She grinned broadly. "I do. I plan to spend the whole evening with a tall, sexy, handsome man."

"Ooh, he sounds like a real stud." I raised my eyebrows.

"He's not half-bad," she said with a chuckle. "He's even going to bring dinner and help me drink some wine."

I kissed her softly. "I'm starting to get a little jealous."

She whispered, "He doesn't know it yet, but I'm going let him ravish me afterwards."

"You little minx," I growled at nipped at her neck as she squirmed and laughed. "What's he bringing? And when?" I brushed my nose with hers.

"Chicken Alfredo from Gianelli's. Extra breadsticks. Cannolis for dessert. Around seven. He's always on time too. And always shows up for me." She licked her lips. "Sexy as hell."

"Too bad you're busy. My rotten luck. Give this incredible stud my regards." I kissed her, holding her body against mine.

Then I walked to the door and said over my shoulder. "Sounds like one hell of a lucky guy."

Her sweet laughter filled my ears as I walked out of her office.

35

LANA

"I knew you were a smart man," I said to Dylan as he came in with the food from Gianelli's. He was a little early, but I'd expected that.

He put the food on the table and pulled me close to kiss me.

"I had it under good authority that I'd better not be late. Didn't want to ruin my reputation of showing up."

I laughed at his arched eyebrow. Then I put my arms around his neck and gazed up at him.

"You did tell me once that if I needed anything, that you'd always show up for me."

Dylan's smile softened as he lowered his head to kiss me. He always had been there for me.

Even during the years when we lived states apart, not communicating aside from one sympathy card I sent. I think I knew deep down that if I'd called him for anything, he'd have dropped anything he needed to show up for me.

I definitely knew it now.

We had dinner with Dylan sitting right next to me, as if he couldn't stand to be too far away.

We talked about the upcoming tasting event a little.

"To you," he finally said, holding up his wine glass. "And your fantastic job with Emberox Spirits."

We toasted, and then Dylan took my hand in his. He pressed my palm against his cheek then brushed his lips over my knuckles.

Dylan pulled me up as he stood and hauled me close against him. He held me like we were going to slow dance, but instead, he stared down into me.

"Still the most gorgeous blue eyes I've ever seen," he said softly. Then he brushed his knuckles against my cheek. "You're so beautiful, Lana."

"You keep saying things like that, you just might get lucky," I teased.

"I am lucky," he said. He kissed me softly and slowly. "Lucky just to be here with you at all."

I started in the direction of the bedroom. He kissed me until my legs came up against my bed.

"I'm so in love with you I can hardly think straight," he murmured against my lips.

My breath caught.

It felt like everything I'd wanted had come true.

Dylan Easton loved me.

"Dylan—"

He stopped me with his kiss. Whether it was to make it clear he didn't expect me to say it back yet, or because he was afraid I wouldn't, I didn't know.

Whichever it was that had him stop me from answering what he said, I was grateful. Because I wasn't ready to say it yet. A small part of me still feared getting hurt. But I felt it. I'd felt it for a long time.

And I wanted to show him so much, even if it wasn't the right time to say it.

He leaned down, pushing me gently backward as he did. But I stopped him and dropped to my knees in front of him. I unzipped his fly while I stared up at him, licking my lips.

He shook his head like he could barely believe what he was seeing.

"So God damn gorgeous, Lana."

When I wrapped my lips around his cock, his whole body jerked. Dylan sank his fingers into my hair as I wrapped my tongue around his shaft, licking it like a lollipop. I licked and sucked like I was determined to taste every spot. Then I sucked him as deep as I could and swallowed while I glanced up.

Dylan made a strangled sound of pleasure, bending his shoulders forward to curl his body over me. He gently massaged my scalp with his fingertips and stroked my hair.

"Baby," he gasped as I slid my mouth up and down his cock, varying the speed and suction. I cupped his balls in one hand, kneading them gently, and wrapped my other around his shaft.

I stroked him while I sucked, my movements getting more enthusiastic as I felt him thicken and harden in my mouth. He was close, and this time he wasn't going to urge me into another position.

"Lana," he groaned as I sucked extra hard.

I moaned around his cock, and he shouted in pleasure as he came. I swallowed, determined to hang on until I'd wrung every drop from him.

When he'd finished, he hauled me up, letting me taste him in the kiss. Then we made quick work of our clothes, and Dylan urged me to lie face-down on the bed.

He moved behind me and gripped my hips to lift my ass into the air. Dylan stroked his hand over my back from my shoulders to my lower back, his hand finally coming to rest on the bottom of my ass and top of my thigh.

"Let me take care of *you* now," he said, his breath against my body.

Then he licked my pussy in one long, upward stroke from clit to the top that turned my thigh muscles to jelly.

He held me open with his thumbs and licked inside me, stroking and massaging my folds until I almost couldn't stand the pleasure anymore. I pressed my cheek into the pillow and spread my thighs as he finger-fucked me while mouthing at my clit. The bed shook a little, and I realized he was stroking himself.

When I felt his hard cock against my calf, I knew he was going to fuck me soon. I squeezed my inner muscles around his fingers, prompting him to suck my clit just right. Pleasure exploded in my lower body, rippling up my spine and making me cry out.

"Yeah, baby," he groaned, his mouth against my pussy, his finger still pumping into my body.

Dylan shifted up to his knees and thrust his cock deep inside me while I was still coming. My body reacted with another wave of intense pleasure that laddered its way up my torso from my core, making my breath catch and a desperate little sound escape my throat.

He thrust hard and deep, ready to blow again. I pushed myself back against him, taking him as deep as possible as my pussy clenched around him.

"Fuck!" he shouted, slamming forward into me and almost flattening me on the bed with the force of it. He came, his hands pulling my hips back against him with each thrust, making wordless sounds of pleasure.

My orgasm finally started to slow and let me catch my breath. Dylan slumped forward over my back and mouthed at my shoulder, leaving a wet trail with his tongue. He licked over to my neck and sucked lightly there.

Finally, my legs gave out and I dropped flat onto the bed with Dylan on top of me. He kissed the shell of my ear, panting as he spoke.

"I love you, Lana." He nibbled the lobe and pushed his cock into me one last time. "I love you so much."

When I could roll beneath him, he kissed me before I could say anything. Again, I was grateful.

I spent the rest of that night trying to show Dylan that I loved him too without having to take the risk of saying the words out loud. I knew I would. There'd be a better time. An easier time.

And until then, I'd make sure everything I did or said helped him realize it even without him hearing those exact words.

36

DYLAN

"And that, my friends, is the beauty of having a mailing list." Maddie brushed her hands together in a 'that's done' gesture. "Lana's idea to start one was genius. Now we can send personalized invitations to the tasting event to your most loyal customers."

Maddie talked about the email invites to our customers for that night. Lana added some advertising opportunities and debated with Maddie whether it should be open to the public-at-large or a ticketed event to keep the number manageable.

I watched Lana's throat move as she spoke, and I enjoyed the tiny peek above her collar of a bruised spot. One I'd left there the night before. I couldn't wait to get my mouth on that spot, and every part of her, again.

She hadn't told me she loved me. I hadn't really expected her to. But things between us had gotten more intense since I told her.

I sensed that Lana just needed time to get there. And I was willing to give her all the time she needed.

Brent got up from the table to go see to some customers.

Maddie excused her and Lana, then she took her across the taproom to point at something on the wall. A poster from Emberox Spirits advertising their vodka. Probably for some design notes or something ad related.

I was watching them when I noticed Todd in the doorway of the taproom. He had a pretty girl on his arm—the Lisa he'd gushed to me about.

Todd hadn't ever just shown up before. He always called, as if he was trying to make up for his more impulsive behavior when he was still using.

I stood to approach him, but he directed Lisa to a table and headed straight for Lana and Maddie.

Shit. He touched her arm before I could take a step.

Todd started to move close like he was going to awkwardly hug her, but he stopped short and just squeezed her arm instead. He looked nervous but genuinely happy to see her.

Lana, on the other hand, looked uncomfortable as hell. She even physically leaned toward Maddie as if for support.

After a few minutes, Todd gave her a nod and headed toward the table where Lisa sat watching him. Lana headed toward my table.

"We've got everything covered on our end," she said quickly. "We're going to take off."

"Already?" I asked, surprised. I figured they'd be there for at least another hour. "Everything okay?" I glanced past her to see Todd staring at us.

"Yeah, everything's fine. I just have some things to take care of at the office." Lana was working on other accounts besides Deft Rock now. I knew she probably did have work to do. But I felt sure that Todd showing up had a lot to do with her leaving early.

"You don't have to leave because Todd's here, Lana," I pointed out.

"I know. It's fine," she said with a deep breath. Then she spoke softer. "I'll see you tonight, okay?"

As she left, Todd watched her. Every damn step. Then his glare turned to me again.

I decided to bite the bullet. I went to Todd's table so he could introduce me to his girlfriend.

"I'm surprised to see you here," I said, hoping to smooth past him seeing Lana again.

"I'll bet you are," he said cryptically.

I ignored that and held my hand out for Lisa. "I've heard a lot about you."

Todd introduced us, and we chatted for a few minutes. Then he took my elbow.

"Can I talk to you privately for a minute?"

I let him lead me away from the table.

Finally, he said, "Why didn't you tell me you and Lana were working together?"

I realized how shaken he was. Seeing her had done a number on him, and I honestly hadn't expected that.

"It seemed like bringing her up would be a bad idea, Todd. And I think I was right. Are you okay?"

"I'd be better if I'd known you two worked together," he hissed.

"You have a girlfriend. You've moved on. I figured it was best not to bring Lana up. At least not for a while." I tried not to feel guilty about the other things I hadn't brought up about Lana.

One day at a time. I'd tell him everything. Eventually.

Brent needed my help in the office for a minute, and I was glad to have the conversation interrupted. I let Carl know that anything Todd and Lisa ordered was on the house.

Then I went to help Brent and guiltily hoped that by the time I was free again, Todd and Lisa would be gone.

∽

I opened the door to Lana, glad that the day was finally drawing to a close. She'd gone home from work and changed into more casual clothes. A duffel bag was slung over her shoulder.

"Planning on taking a trip?" I teased. "Going to rough it in the park?"

"Nope, going to live in the lap of luxury in your bed," she said, but her usual teasing and cheeriness seemed a little forced.

"You can rough it in my bed too, if you want. If that's how you like it," I said, trying to draw either a smile or a heated smirk from her.

Instead, she dumped the duffel inside the doorway, and as soon as I sat on the couch, she let me pull her into my lap.

"You okay?"

"I've felt a little off since I saw Todd earlier, if I'm honest." She licked her upper lip. "Just worrying about what he'd think if he knew."

I tucked a few blonde strands behind her ear. "What did he say to you? You looked uncomfortable."

"He said he was surprised to see me. *Happy* to see me. Then he wanted to know what I was doing there. I figured honesty was the best policy—at least for that. And when he found out we were working together, he didn't really have anything to say after that. Just that he was surprised." She sighed and leaned her forehead against my temple. "I don't think he took it very well."

"Maybe it was just shock at seeing you. I should have told him about the Berman account and you running it." I kissed her softly. "It just seemed like bringing you up might not be a great idea."

"Judging from his reaction, I think you were right." She picked at the buttons on my shirt. "Do you really think he's doing okay?"

"I do. But I think he's still fragile. It's almost like he needs everything in him to fight his addiction, so he doesn't have much left to deal with other things, you know?"

Lana nodded. "That makes sense. But we can't sneak around forever. He's going to find out about us one of these days. Maybe it would be better if he heard it from us, privately. Where we can handle his reaction and reassure him if he doesn't take it well."

"You're so sweet, you know that?" I said, brushing my lips against her cheek.

After the way Todd treated her, nobody would blame her if she didn't really worry or care about him and his reactions. But there she was, trying to make sure he was going to be okay about something that truly wasn't any of his business in the first place.

"I think he should hear it from us, or one of us. Probably me. But I think he needs some time to come to grips with us working together first. I don't want to throw too many surprises at him and have him fall apart again."

"You're right," Lana agreed. "It's only right to give him some time. I'd hate for him to get reckless and upset and jeopardize his new relationship. What was her name again?"

"Lisa."

"She's beautiful. I noticed she had a nice smile too,

because she smiled at Todd like he hung the moon." Lana kissed my forehead and sighed. "I hope it works out for him. I really do."

"I know you do." I took her face in my hands and kissed her deeply. "I think deep down Todd would be happy to know that you still care about him."

He really would be. But part of me still worried he carried a flame for Lana, despite the new girlfriend and all his claims that he'd moved on.

As flustered as he'd been earlier that day when he saw Lana, it was easy to believe that he still pined for her, at least from time to time.

"He's going to be okay," I assured Lana.

She nodded. "I'm sure he will be."

Once we had that out in the open, I was ready to move to a different topic.

"Hey, I heard a rumor about somebody roughing it in my bed. Know anything about that?"

"Can't say I do." She laughed as I grunted and hoisted us both off the couch to carry her to the bedroom.

37

DYLAN

With everyone from Berman at the brewery, I knew I couldn't put off talking to Lana about Todd any longer. If he showed up before I said anything, the whole thing would be so much worse.

"Hey," I said to her and instantly got the sweetest smile.

"Hey yourself," she said.

The last couple of weeks had been amazing with Lana staying with me or vice versa most nights. The only part that wasn't amazing was the worry about Todd finding out, which I knew was coming.

I was going to have to tell him. But I hadn't been able to bring myself to do it yet.

And I wasn't ready to do it on this day either. I needed a little more time, that was all.

"Can we talk?" I asked Lana, gesturing for us to move away from the group for a second.

She followed me with a little smile still on her face. I hated to make it disappear, but I didn't have a choice.

"Todd called a little while ago," I started.

"Yeah? How is he?" Lana glanced back at the group who

were preparing for the tasting, hoping we'd knock Emberox Spirits' metaphorical socks off.

"He's . . . on his way here." I watched Lana's smile disappear. "He wants to help, Lana. To be a part of this. I couldn't say no. But I didn't want him showing up and surprising you."

Lana inhaled sharply and nodded.

"Okay. Yeah. I think it'll be fine." She managed to smile, but I knew she was conflicted about seeing him again. "If he wants to help, that's a good thing."

"It is," I agreed. "Maybe we can get to know Lisa better."

"She does seem nice," Lana said, smiling tightly. I'd have kissed her then and there if we'd been alone or at least better hidden. She touched my arm and headed back to the group.

I tried not to let Todd coming dampen my enthusiasm for making this tasting a success.

Everyone was sure we had the deal in the bag. But I'd been sure about my marriage and my relationship with my brother once upon a time too. I tried to think positively, though.

Within minutes, Todd appeared.

Todd, *alone*.

"Where's Lisa?" I asked as I greeted him and motioned for him to come over and join the group.

Todd grimaced and glanced down at the floor. "We broke up. But it's okay. These things happen, right?"

He'd been head over heels the last time I'd talked to him. But he was acting like it wasn't a big deal. Either he'd never been in love with Lisa, or he was covering up some serious pain.

"Todd—"

"I've rented a room for the week," Todd said, interrupting me. "Figured I'd stay close, see if you needed my help. Nice to change up the routine after the breakup too."

While Todd spoke to me, his gaze leveled on Lana across the room. Something in his expression went soft. And my hackles went up instantly.

"Are you sure that's a good idea?" I asked. "Too much change at once..."

"I'm sure," he said, staring at the woman *I* loved. "I think it'll all work out for the best."

Someone touched my shoulder. I turned to see Carl, frowning at a piece of paper in his hands.

"Dylan, can you come check this inventory list? I'm not sure it's right, and the last thing we want is to run short on the big day."

"Sure," I said.

I glanced back at Todd, but he was already walking across the room toward Lana.

38

LANA

I felt like I handled it pretty well when Dylan told me Todd was coming. But watching him walk toward me, smiling, made me wonder if Dylan had made a mistake by letting him come.

Lisa wasn't with him. And Todd didn't know about me and Dylan.

Could we really hide it well enough that Todd wouldn't catch on?

"Lana, can we talk?" he asked, motioning with his head for us to step aside. I went with him, guilt and worry rising up inside me.

"I wanted to tell you how sorry I am. For everything. How things ended between us, what I did, is one of the biggest mistakes I've ever made in my life, and I'm sorry. I wanted to make sure you knew that."

He seemed sincere, so I figured the least I could do was make the same effort.

"Sure, Todd. I appreciate you saying that."

He blushed and glanced down. "Working the steps, you know? Making amends."

I put my hand on his arm, genuinely happy that he was still actively working at his recovery.

"I'm so glad, Todd." I almost asked about Lisa, but I bit my lip and didn't. If he wanted to tell me where she was, he would.

Brent cleared his throat to get everyone's attention and started handing out tasks. I needed to get some decorations purchased specifically for the tasting and hang them in places we'd all decided on at another meeting.

As soon as Brent suggested that as my contribution, Todd volunteered to help me.

"I can hang that if you want," Todd said about a lightweight Emberox Spirits logo sign. He put his hand on my arm as he spoke.

"That's okay. I can get it if you want to keep the ladder from wobbling," I said with a smile.

As I went up it, Todd put his hand on my hip. The touch pinged as something unnecessary, but I wrote it off as innocent.

On my way back down the ladder, however, he put his hand on my hip again.

It could have been innocent. Todd might have been overzealous in trying to make sure I didn't slip or unbalance myself.

But it also could have been something else.

I had my answer when I went up the ladder a second time, and again Todd touched my hip again. When I came down, he didn't move away enough to keep our bodies from brushing. It was awkward and uncomfortable for me, so I took a few steps back.

"Todd," Dylan said. "Come here for a minute."

His voice was sharp, with just a hint of anger. I took the opportunity to walk away and regain my composure.

"What?" Todd snapped, not moving from the ladder.

I could hear the challenge in his voice and hoped nothing was going to happen.

Dylan had to approach him, and by the time he got there, he was pissed.

"What you're doing with Lana," he said in a low voice. "Knock it off."

"What I'm doing?" Todd snapped back. "Helping?"

"You know exactly what you're doing. And this is my place of business, where we're all working to get this done." Dylan took a deep breath and let it out slowly. "You're not here to help, are you?" he finally said.

I glanced around at Brent, the servers, Maddie, and Chelsea. Chelsea was staring at Dylan, a frown on her face, like she was trying to figure out what was happening.

Todd said something under his breath and walked away, opting to help Brent unload some cases of liquor.

Dylan glanced at me with raised eyebrows, then he winked and gave me his most handsome half-grin. But I caught it dropping and his jaw clenching as he turned away.

I went back to work, Maddie helping me instead of Todd, and was grateful that Todd stayed away from me the rest of the time he was there.

$\sim$

"Get in here," Dylan said, pulling me through the doorway and closing it behind me. He pulled me into a tight hug, then he kissed me slowly. "I hate being in the same room with you and not being able to kiss you."

He raised his eyebrows and glanced down between our bodies. "Or do other things."

I playfully slapped his chest. "Even if people knew for sure about us, we wouldn't be doing those other things."

"I know, but it's hard having to pretend that I don't want to pull you into my arms every few seconds."

He sighed and let go of me enough that we could walk into his living room. Then he pulled me down into his lap on the couch.

"I'm looking forward to everyone knowing. I can't pull you into my arms all the time, but at least I won't have to pretend like I don't want to." Dylan slid his hand down my thigh to my knee and back again, pushing the short skirt I wore up as he did so.

I giggled and stopped his hand.

"You don't want me to?" he asked with a grin.

"Oh no, I really do. But I came here to ask how you were doing." I followed his gaze down to where he stared at his crotch, at how his pants were starting to tent as he got hard. I laughed. "Doing fine, I see. But I meant about Todd."

Dylan bit his lip, nodding. "He's pissed at me, I think, for calling him on his bullshit today."

I felt bad about that. Maybe I'd overreacted. I knew it was possible.

"He might not have meant anything, Dylan. The fact that we were together a long time ago . . . maybe that just made him more familiar than he should have been."

"You're being too easy on him, Lana. I think he knew exactly what he was doing." He tucked my hair behind my ear and kissed me again. "Leave Todd to me, okay? I can't deal with him right now, but after the tasting, he and I are going to have a serious talk and get things straight between us."

I took his face in my hands, staring into his deep brown eyes. "I thought you two were doing so well."

"We were. Until he acted like he was trying to get somewhere with you today." Dylan kissed my palm. "I'm thinking of it as his mistake, and I'm going to give him the opportunity to fix it. *After* the tasting. For now . . . I don't want to think about Todd anymore tonight."

Dylan slid his hand underneath the front of my skirt and slipped a finger between my legs to press against my panties.

"If that's all right with you, of course."

He grinned as he said it, as if I might protest, when he knew I wouldn't. I let my thighs fall open a little and pressed myself against his finger.

"Whatever you want is alright with me," I said softly, moaning as his finger shifted to rub my clit through the fabric.

"That's what I like to hear," he breathed, hooking his finger into the crotch of the panties to pull it aside and slip a finger slowly into me.

"*Dylan*," I whispered as he buried his finger to the knuckles and used his thumb to tap and brush my clit.

He did it with no rhythm, keeping me on edge and not knowing what to expect.

"Your blouse," he said, licking his lips.

So I unbuttoned it, still trying to push my pussy against his fingers and tighten my inner muscles around him. He dragged the shirt out of the way and yanked the cup of my bra down to suck my nipple into his mouth. His teeth gently raked the sensitive flesh, sending a rush of wet heat down my body to pool between my legs.

"God, baby," he groaned. "You're so damn wet for me already."

"Because I want you so much."

Dylan had that effect on me. All I had to do was think

about him touching me and I could self-consciously slick between the legs.

I worked his fly open and pulled out his cock, already rock hard. I stroked him while he fingered me, his head quickly getting slick as I spread the glistening drops that formed at the tip over his skin. Hearing him hiss and moan in pleasure had me wanting him so much I could barely wait.

Dylan glanced around the living room at the closed curtains and the door. Then he pulled me down into a kiss that stole my breath.

"Ride me, baby. Right here, just like this," he ground out.

I squeezed his thick cock as I stroked him, root to tip.

"Yes, Dylan." I wanted him so much I'd have done anything he asked.

He gripped my hips with both hands and helped move me into place, then he pulled my panties to the side and pressed his cock head against my opening.

I gasped as I lowered myself onto his cock, letting it spread me open inch by inch. Halfway down, I sucked my bottom lip into my mouth.

"You did lock the door?" I asked to be sure.

Dylan laughed, the rumble passing from his body into mine. "I don't remember. Think of it as an adventure."

The only person who might open Dylan's door and walk without at least knocking had been Todd, but he might not do that now that things were tense between them. If he was going to be that bold and rude, then maybe it would serve him right to see us together.

A flash of guilt reminded me that Todd was fragile, in recovery, and I certainly didn't want to do anything to jeopardize that.

But Dylan's cock filled me as I sat fully in his lap. I couldn't have stopped then even if I'd wanted to.

"*Baby,*" he gasped, pushing my hips to lift me then sliding me back down his length. "You always feel so *fucking* good."

I moaned, and Dylan obviously loved that because he bucked up into me, bouncing me on his lap. He caught one of my nipples in his mouth and sucked hard, making my clit throb even more.

I reached down to touch myself, to rub my clit and bring my orgasm on faster. I just needed him in that moment. But Dylan pushed my hand away and took over, his other hand gripping my ass tightly and moving me on his cock.

"This what I needed after today," he said softly, kissing my chin and then my mouth. "You're what I need. Always."

His thumb brushed my clit with a circular motion and his sweet, sexy words pushed me over the edge. "Dylan!" I cried out as my orgasm rippled through me.

Dylan cursed and grunted, his cock thickening inside me. He came groaning my name, feeling twice as big and hard as he was as my muscles tightened rhythmically around him until my muscles gave up and let me go limp in his lap.

I rested my head against his shoulder and pressed my lips to the side of his neck. We both took deep breaths until we'd recovered, and he started slipping from my body.

"I could sleep right here," I said honestly. We hadn't been getting much sleep lately, usually staying up to make love at least a couple of times. And the stress of the day had taken its toll too.

"Me too. And we'd both be miserable in the morning." He gently patted my behind to urge me to get up, so I did.

"Come on, baby," Dylan said, taking my hand when he

stood and leading me to his bedroom. We shed the rest of our clothes next to his bed and crawled under the covers.

"I didn't bring clothes for tomorrow," I pointed out.

"You left some here last week that I washed for you. So don't worry about it." He kissed my forehead, and I relaxed into it as if my body instinctively knew that I was safe with Dylan, and everything would be perfectly fine.

39

LANA

"So there's nothing going on that I need to know about?" Chelsea stared at me from where she sat behind her desk. "I'm just trying to be sure, Lana."

She'd summoned me into her office first thing. I felt like my insides were going to shake apart as I sat there.

She'd asked what was going on with Dylan and Todd at Deft Rock yesterday. I didn't give details, but I pointed out that they had a history of tension and had only recently started to get along again.

She didn't outright ask me if I was seeing Dylan. I knew that's what she was really asking. But because she didn't ask point blank if I was dating or sleeping with Dylan, I felt like I could say no—nothing was going on that she needed to know about.

Deep down, I knew it was a lie. Or at best, a lie by omission. But I didn't feel like I could or should tell her.

"No. Everything's fine. Dylan intends to talk to Todd soon and smooth things over." I swallowed hard, trying to push down the guilt it was causing me to say those things.

"They often have words with each other. That's just been their relationship for years."

"Dylan seemed pretty worked up over Todd talking to you, that's all." She stared at me, waiting for an answer.

"He knows what went on between me and Todd when we were together. He's just being protective." Not a complete lie.

Chelsea said, "Okay. Just making sure. You *will* come to me if anything arises, yes?"

"Of course," I assured her, then I hurried back to my desk.

I kept to myself for the rest of the day, mostly because of guilt. But I did have a lot of work to finish too. The tasting event was the next day, and I was determined that everything would be perfect.

As I left for the day, planning to go to Dylan's with my clothes for the event, I saw Todd standing next to my car.

One more day, Lana. Just keep him happy for one more day, then Dylan's going to talk to him.

"Hey. What's up?" I said as cheerfully as I could.

"I wanted to apologize. Again," he said with a sheepish grin.

"You already did, Todd. I accepted your apology, so there's no—"

"And I wanted to tell you that I've never gotten over you," he blurted, then he looked at me with pleading eyes.

I wanted to call Dylan. I wanted to *be* with Dylan. But I wasn't going to storm off, no matter what Todd said. I wanted to resolve our past like mature adults.

"It's all water under the bridge. I've moved past it, Todd. I hope you will too," I said sincerely.

"I know our breakup was my fault, and I've regretted that every day since," he continued.

"You cheated on me, Todd. I don't think you cherished our relationship as much as you imagine now," I explained calmly.

"Like I said, biggest mistake of my life." He stepped closer. "And I'm here to ask you for another chance. Can you give me that, Lana?"

Dylan mentioned that morning that he'd broken up with Lisa, because I'd asked where she'd been the day before. I still hadn't expected this.

"I cared about you, Todd. I still do," I said honestly. "But no. I'm not prepared to do that. I've moved on and you need to do the same."

The innocent, soft expression he'd worn turned suspicious and hard.

"Is there something going on between you and Dylan?"

"What?" I tried to breathe slowly to keep myself calm. I stared at him, unsure of how to respond. "Todd, I—if you—"

"Fuck, I knew it," he hissed, shaking his head. "Moved on with my brother, you mean."

I hadn't meant to let it show on my face. But his question had caught me off-guard.

"Todd, wait!" I said, rushing after him, but he was already in his car speeding away.

I dialed Dylan as I got into my car, taking deep, slow breaths while I waited for him to answer. It was his voicemail.

"Todd just asked me if there was something going on between us, Dylan. Please call me when you get this," I said.

Then I fired off a quick text.

Todd knows.

I waited for my heartbeat to slow enough that I no

longer felt faint, and I drove away, hoping that Todd didn't do or say anything stupid while he was upset.

DYLAN

"You sure don't waste any time, do you?"

The sudden question startled me. I was knelt behind the bar installing a keg, but I stood to see Todd leaning on his hands against the other side.

"What?" I asked, confused. But with a growing dread at the look in his eyes and the defensive way he stood.

"Is it true?" he asked. "About you and Lana? Because if it is, you *didn't fucking tell me.*"

I didn't know what he'd heard or what he'd guessed, but I figured I'd bide myself at least a little more time.

"What about me and Lana?" I asked.

"Don't fuck with me, Dylan. Are you and Lana together?" He glared at me, one eye narrower than the other.

There didn't seem to be much point in denying it at that point. I didn't want to have the conversation the day before the big event, but it seemed like I didn't have a choice.

"Lana and I are together, Todd, yes. But you should know that—"

"Motherfucker!" he said, causing Brent to glance over at us. "I should have known. So, were you fucking her when we were together? Or did she just hop into your bed the minute we broke up?"

"Todd, it's not like that. We weren't together when you were dating her. But since she came back, we've gotten closer, and things just happened."

I left out how we'd spent the night together before she left for New York. And I also left out how I'd been pursuing her like mad since she came back.

One step at a time.

Todd cursed and paced in a tight circle basically telling me what a terrible brother and human being I was. His rant was loud and long enough that everyone started paying attention.

Todd became aware of that and finally just called me a rotten son of a bitch before he stormed out, almost in tears he was so furious.

Fuck! Just fucking perfect.

Just what I needed the day before a business deal that could really put Deft Rock on the map.

I pulled out my phone to call Lana and saw that she'd left a text and a message. I didn't check either but called her anyway.

"Did you talk to Todd?" she asked. "He's so upset."

"What the hell did you say to him?" I asked, my voice sharper than I intended.

"Nothing. He asked if there was something going on between us..."

I heard her clear her throat as she sounded like she was fighting tears.

"I didn't say anything, but he knew, Dylan. I think he could see it—"

"Damn it, Lana. You couldn't hide it for another day?" The words were out before I could stop them.

"Dylan, that's not fair. I tried. I didn't want to hurt him, so I was going to find a way to deny it, but he suddenly knew." She sniffed. "I wasn't prepared to tell him yet either."

"I just don't understand how you couldn't hide it. Just another day, Lana," I raked my fingers through my hair. "Now I've got to worry about him going off and doing something stupid and hurting himself."

"That's not my fault!" she said. And I knew it wasn't, but the frustration had gotten the better of me. "I'm not going to be held responsible if—"

"Of course not. I didn't mean that you would be. I'm just—"

"That's not how it sounded. Dylan," she said angrily.

I blew out a breath. "Sorry. Lana, I can't talk right now. I've got to find Todd and calm him down."

"Dylan, I—"

I hung up and dialed Todd. I had to get a hold of him and calm him down before he ruined all his progress by going off the deep end.

Voice mail.

Great. Not only did I have to worry about Todd making a terrible mistake while he was upset, but Lana was now pissed off too.

All on the day before the most important event for Deft Rock.

What else could go wrong?

40

LANA

I glanced around the taproom to see the guests nodding their heads to the beat of the music and enjoying themselves. The DJ had kept the music playing, and the drinks seemed to be going over really well.

Shane and Vera had been impressed when they showed up a couple of hours before the event.

Dylan and Brent had shown them around and now stood next to their table talking to them. Everyone was smiling.

The night was going perfectly for Deft Rock. I was a shoo-in for the next promotion at Berman thanks to this account.

If only things weren't tense between me and Dylan, I could have relaxed and even enjoyed myself.

I sipped my ice water. I really could have used a drink, but it was important to stay completely professional. Alcohol also might have tempted me to try to talk to Dylan, and that had to wait. I didn't want to distract him or throw him off in any way. Not today.

Dylan glanced at me from where he talked to Shane and

Vera. He gave me a nod and started to smile, so I nodded back and gave him a big smile.

I didn't want him to worry about our conversation during the event.

I hadn't talked to Dylan since the discussion about Todd over the phone. I *had* felt like he was accusing me, and that still stung.

I'd almost called him right back after he hung up. Then I realized he had a lot on his mind worrying about Todd, and I decided to give him some space, at least until after the event. I wanted to help him, not add more stress.

The most important thing was that the tasting went off without a hitch first.

Someone shouted, a sort of high-pitched cheer that drew my attention. Several heads turned toward the doorway where the sound came from.

Oh no.

Todd stepped further into the room. He seemed to be talking to people as he passed them, his voice loud but not loud enough that I could make out most of what he said. I heard Dylan's name a couple of times, though.

People were smiling awkwardly and looking at each other as he passed them. He stumbled but caught himself.

He'd clearly gone off the wagon. *At the worst possible time.*

Dylan spotted Todd and said something to Shane and Vera, then he hurried up to Todd and grabbed his shoulders.

It was difficult to hear him over the music, which was just loud enough to swallow up most of what he said. Between straining to hear and watching his lips, I thought he said, "Come on, Todd. Let's get you into the back and get some coffee in you."

Todd pushed Dylan away from him, then held his hands up.

"I'm fine, Dylan. Just here to see your triumphant night." Then he looked around the room and I couldn't figure out what he said because I couldn't see his mouth the whole time.

While Todd glanced around, he spotted me. His mouth twisted into a mockery of a smile, and he started my way.

No, this wasn't going to happen on Dylan's big night. I could tell by the look on Todd's face, I was in for an angry confrontation.

I headed for the doorway, thinking that maybe I could lead Todd outside, away from the other guests in case he got loud enough to draw people's attention.

Todd caught up to me before I could get outside.

"Lana, don't you look lovely tonight," he said with a sneer. "Dressing to impress, huh? I'll bet it *does* impress Dylan, doesn't it?"

"Shh," I hissed, stepping closer. "Keep your voice down, Todd."

Only a couple of people looked our way, but it wouldn't stay that way for long if he kept it up.

"Oh, keep my voice down, huh?" He said louder. "You don't want anybody to know about what's going on, do you? I don't blame you. It reflects poorly on a woman like you. So prim and proper with your fancy job but fucking your client behind everybody's back." He chuckled. "I never would have thought you'd do something like that, Lana."

His breath smelled like whiskey, and his eyes were wide and glassy.

Part of me felt bad for him because addiction had to be hell.

I tried my best to be understanding, but then he leaned close, his face only inches away from mine.

I could see Dylan looking our way, his face angry, and body tense. I hoped whatever happened, it didn't cause a scene.

"How's Dylan liking my sloppy seconds these days?" Todd said, directly in front of my face.

I gasped, shocked at the open hostility.

"You're drunk," I said, not hiding how I felt about that. I pulled him by his arm to try to get him outside. "Let me call you a cab to take you home."

He grinned, an ugly expression, as he snatched my hand and yanked me toward him. "I never would have thought you'd be such a whore."

"Todd, please," I hissed, trying to pull away.

He leaned in closer.

"How did you like fucking my brother? Did he get you off better than I did?"

His words cut through me, and before I knew what I was doing, I threw my water in his face.

I regretted it immediately. It was an instinctive reaction.

At least it was better than slapping him, I reasoned.

Todd grabbed my arms and jerked me forward, his face screwed up in anger. Then Dylan was there, grabbing Todd and pulling him away from me.

My arms throbbed where he'd grabbed me, and I wondered if I would have a bruise.

Todd, for all his problems with drugs and alcohol, had never put his hands on me when we were together. I didn't think he realized how rough he'd been just then.

Todd tried to pull away from Dylan, looking furious.

"You want to know how she likes to be fucked?" he shouted. "I can teach you—"

"You fucking—"

Todd tackled Dylan, ramming his shoulder into Dylan's midsection and pushing him back a few feet. Dylan didn't go down, though. He was bigger than Todd and sober, so he kept himself upright easily.

"Stop it, right now!" Dylan shoved Todd off him, but Todd came back for more. Dylan's punch drew the attention of everyone who wasn't already watching. Todd staggered back, knocking over a table, as blood gushed from his nose.

I stood frozen, my hands covering my mouth in shock. Everyone else stood just as still, stunned into silence after the sudden outburst.

Brent's face was bright red, like he might explode from anger. Chelsea and Alexander were wide-eyed, slack jawed. And Shane and Vera both watched with the same expressions.

And Dylan. My chest ached at the sight of him. I couldn't breathe.

He just stood there, chest heaving, his hand still curled into a tight fist by his side. His jaw was rigid, eyes cold and hard as he glared down at Todd. He seemed coiled tight, ready to lash out again at the slightest provocation from Todd.

My heart pounded as the silence stretched on. I wanted to say something to diffuse the situation, but everyone's eyes darted from Dylan to Todd and then to me.

But what if I made the situation even worse than it already was?

I felt like I was suffocating. I had to get out of there. I ran out.

I should have gotten out before Todd confronted me. And I shouldn't have thrown my water in his face.

I got in my car and went home, crying the whole way at how I ruined the entire event. What was supposed to be a big celebratory night for Dylan turned out to be a complete disaster. And it was my fault.

DYLAN

I pulled Lana's number up and stared at my phone.

After the event ended, I'd driven by her house to make sure her car was there. I needed to know she'd made it home safely.

She had. I almost pulled in and knocked. But I wasn't sure I was ready to talk to her yet.

I backed out of my contacts and put my phone down. I still wasn't ready, mostly because I didn't know what the hell to say.

If I knew everything was going to be okay despite what had happened, I would have called her and at least told her that. But I didn't want to have to tell her how badly things had gone after she left.

"You'll have to excuse us," Shane had said abruptly after Carl and Jason had managed to get Todd into a cab.

"If you'll let me explain," I'd said, but Vera had shaken her head. "We can't have our brand associated with this kind of thing, Dylan. Drunken brawling? I'm sorry, but we need to go."

I couldn't convince them to stay and let me explain, but I

hoped that tomorrow they might listen to me. I was sure they were shocked, and I didn't blame them for not wanting their company name associated with anything like that.

The news all seemed pretty bad, and that was the last thing I wanted to share with Lana. And I didn't know what to say about people at Berman finding out about us.

It was pretty damn obvious that the fight between me and Todd was over Lana. Todd had been loud enough for everyone to hear, even over the music. I leaned my head back, groaning at the memory.

Lana had been so worried about people at work finding out about us, and exactly what she had feared had come true. In the worst, most dramatic way possible. The possibility of her getting fired over this formed a knot in my chest.

What if she was right? I suddenly wondered.

What if this is all a sign that we weren't meant to be after all?

I hated having that thought, but it felt like everything good that happened recently was falling apart before my eyes.

I pushed away the intrusive thought, refusing to go down that path.

I also didn't know quite what to say about Todd except that I was sorry for the way he acted.

And I was sorry for our conversation the night before.

I really hadn't meant to accuse her, and I knew how I'd sounded. She hadn't told Todd, and it wasn't really her fault that he'd figured it out by looking at her.

How could she control something like that?

No, the fault lay solely with Todd here, for letting himself go back to his bad habits the minute he was upset about something. It wasn't going to be an excuse to get away with his behavior. Not anymore.

That was a conversation that had to wait too. There was no point in trying to reason with Todd until he was sober again.

As soon as he was, he and I were going to have a talk. And I was going to draw a hard line on what behavior I would find acceptable from him from there on out.

If he couldn't abide by that, he'd need to steer clear of me until he could.

'Tough love' they call it in addiction circles. And it was that. Because it was pretty damn tough on the person trying to give it too.

I hoped Todd could understand that someday.

I pulled up a photo of Lana on my phone and touched the screen just under the apple of her cheek. I'd gotten so used to having her with me almost every night, and I missed her.

I decided to go to bed and try to sleep. And hope things looked brighter in the morning.

41

LANA

"What the hell happened last night?" Chelsea sat at her desk, fingers laced together in front of her, her expression stern.

I knew this was coming as soon as I walked into the office that morning. Everyone turned to look at me, and Maddie looked like she wanted to cry.

I understood how she felt. I'd barely slept, and I'd cried so much that I felt wrung out.

I knew what I was walking into, and I knew what I had to do. But it hurt, and not crying in front of Chelsea was going to be some kind of miracle if I pulled it off.

"When you asked me if anything was going on that you should know about," I started, "I wasn't entirely truthful. Dylan and I have been seeing each other."

"Lana—"

"I know, I know," I said, putting a hand up. "But I didn't think you needed to know since it wasn't causing any issues."

When she tilted her head and raised her eyebrows, I said, "At least, it wasn't at the time."

I explained what happened in as much detail as I could stand, down to the things Todd said to me that caused me to throw water in his face.

Chelsea, to her credit, listened calmly and without interrupting me. Then she sighed.

"That's a hell of a story. He had no right to say those awful things to you, so I don't think your reaction was out of line. But think of how it looks for the agency, Lana!" She tapped her desk. "You can't keep things like this from me. We could have had security outside to keep Todd from getting in, anticipated problems and tried to stop them, if *only you'd told me.*"

She was right. I should have confided in her when the reputation of the agency was on the line.

"I'm sorry, Chelsea. It was a mistake not to tell you. Do you think the collab's still going forward? Have you talked to Shane or Vera?"

Her expression darkened. "They canceled the meeting we had scheduled for this afternoon. I tried to get them to come in so we could discuss things, but they opted to leave for Colorado early."

Fuck. That was it. They'd clearly changed their minds.

I nodded, struggling not to cry.

"I'm so sorry, Chelsea." I stood and smoothed down my blouse. "Thanks for giving me the opportunities you have here at Berman. I need to go, but I'll email you a formal resignation by tomorrow."

"Lana, I'm not sure you need to resign over this. I personally don't want to lose your talents here at Berman. Maybe take some personal time, let me talk to Alexander again and see how he feels."

She stood and walked around the desk to touch my arm, almost causing the tears to come in earnest.

I shook my head. "Thank you so much, but there's no need for that. We both know I can't work here after what happened," I said, my voice breaking. "I'll email tomorrow," I blurted, then I turned and rushed from the office.

I'd screwed up my relationship with Dylan, and I'd screwed up Deft Rock's collab, hurting both the brewery and my career.

I drove home, tears in my eyes, feeling more like a failure than I had in years.

I needed to figure out if anything could be salvaged and then do something about it. And hope it wasn't too late.

~

I was staring out the cab window when my phone rang with a call from Dylan. I almost didn't answer it, but I forced myself.

Dylan deserved to hear what I had to say as soon as possible. As painful as it was, there was no need to put it off.

"We should talk," Dylan said when I answered. "Let me come over so we can talk in person?"

"I'm out of town, Dylan. And we do need to talk, but we can do it on the phone. I wanted to tell you how sorry I am about everything that happened last night. I didn't handle it well," I admitted, "and I know I made everything worse. I'm so sorry, Dylan."

He sighed. "No, baby, it wasn't you. None of that was your fault. Todd had no right to talk to you like that. Anybody would have reacted the way you did."

"I'm not so sure about that, Dylan."

"I am." Dylan took a deep breath. "I'm sorry I made it seem like I was blaming you for Todd finding out last time we talked. I was out of line. Todd's behavior isn't on anybody but Todd. I feel like I've been giving him passes for years and blaming everything and everyone else, and I'm sorry if I did that to you."

I sniffed. It was wonderful to hear all that, but it didn't really matter anymore.

"I appreciate that, Dylan. But he's your brother, and he always will be. Given how he reacted to me and the idea of us together . . . I think we need to stop seeing each other." It hurt so much to say that I could barely get the words out.

"No," he said sharply. "Lana, *no*. We can't let Todd's reactions dictate what we do. I won't accept it."

"Dylan, I can't keep causing a rift between the two of you. I should never have let that happen," I explained.

"You didn't. That's Todd and his unwillingness to face facts. It's not your fault." He inhaled sharply. "Just come home and let's talk about it. Where are you anyway?"

When I didn't answer, he continued, "Don't make a rash decision after what happened yesterday. Everything's going to be ok. Please, just come home."

I wanted to say yes. I wanted to agree to go back and throw myself into Dylan's arms. But I knew I couldn't. It just wasn't right or fair to do that.

"I've made everything such a big mess for you. And for Brent. Your business prospects. Your relationship with Todd. I just don't think we can keep doing this, Dylan." My voice broke on his name, so I covered my hand with my mouth and tried not to sob.

"Baby, stop talking like this. Where are you? I'll come to you and—"

"I'm so sorry, Dylan. I have to go." I hung up and turned my phone off so I wouldn't be tempted to answer if he called back.

Then I took a deep breath and braced myself for what was coming.

I needed to look together and not like I'd been about to cry like a baby in the back of a cab.

∼

"They'll see you now," the receptionist said, leading me to the meeting room where Vera and Shane had agreed to talk with me.

I took slow, deep breaths on the walk there.

The worst they can say is no, and then at least you can say you tried.

"Thank you so much for agreeing to meet with me," I said as they shook my hand and I sat.

"We were surprised when you called," Vera said. "It shows a lot of initiative that you'd come all this way after what happened."

"I just want to explain and hopefully make it clear that what happened isn't representative of Deft Rock. Not at all." I did my best to look them each in the eyes as I explained what happened was completely unacceptable to Deft Rock and that it would in no way be associated with the Emberox Spirits brand.

Vera steepled her fingers together. "Look, Lana, we were really impressed. The tasting was a success as far as we were concerned. At least until the brawl."

Shane nodded. "Until that point, we were ready to sign on."

"Surely," I said, trying to appeal to their common sense, "you can't hold Deft Rock responsible for a fight breaking out in the taproom. That could happen anywhere at any time."

"True," Vera said. "But it was one of Deft Rock's owners and his brother, not random guests. That would have been different."

"We loved Deft Rock and the drinks you all created. And we think retail distribution and our merged branding would ultimately be incredibly profitable," Shane explained.

"But we hesitate to do business with temperamental people. People who would punch their own brother in their full establishment. I didn't take Dylan to be that type, but I guess I read him wrong."

"But if you understood exactly what happened..."

Did I want to share that much with Vera and Shane? It had been hard enough to tell Chelsea.

They both looked willing to listen, so for the second time in as many days, I explained the situation with Todd, Dylan, and myself. I told them about how Dylan had taken care of Todd and tried to help him, and how Dylan had grabbed me and slammed into Dylan. He had to defend himself, and things had gotten out of hand.

By the time I was done, Vera had a strange, slight smile that I couldn't decipher.

Did she believe me, or did she think I was lying and trying to trick her?

She didn't look suspicious, but of all the reactions I'd expected from the story, a smile hadn't been one.

"So, it's you," she said, still wearing a strange smile. "I can't believe I didn't see it before."

"I ... I don't know what you mean," I admitted, glancing between her and Shane. He looked equally confused.

"I suppose there's no harm in telling you," she said with a soft laugh. "I was so impressed with Dylan the day we met, that I suggested he and I spend some time together. Alone."

"Vera," Shane said with a soft laugh.

"What? As far as I knew, he was handsome, successful, and available." She shrugged, then turned to me again. "He set me straight about the last part right away by explaining that it was complicated, but he very much was *not* available."

I sat speechless, unsure of what to say.

"Dylan told me all about this wonderful woman who had his heart after he turned me down. And a man would only fight his brother over a woman he loved very much."

I blinked back tears. I hadn't known he'd told her about me.

"Dylan's protective. Honorable. Just a good man all-around," I said earnestly. "He wouldn't have fought with Todd if Todd hadn't forced him to."

Vera nodded. "I can see that. Seems he's less temperamental than I thought. He was backed into a corner, and did the only thing he thought he could, is that what you're saying?"

"That's what I'm saying."

Vera and Shane glanced at each other, then she turned back to me. "How lucky you are to have a man who'd fight like that for you."

Had a man like that, I told myself.

How lucky I *was*.

I bit my lip to keep from crying.

"But he's lucky too, to have someone who cares about him so much that she'd come all this way and give such personal details to try to save the deal," Vera added.

She and Shane exchanged another look. Then Shane stood and held out his hand for me to shake again.

"We need to talk in private, Lana. We're going to reconsider our position. Weigh some pros and cons and see how we feel then."

"Thank you," I blurted, sighing in relief. "For talking to me and reconsidering. Thank you so, so much."

When I got into the cab, intending to go to the airport, I decided that maybe I needed to clear my head for a couple of days before going home and trying to find another job. And having to face Dylan, who would probably still try to talk to me.

Maybe Vera and Shane would go through with the collab and at least something could be saved.

"The nearest hotel's fine," I told the driver.

I pulled my phone out to turn it back on, but I decided to leave it dark. I needed some time and having to deal with texts and voicemails would only make things worse.

I'd spend a couple of days relaxing and thinking, and then maybe I'd be able to talk to Dylan and make it clear we were over without completely falling apart.

I knew how hard it had been for Dylan and Todd to get back to speaking terms again. And how hard Todd had to work to get sober again.

I'd moved on from this and I felt like I was back to the same drama that I desperately wanted to leave behind.

All that I'd feared came true.

I fell in love with Dylan and it crashed and burned like I feared it would. And my career at Berman was over.

There was no way I could go back and pick up where I left off. My reputation was already tarnished. I wouldn't be able to recover and get my career back on track there.

I would need to look for a new job, have a fresh start. And that was fine. I knew I could do that.

But that wasn't what I was worried about. I wasn't sure how I'd put my heart back together after Dylan.

42

LANA

I'd returned to Everbrook the prior day, so I went to see Grandpa and make sure he was doing okay. I still left my phone off most of the time. I wasn't ready to deal with texts and calls.

And the thought that maybe Dylan had stopped sending messages filled with me equal dread. If he gave up too easily, it would somehow feel even worse.

As soon as I walked into Grandpa's room, he grinned. "Another visitor already? It must be my lucky day."

I hugged him tightly and sat on the edge of his bed across from where he sat in his recliner. "Another visitor?"

"Your ex-boyfriend just left here again. Couldn't have been more than a minute before you got here," he explained.

He must've meant Dylan. I shook my head, a knot forming in my stomach. Dylan was just here?

"Grandpa, did you mean Dylan all this time when you said my ex-boyfriend had come to see you?"

"Yes, who did you think I meant?"

"Grandpa, Todd's my ex-boyfriend, not Dylan."

"Sorry, sweetheart," he said. "I know that. But I always thought Dylan should have been your boyfriend, and I guess I got that into my head." He patted my hand. "Still think you two should have been together. And the fact that he still comes here to see me, well, I figure I'm right. I still keep hoping the two of you will get your act together one day."

He winked at me, and I felt a tear slip down my cheek.

"If you didn't pass him, he probably took the hall that leads to the side entrance instead of the main one," Grandpa said, then he glanced at the window. "Sure is a beautiful day out there. I think I'll go out to the sun porch."

If Dylan really had left only a minute earlier, maybe I could still catch him.

For what, Lana? You decided it was over.

"I'll meet you out there, Grandpa. I just need to take care of something first."

I walked down the main hall toward the entrance. If I didn't catch Dylan, I needed to stop into the admin office anyway to be sure Cheryl knew I was going to make another payment next week.

It was going to be rough for a while until I found another job, but I was determined not to have to move grandpa to a less expensive facility, even if it meant I had to wait tables again to make ends meet.

I didn't find Dylan in the hallway. I stood in the lobby looking out of the glass front to see if he was in the parking lot. Only cars, no people walking around that I could see.

I stepped into the admin office doorway as Cheryl came out of her office with paperwork in her hands.

"Hello, Lana," she said with a smile.

"Hi Cheryl," I said. "I was planning to stop by and tell you that I can make a payment next week on Grandpa's balance. I know it must have started building back up since we talked."

"It would have," she said cheerfully, "but the bill's just been paid."

"Again?" I said with a gasp. "You have to tell me who's doing that so I can thank them."

I realized then that she hadn't said *the bill's been paid*. She said the bill's *just been* paid.

"Sorry, Lana. They still want to remain anonymous."

"*When* was it paid?" I asked.

"Just minutes ago. What a happy coincidence!" Her grin broadened.

Was it Dylan? He'd just been here.

"Please tell me who," I begged. "I'll never out you as the one who let me know."

She chuckled and shook her head. "I can't. I—" Her eyes went wide as she looked over my shoulder. "I—excuse me, Lana."

She narrowed her eyes and then raised her eyebrows as she glanced over my shoulder again, like she was trying to signal me, so I turned.

Dylan had just come out of the men's bathroom. He stopped when he saw me, his eyes as wide as Cheryl's.

"Lana," he said softly.

I burst into tears. How had I ever deserved someone as wonderful as Dylan? And how had I let it all go to hell?

"*Lana*," he said, rushing forward to pull me into his arms.

DYLAN

"Shh, baby, it's okay." I held Lana tightly as she cried on my shoulder.

When she was calmer, I moved us so that we stood outside the lobby in a little enclave with a bench and an awning.

I held her hands while we sat and she sniffed deeply, shaking her head.

"You've been paying his bills all this time?" she asked, wiping a tear from her face.

I kissed her hand. "Grandpa would've wanted to, so I did it for him since he couldn't."

Lana licked her lips and took a long, slow breath. "I can't pay you back right away, but I will eventually. I appreciate—"

"Stop, just stop," I said. "You're not paying anything back. This is why I didn't just offer you the money. I figured you wouldn't accept it."

"You're right. I won't." She straightened her neck. "I appreciate what you've done, so much, but I always pay my bills. I'll figure it out."

"Damn it, Lana." I cupped her cheek. "It's technically from money that grandpa left me when he died, so it's like he's paying for it. Please don't think another thing about it."

I could see that argument was getting through to her. My grandpa would have paid James' bills if he'd still been alive when they started piling up. She had to know that too.

"It would make Grandpa happy to know he was helping James," I said. "So let him help, Lana."

She started to sob again, so I pulled her close, my arm around her shoulders.

"I'm so sorry about everything," she said, clearing her throat. "I resigned after what happened at the event. I'm so sorry about—"

I touched my finger to her lips to stop her. "About flying to Colorado to try and fix things? Vera called this morning."

She nodded, still looking glum. "I did the best I could. I'm so sorry, Dylan."

"They're going ahead with the collab, baby. You won them over. We're meeting with them about the first test run next week. I was going to call you or just show up at your house if you wouldn't answer your phone to tell you after I left here." I stroked her hair and cupped her cheek. "Nothing that happened at the event was your fault, and you still managed to pull the deal out of the fire. The agency should be begging you to come back if they have any sense."

The look of joy and relief on her face made her even more beautiful than she already was. Her blue eyes shone with tears, and another tracked its way down her cheek.

"*I'll* beg if I have to," I finally said. "Because I have sense, even if they don't. I need you, Lana. Whatever you think is so messed up between us, it can be fixed, just like you fixed the collab with Emberox. We can get through whatever comes, as long as we're together."

I brushed my thumb over her perfect, pink lips, then I leaned over and kissed her.

My throat tightened in relief when Lana wrapped her arms tightly around my neck and kissed me back.

∼

I stood behind Lana as she unlocked her door, my hands on her hip. I dipped my head to nuzzle the back of her neck, causing her to giggle and shrug her shoulders.

After we'd kissed on the bench outside Crystal Fountains, we'd gone to the sun porch where James was waiting for her. He beamed when he saw us together, Lana's hand in mine.

"About damn time," he said with a laugh.

It had been a shorter visit than Lana had intended, but James had gotten into a game of cards with one of his friends anyway.

We promised to come back and visit together next time, and that made James happy.

The lock clicked, so Lana pushed the door open. When I closed it behind me, I pressed my back against it and pulled her close.

"God, I've missed you," I breathed against her lips, then I kissed her deeply.

Lana took my face in her hands, and I stared into her gorgeous blue eyes.

"I should have said it a long time ago, Dylan. I shouldn't have waited, but I was afraid." She kissed me again and said, "I love you, Dylan. I've been in love with you for so long."

Hearing her finally say it was good medicine for all the hurt and misunderstandings. Could anything really be wrong if Lana loved me?

"I love you, baby," I said back to her. "So much."

I grabbed her ass and lifted her to straddle my hips, then I walked us to her bedroom, kissing her the whole way. I felt almost frantic with the need to feel her body beneath mine. To feel her wrapped around my cock.

To hear my name from her lips as she came.

We were in such a hurry to get our clothes off, a button pinged against the wooden floor, and I didn't know if it had popped off her shirt or mine.

And I didn't care.

She lay back on the bed, so I lay on top of her, already rubbing my hardness between her legs and moaning at the heat I found there. But it had been too long since I'd tasted her. There was nothing like feeling her come against my tongue and knowing that I could undo her so easily.

I kissed my way down her body, loving her quick little breaths of anticipation.

"Dylan," she moaned as I teased around between her legs with my tongue, licking the crease where her thigh met her body, kissing her outer lips, but avoiding the place I knew she wanted my tongue most. I wanted her so bad and I struggled not to hurry. I wanted it to last as long as possible.

Finally, with her squirming because she wanted it so badly, I couldn't resist anymore. I licked up from her opening to her clit and pressed my lips in a pucker around her little pulsing button to suck lightly.

She arched off the bed, making my cock throb.

She was already slick and quivering, so I pushed two fingers inside her to increase her pleasure. I sucked her clit, tapping it and twirling my tongue around it. Each time I could tell she was close, I slowed down and backed off enough to keep her from going all the way.

After several minutes of this teasing, she sank her fingers into my hair and groaned. "Need you to *fuck me*, Dylan. *Please.*"

I needed that too. My cock pulsed at her words. I teased her clit with purpose then, with my tongue and a thumb. "Come for me, baby, and I'll fuck you all night long if you want."

That promise worked. Lana cried out and came, her pussy pulsing against my lips and tongue. I groaned at the feeling of it, knowing that I had given her that much pleasure.

I couldn't wait any longer. I already knew it was going to be a struggle to hold back, but I was determined to go as slowly as possible.

I crawled up and kissed her, letting her taste herself on my tongue. She wrapped her legs around me, spreading herself open and lifting her hips.

I slid into Lana like a hot knife into butter. We just fit together in a way that had never happened to me with anyone else. I could anticipate her moves and join them, and she always seemed to be in sync with what I wanted too.

We both groaned as I thrust into her again, her pussy still tightening in the throes of her orgasm.

"Dylan!" she shouted, her fingers digging into my shoulders as another wave hit her. I had to grit my teeth to hang on and not lose it then and there.

"Oh, Dylan," she said, shuddering beneath me. "I love you so much," she said softly.

I kissed her, trying hard to delay my own orgasm, but hearing that again made it impossible to resist. "I love you too, baby," I whispered, and when her pussy tightened around me again, I slid a hand between to thumb her clit.

Lana exploded, her back arching as she shouted wordlessly in pleasure. She clamped around me and I came, unable to hold back any longer. I kissed her chin, her neck, then I sucked against the side of her throat as I spilled deep inside her.

This was it for me. Lana was all I wanted. She was home. And anything that would stand in the way of that had no part in my life.

I knew I was never going to give this woman up. Not for the brewery, or for any friend or family. Not even for Todd.

When our pleasure started to fade, I rolled onto my back and pulled Lana with me, unwilling to let any space get between us. After our breathing slowed and the light seen of sweat on my body started to dry, cooling me off, I pulled the sheet up and over us.

Lana hummed contentedly as she rubbed her cheek against my chest. I combed my fingers through her soft, blonde hair. For the moment, everything was right with the world, and I just wanted to bask in that while I could.

After a while, Lana lifted her head and looked up at me, chin on my chest. "I don't want to ask, but I need to know."

"Todd?" I said, guessing what it was about.

Lana nodded. "What if he can never accept us being together?"

I stroked her face. I'd thought about that a lot, long before he found out and had his blow-up at the brewery. I was more confident than ever about the answer I'd come up with.

"I was right when I said Todd was fragile. And I figured he'd be upset if he found out about us. I was right about that too. So, I hope you'll trust me about this—Todd will be okay, eventually. I think he'll come around."

Lana pulled herself up, bringing our faces closer. "I do trust you. But how can you be so sure?"

I sighed. "I'm not sure, but I think that's what will happen. And if it doesn't..." I kissed her softly. "Then that's on Todd. He's an adult. He has all kinds of resources available to help him. Rehab. Therapy. I'll even go to family therapy with him if that's what he wants. I'll be there for him any way he needs, but I won't be responsible for him. That's up to him."

I kissed her again. "And I won't let him come between us. If Todd decides he can't handle the fact that I'm head over heels in love with you, then Todd can deal with that on his own, somewhere else. I think he loves me enough that he wouldn't break up the family over his jealousy. I'm going to trust him that it's true, at least. Give him the benefit of the doubt."

Lana smiled at me so sweetly, my heart ached. She touched my cheek. "And I trust you to make the right decision."

I kissed the palm of her hand. "I'm going to do whatever it takes, Lana, for us to be together." I brushed my thumb over her cheek.

She rubbed her cheek against my palm. "You told me once that you'd always show up for me. And even when I didn't call you or ask for anything, you still did. I love you, Dylan. I always will."

I'd always show up for her. I knew it back then, and I knew it while she kissed me, letting her legs spread around my hips to sit atop me.

"I believe you said something about, um, let me see ... Fucking me all night long. Unless I'm remembering wrong or something, that sounded like a promise." She grinned mischievously and rubbed herself against me.

My cock took note and started to thicken beneath her. I pulled her down to press a peck to the tip of her nose.

"A promise I fully intend to keep," I said as she laughed then kissed me again.

EPILOGUE
LANA

I stopped the video with the remote I held.

"What do you think?"

Dylan sat at the table next to me with his arms crossed.

He nodded. "Sharp. Professional. But I expect nothing less from you anyway."

We'd just watched the new TV ad spot for the Deft Rock and Emberox Spirits brand of hard seltzer. I'd pitched the idea to Vera, who loved it. Brent thought it was great too.

"It obviously fits with the other commercial, it feels like part of the whole, but it still brings in something new," Dylan said. "The 'serious refreshment for fun-loving adults' is great."

"Thanks. Vera loved that too and is thinking about making it the brand's new tagline," I admitted, a little proud I'd come up with it.

Since we were alone in the room, Dylan leaned over and pulled me close to kiss me. "I love it too. And you, of course. But if it had sucked..."

"You'd have told me. I know," I added with a laugh, pushing him away. "How are the latest numbers?"

"They're fucking fantastic, baby," he said, turning serious. "We've got sales numbers for the entire first year of our collaboration, and profits are continuing to go up. There's nothing slowing down this train. With the branded merchandise hitting the shelves before Christmas and the hard seltzer already taking off out of the gate, I think the second year's going to blow the first one away."

"That's what I like to hear," I said with a grin.

"And the line of non-alcoholic drinks rolling out after that opens the market up even more," he added.

We'd been working on the non-alcoholic drinks for a while, unsure whether it was going to be a good business move or not. But we both felt strongly about it, in no small part because of Todd.

It seemed like a way to honor him as Dylan's brother to have those kind of drinks available, not just in stores, but in the taproom too.

Vera and Shane had fortunately been on board with the idea, and all the market research we had said it was going to be a good financial move too.

Dylan's phone buzzed, and I could tell by his smile that it was Todd. I stood and busied myself doing other things to give him a little privacy, but I could still hear Dylan's side of the conversation.

"Next week? That'll be great. Tell Lisa we're looking forward to seeing her," he said.

Todd had gotten back together with Lisa not long after his and Dylan's fight at the tasting event. And it had taken most of the year, but he and Dylan were on much better terms.

He'd accepted that Dylan and I were together and had apologized to me with such sincerity that I forgave him.

I apologized to him too, admitting that I'd been attracted

to Dylan before Todd had even shown up, and that I could've probably handled things better when we were dating..

The conversations had been difficult, but we all felt so much better afterward. I was so relieved that Dylan and Todd were getting along, especially since I thought Dylan was going to ask Todd something that he never would have had things still been tense between them.

"Are you going to ask him during this visit? There's not much time left, you know," I said when he got off the phone. "Barely a month."

Dylan got up and sauntered towards me. "Barely a month? For what? Hmm, what am I forgetting about?" He wrapped his arms around me, pinning me to him at the waist and leaning me back to kiss me. "Has something slipped my mind?"

"It's nothing important," I replied cheekily.

He gasped, feigning shock. "How could you? Nothing important?"

I turned my head with a laugh, but he kissed my cheek anyway.

"I'm going to ask him this time. He really has accepted our relationship, so I believe he'll say yes." Dylan smiled at me, his deep brown eyes sparkling. "If not, I'll ask Brent."

"I don't think you'll have to. I doubt there's anything that could make Todd miss out on being your Best Man. He's going to be thrilled that you're asking him."

I'd asked Maddie to be my maid of honor, and I could barely believe how excited we both were that the wedding was less than a month away.

Dylan reached for the counter behind me and slid the papers he'd grabbed into my hands.

"Sales numbers. See for yourself what a success you've

helped bring about as Deft Rock's marketing and event manager." He beamed and waited for me to look at the papers.

The collab hadn't just been successful, it had been wildly successful. It put Deft Rock on the national stage and on its way to being a household name.

"Being the brewery's marketing and event manager does lack the prestige of working at a top ad agency, but it's rewarding to work on just one company's marketing."

I laughed and slapped his behind. "Not to mention the perks."

"Fitting that you're going to end up owning part of the place after I slip a ring onto your finger next month since you helped make the place a success." He pulled me into his arms again.

"Oh, so you remember the wedding now?" His constant act of forgetting had been a running joke for the last few months.

"How could I forget. Especially when I keep thinking about the wedding *night*. Having you as my wife. Hell, every night with you is like a honeymoon already, though, isn't it?"

I kissed his grin, then he pressed his lips against mine and took our typical workday flirting into something heated and impatient.

"Get used to it," I said. "Because you're going to be well and truly stuck with me after you say your vows."

"I'm going to do everything I can, baby," Dylan said, staring into my eyes, "to make you happy every day of the rest of our lives. You get used to *that*."

∽

"Have I told my wife how much I love her?" Dylan murmured into my ear.

I smiled at him teasingly. "Only about a hundred times. But I'll never get tired of hearing it."

I would never in a million years get tired of hearing those words from Dylan. Or him calling me his wife.

Our wedding reception was in full swing at Deft Rock. Dylan and I couldn't think of a better place to celebrate. Our friends and family filled the space, laughing, eating, dancing joyfully. The clinking of glasses and happy voices echoed through the room.

I caught glimpses of Vera chatting with Maddie near the bar. Brent was trying to teach Grandpa the latest dance moves, much to Grandpa's amusement. Todd and Lisa were taking pictures together at the photo booth. Seeing everyone together and happy filled my heart with gratitude.

Todd had been thrilled when Dylan asked him to be the Best Man. He was truly happy for us. Having his sincere support was better than any wedding gift we could've ever received. Because I knew how important it was to Dylan. To have his brother by his side. The day wouldn't have been complete without Todd as the Best Man.

Todd tapped his glass, calling everyone's attention for his speech. The crowd fell to a murmur, quieting down and settling in their seats.

"When Dylan first asked me to be his best man, I'll admit I was hesitant. Given what a pain in the ass I've been to Dylan, I didn't feel worthy of giving this speech." Todd began, smiling at his brother. "Like that time I drew a beard on his face with a Sharpie, just in time for his school photos." Todd wiggled his eyebrows. Dylan chuckled, shaking his head at the memory.

"But then I realized I might be just the right person." Todd's voice grew serious. "Because no one knows these two amazing people better than I do. And I can say from the bottom of my heart, how good they are for each other." Dylan smiled at Todd, touched by his words.

"Dylan, my whole life, you've always looked out for me. Whether it was standing up to the schoolyard bullies or giving me a kick in the pants when I needed it. Even when I resented it in the moment. Thank you for always having my back. I know I haven't made it easy for you."

I saw the pain and regret in Todd's eyes as he looked at his brother.

"You believed in me and supported me when I didn't deserve it. Even when I thought I didn't need it, you knew that I did. And I thank you for that, brother. I wouldn't have made it this far without you."

Dylan seemed to be fighting back tears, blinking rapidly and tightening his jaw. I squeezed his hand.

"This might be the first time I've said this. Dylan, you're the best big brother anyone could ever have," Todd said sincerely. "And you've got yourself an amazing woman." His gaze turned to me as he smiled softly. "Lana, your kindness and big heart have truly humbled me. Despite the pain I caused, you found it in yourself to forgive. That takes a strength of character I can only aspire to. Seeing you two here today, so incredibly happy and in love fills me with hope. Lana, thank you for making my brother so happy. He deserves it. And I know he'll spend his whole life making you feel the same. I wish you both a lifetime of joy, adventure, and love. Thank you for allowing me to stand here and be a part of your special day."

Dylan smiled appreciatively at his little brother. Todd raised his glass in a toast. "To Dylan and Lana!"

The guests echoed the words and toasted. Dylan pulled Todd into a tight hug, patting his back. Watching the two brothers, my heart swelled with emotion. I blinked back tears as I hugged Todd.

"That was beautiful. Thank you, Todd," I whispered.

"I meant every word, Lana." Todd gently squeezed my shoulder as he reached for Dylan's. "I love you guys."

Dylan and I kissed sweetly amidst cheers and whistles from our family and friends. After more toasts and words of congratulations from everyone, we made our way to the dance floor.

Dylan and I swayed gently to the music, arms wrapped tightly around each other, lost in our own little world. Everything else seemed to fall away. At that moment, it was just the two of us.

I gazed into Dylan's eyes, feeling like the luckiest girl in the world. My heart was so full it could burst.

Dylan leaned down and kissed me softly as we revolved slowly on the spot. He spun me out slowly, then pulled me back into his arms. My foot caught on the hem of my dress as I twirled, and I stumbled, catching myself on his chest.

"You okay?" Dylan asked, chuckling.

I laughed as the memory of our first meeting came flooding back.

"You caught me again," I said softly, leaning my head on his shoulder.

"Always will," he murmured into my hair.

"You know, I've been meaning to ask you." I paused, looking up at him.

"Hm?" He hummed brushing my nose with his.

"That day we met in the parking lot. Did you really trip me on purpose?"

He pulled back to gaze down at me, a mischievous twinkle in his eye.

"Have you been curious all this time?" He asked, the corners of his mouth twitching.

"Yes, I have been actually." I nodded, a little excited that I was finally about to find out.

He smirked. "Maybe."

I pushed at his chest playfully. "Tell me. Did you really?"

He chuckled softly, holding my hand against his chest as we continued to sway. "What do you think?"

"I can't imagine you'd do something like that intentionally," I narrowed my eyes, trying to figure out the truth hidden behind his goofy grin. "I don't think you did."

"Well, Mrs. Easton, I'm glad I can still keep you guessing," he said, kissing me softly. Then he whispered in my ear, "Because I did."

I gasped in surprise and laughed. "Dylan!"

Dylan threw his head back in laughter. I looked at him incredulously, unsure if he was serious or just pulling my leg.

"It's not like I planned it. I saw an opportunity and I took it." He shrugged, a sly grin on his face. I looked at him expectantly, waiting for him to explain. "It occurred to me at the last minute that I should move my foot to let you pass and I decided not to, knowing you'd likely trip. I wasn't going to let you fall, so I thought, what's the harm?"

I smacked his arm as I shook my head and smiled in disbelief. "I can't believe you did that. I thought I was a complete basket case that day."

He laughed softly and kissed my forehead. "You were irresistible. And I have no regrets," he said smugly. "I took one look at you and just knew I had to have you in my arms."

"By making me almost fall flat on my face?" I asked, trying not to laugh.

"By any means necessary." He winked. "Worked, didn't it?"

"I guess it did," I replied, smiling widely and nestling back into his chest.

I'd finally found where I belonged. There in Dylan's arms, I was home. And I couldn't wait to see what the future held for us. Because I knew, no matter what, we would face it together.

He brought my hand up to his lips and kissed my fingers.

"I loved you, Lana," he whispered. "So much."

My heart fluttered as I reached up to caress his face. "I loved you too, Dylan. More than I ever thought possible."

"I'm going to spend every day making you happy, taking care of you, loving you with my whole heart. No matter what life has planned for us. I'll always show up for you, baby."

He kissed me again, and I knew in my heart that he meant every word.

My husband, my partner, my rock.

THE END

Thank you for reading **Falling For My Ex's Brother**.

If you love off limits romance, then you'll love Protected By My Grumpy Hero.

. . .

An age gap romance filled with flirty banter, spicy love scenes, and a swoon worthy happily ever after.

Their undeniable chemistry is put to the test when they're stuck under one roof. Will their fake relationship seal the deal?

SNEAK PEEK

PROTECTED BY MY GRUMPY HERO

Here I am, trying to resist the woman of my dreams.
And what does she do? Handcuff us together.

It was clear from the start. She can't be mine.
She's younger, my boss' daughter, and under my protection.
Her life is threatened and I need to stay focused to keep her safe.
But her tight body and sweet smile is distracting as hell.
Keep it professional. Just follow the rules.
Don't let her get close.
Don't sleep with her.
Definitely don't fall in love.
I've broken all three and now my heart is on the line.

~

Chapter 1
Blake

My team and I were at the gala to protect the governor and his family. I couldn't afford to be distracted and usually wasn't. I'd done security work for years with no problems.

But the stunning woman in the sleeveless, black cocktail dress was making it almost impossible for me to focus on anything but the thought of my hands roaming over her mouth-watering body.

I couldn't stop zoning in on her no matter where she was in the room. Normally, I kept a bead on my target at all times, like an automated laser sight programmed to a singular focus.

Every time this woman moved, it drew my eye. Her graceful movement was impossible to ignore as she effortlessly glided across the floor.

There was an energy about her that pulled me.

I watched from the first-floor balcony for an overview of the entire ballroom. I was tempted to go down into the crowd to approach her for a better look.

I wouldn't. That would be irresponsible. But my dick kept trying to convince me to do it.

Just looking at her made me sweat, and I'd only seen her from the back.

I wanted her to turn around so I could see the rest of her. I'd only caught glimpses of the side of her face. But she had the most perfect, fantasy-inducing body I'd ever seen.

Her presence was proving dangerous because I would have rather admired her all night than watch the crowd I was paid to monitor. My only hope was that she'd leave early. If not, I was going to have a hell of a hard night trying to keep my eyes on the governor instead.

The woman brushed her long, brown hair over her shoulder and took a step backward. She started to turn away from the man she was talking to, but he touched her arm and stopped her.

She was clearly uncomfortable. As he talked and moved closer, she stepped backward again.

The guy had a pink face, like he'd gone overboard with the alcohol. His hand stayed on her arm as she lifted it and tried again to step away. His grip tightened.

Hell no.

Andrew, my top man, glanced up at me as I moved to the staircase. I pointed at my eyes and then at the governor to let him know to watch him.

I was halfway down the winding stairs when he signaled back. Within only a few seconds, I was almost in front of the drunk idiot putting his hands on the woman I couldn't stop looking at.

She pulled her arm away, and he reached to put a hand on her shoulder. She took a quick step backward, too quick, and her heel tilted. She stumbled, but I was behind her in a second and caught her with my hands on her hips.

That perfect heart-shaped ass landed against my crotch and I almost thanked the asshole who'd made her trip.

Almost.

"You alright, ma'am?" I said. "Did you turn your ankle?"

She took a quick, sharp breath and straightened to test it. "No, thank you. I-I'm fine."

The man stared at her. I didn't like the look in his eyes.

"Sir, the lady has other guests to speak with, as I'm sure you do too," I said in a tone that made it clear he didn't have a say in it. I put a hand on her shoulder and led her away from him.

"Are you alright?" I asked, softer, my eyes still on the creep who was already grabbing another drink.

She said yes, so I finally stopped and looked at the woman I'd helped.

Her bright blue eyes gazed right into me as she smiled. "Thank you so much. He seemed incapable of taking a hint. I thought I was going to have to karate chop him in the neck." She chuckled and tucked a long, curled lock of hair behind her ear.

She was so fucking gorgeous. I almost forgot how to speak. Her brown hair had just enough red in it to stand out from all the other shades in the room. And her cute little nose sat above full, pink lips that I suspected could bring most men to their knees.

They could have destroyed me in mere seconds. I could almost taste them and feel them against mine.

She frowned slightly, her blue eyes narrowing. I finally got my wits about me.

"Next time, start with the karate chop. Best bet for men like that. If you're really alright..."

"I am. Thank you again."

"Good. Excuse me, ma'am." I gave her a quick smile and a nod.

Every step I took away from her was like walking through quicksand. Part of me wanted to quit on the spot, throw her over my shoulder caveman-style, and take her home to my bed.

Mostly, I wanted to get her number and see what she was doing after this shindig was over.

Fortunately, the conscientious chief of security inside me kept me professional. But I knew I'd be thinking about her later that night when I was in my bed.

"Check," I said softly into my mic as I reached the balcony again.

Andrew spoke over the comm channel. "I've got eyes on

Bloom One." I watched Andrew zone in on Sally Ellis, the governor's niece.

"Copy that, I've got Petal Two," Trevon said.

The rest of my team answered in their assigned order.

I said, "I've got eyes on Flower One again."

Governor Ellis stood next to his wife, Beth Carmichael, otherwise known as Flower Two. I hated the code names Jack had picked, but they were easy to remember.

The governor and his wife were Flower One and Two when separate and Flower Power when together, a name that at least made me smile. The governor's siblings continued on under the Flower moniker.

Vincent's and Beth's children were Petals.

There were only two Petals because each of them had a daughter with another spouse. Vincent's daughter was in Europe and had been since I took the job. Beth's daughter Alicia was being shadowed by Trevon even though she'd insisted that no one follow her around.

The blue-eyed beauty of my dreams spoke to the governor, getting a hug, then spoke to his niece briefly before mingling again.

I tore my gaze away from her gorgeous smile and perfect body and focused on the governor.

At least, I tried to. Every time she moved, it was as if my entire body was drawn toward her like an antenna trying to find a signal.

And almost every time I watched her moving among the people, I caught her staring back at me.